DUTY CALLS AT GOODWILL HOUSE

GOODWILL HOUSE SERIES BOOK THREE

FENELLA J. MILLER

Boldwood

First published in Great Britain in 2022 by Boldwood Books Ltd.

Copyright © Fenella J. Miller, 2022

Cover Design by Colin Thomas

Cover Photography: Colin Thomas

Every effort has been made to obtain the necessary permissions with reference to copyright material, both illustrative and quoted. We apologise for any omissions in this respect and will be pleased to make the appropriate acknowledgements in any future edition.

A CIP catalogue record for this book is available from the British Library.

Paperback ISBN 978-1-80162-844-0

Large Print ISBN 978-1-80162-845-7

Hardback ISBN 978-1-80162-843-3

Ebook ISBN 978-1-80162-846-4

Kindle ISBN 978-1-80162-847-1

Audio CD ISBN 978-1-80162-838-9

MP3 CD ISBN 978-1-80162-839-6

Digital audio download ISBN 978-1-80162-842-6

Boldwood Books Ltd
23 Bowerdean Street
London SW6 3TN
www.boldwoodbooks.com

For Rachel Bevan and her daughters, Emma and Hannah. Your love and support are so important to me.

1

GOODWILL HOUSE, JULY 1940

Lady Joanna Harcourt was finding the house unpleasantly quiet without the constant chatter and bustle of the WAAF girls.

'Elizabeth, shall we venture into Ramsgate on the bus today?'

Her mother-in-law, the other Lady Harcourt, looked up from the newspaper she was reading. 'I did enjoy our excursion on the bus last week when we went to the memorial service for David and the other men who died at Dunkirk. So, my dear, yes, I should be delighted to accompany you. I think I'll ask Jean to come as well.'

Jean – formerly known as Baxter – had been Elizabeth's personal maid but was now seamstress for the family. In fact, the elderly spinster was a firm favourite with the twins, Liza and Joe, who referred to her as Auntie Jean.

'There are several haberdashers in Ramsgate, which will be of interest to her,' Joanna replied. 'Joan and Val are busy upstairs spring cleaning the rooms ready for the next invasion of girls and I'm sure that they'll be happy to answer the telephone should it ring in our absence.'

'Those two ladies from the village have proved invaluable, and now Betty can concentrate on being our cook and not have to worry about housekeeping.'

'She told me yesterday that we're likely to get a contingent of land girls at the end of the summer,' Joanna said. 'I did so enjoy having girls living here, I thought I might put a card in the window of the newsagents in the village and take a couple to put in windows in Ramsgate...'

'Good heavens, Joanna, that would be unconscionable,' said her mother-in-law. 'Having WAAFs or land girls living here is one thing, but having complete strangers lodging with us is not something I approve of.'

'Very well, Elizabeth, I'll bow to your wishes on this occasion. Would you object if I invited the twins to come with us as well? Liza and Joe are almost like family now.'

Spending time with the children helped to fill the gap that Joanna's daughter, Sarah, had left in her life.

'I should be delighted to have them with us, my dear. They are delightful young people. Joe has grown at least an inch recently, as has his sister. When will they be celebrating their fifteenth birthday?'

'September – I intend to have a small party for them. Joe's still determined to join the RAF, but I pray that this wretched war is over before he's old enough to do so.'

Elizabeth nodded. 'I think we're going to have to monitor Liza's movements, as she is turning into a very pretty girl. She'd be quite a catch for one of the local boys and I want her to marry well. Which reminds me, my dear, have you heard from Sarah recently?'

The conversation was interrupted by the bouncy arrival of Lazzy, the enormous puppy that Joanna had rescued from the unused Victorian wing of Goodwill House a few months earlier. The dog had more than doubled in size and was a gentle giant, loved by all.

'No, bad boy, no jumping up. I'm very pleased to see you but neither of us want to be smothered by your kisses,' Joanna said as she fondled his long grey ears.

'Oh dear, he's left muddy paw prints on your frock. I fear you're going to have to change before we go out.'

'Absolutely not – I'll sponge them off. Excuse me, Elizabeth, I'm going to find the twins and see if they want to come. I also need to ask Betty when the next bus will pass by the end of the drive.'

She found all three of them, plus Jean Baxter, seated around the kitchen table drinking tea. Joe, Liza and Jean were eager to come with them on the trip to Ramsgate.

Betty finished her tea with a smile. 'I'm finishing early today, remember, my lady. My Bert insists that I see the doctor.'

'Oh, I'm sorry to hear that. I didn't know you were feeling unwell.'

'No, it's the other trouble I've got.'

Joanna was puzzled for a moment and then realised that her housekeeper was talking about the lack of a baby in the family. 'It's none of my business, Betty, but I'm not sure there's anything Dr Willoughby can do about that. I remember Sarah telling me, before she went to medical school in London, that the best time to conceive is in the middle of your monthly cycle.'

Betty laughed, as well she might. 'Funny old conversation to be having with an unmarried girl, but Miss Sarah knew more about medicine and such than some doctors do.'

'I'm so proud of her. She joined halfway through the first year and yet when I spoke to her recently, she told me she'd come top in her exams.'

'I'm not surprised. Is her fiancé still based at Hornchurch?'

'At the moment, his squadron is there, but he's expecting to be moved at any time. Hitler's preparing to invade, so I suppose it makes sense for all the fighter planes to remain in this part of the country in order to protect London.'

'My Bert was complaining about the signposts being taken down. He doesn't like change.'

'If it makes it harder for the Germans when they land, then it makes sense to do it. At the last WVS and WI meetings, you'll recall that it was suggested all children and mothers with young babies should be evacuated from the larger cities.'

They'd been lucky, as no bombs had been dropped on the base or on the surrounding villages so far. She was safe, but what about Sarah in London? The men were doing the actual fighting but the women and children had to be brave as well.

Betty snorted. 'That won't happen. I reckon the little ones are better off here with their own families than living with strangers. Are you catching the bus in half an hour?'

Joanna glanced at the clock ticking noisily on the French dresser. 'As we've got only half an hour to get down to the bus stop, so I'd better round up the cavalry and put my hat on.'

Ten minutes later, the five of them were walking companionably down the short drive to the road where they would catch the omnibus to Ramsgate.

Joe pointed to the potato field. 'You wouldn't know a car had driven through there a couple of weeks ago, would you? I expect they'll be harvested soon, as I can see flowers on some of the plants already.'

Joanna smiled proudly as she listened to him speaking. Unlike his sister, he was already beginning to sound like a Harcourt and not Joe Tims from the East End.

'Betty dug up a few yesterday, but they aren't quite ready. It's a lot of extra work for one of my tenant farmers to come here as well as doing their own crops. The sooner we get some land girls, the better.'

Liza dropped back to walk beside them. 'I reckon there'll be bombs dropping on Manston any day now, so why would the RAF want Millie and Di and the WAAFs on the base when it's going to be so dangerous? They'd have been better off staying with us.'

'I agree – but they have to follow orders. Millie's in charge of the other WAAFs now and Di is her second-in-command. The house seems empty without all of them, but the land girls will join us in a few weeks. Quickly, I can hear the bus coming and unless they can see us, they won't wait,' Joanna said as she encouraged Elizabeth to hurry.

* * *

Leading Aircraft Woman 356, Diane Forsyth, a member of the RAF motor pool, was designated to drive an unnamed officer from Manston to Hawkinge. She would then have to hang about at a base near Dover and drive him back.

Di parked outside the Officers' Mess and got out of the car – today she was driving a smart black Hillman, so whoever it was must be someone senior. It was relatively quiet on the base and the kites had only been scrambled once earlier in the day. Thankfully, it had been a false alarm and all had returned safely half an hour later.

Freddie Hanover, recently promoted to squadron leader, had become a good friend; she wasn't in love with him, but she certainly enjoyed his company. Who wouldn't? He was slightly above average height, less than six feet, but taller than her. He had broad shoulders, sandy-coloured hair and green eyes. Definitely a winning combination in her humble opinion.

Millie, her best friend, had met and fallen in love with Flying Officer Ted Thorrington and had then married him within just a few weeks. Di couldn't imagine herself doing anything so impulsive.

Anyway, being in love with a fighter pilot, or any sort of pilot, for that matter, wasn't a sensible thing to do, as their life expectancy was shockingly short.

She thought it would be best to be standing outside the vehicle, ready to open the door for the officer when he emerged. She checked the seams of her stockings were straight, her cap pinned on securely and gave her jacket a tug to make sure it was pulled down and unwrinkled.

'Jolly good, I hoped it would be you – in fact, I knew it would be you, as I asked particularly that you'd be my driver today.'

'Good heavens, Freddie, I thought it was going to be someone important.'

He laughed and didn't take her comment seriously. 'I'm not sitting in the back, so don't bother to open the door for me. Have you been avoiding me? You've been conspicuous by your absence this past week.'

'You can't sit next to me, Freddie, it will look decidedly odd if you do. Officers and other ranks aren't supposed to fraternise, as you very well know.'

'I don't give a damn about that. You're not a bloody taxi driver and I can sit where I want.'

'Yes, sir, of course. You must sit wherever you want.' She politely held open the door on the passenger side and he nodded, his expression solemn but his eyes twinkling, and folded himself onto the seat.

The engine was still running. Di engaged the gears and moved smoothly away, keeping her eyes firmly to the front. Their burgeoning relationship was a secret – apart from to Millie and Ted – and she couldn't risk being seen talking to him in a friendly fashion until they were safely away from Manston.

'It's all right, old girl, we can talk freely now. I thought we could have a spot of lunch together before we return.'

'We're frightfully busy and I don't want to be away any longer than I have to be.' She risked a smile in his direction. 'I'd not object to you treating me to a wad and a cuppa at the NAAFI.'

'Good show! I think I can run to a cup of tea and a bun but would much prefer to get you something more substantial. Maybe, if I get a few hours free at the same time as you, we could venture into Ramsgate?'

'I don't think that would be a good idea. I'd prefer to keep things informal between us at the moment. I'm not like Millie, I don't rush into things.'

'I must admit that their whirlwind romance took us all by surprise,' Freddie said. 'I do like you, in fact, I like you a lot, and hope that my natural charm and good looks will win you over.'

'They just might, but let's let the dust settle from the wedding last week before we stir things up again.'

Di did find him easy to talk to, he was certainly good-looking, but she wasn't sure she was ready to become involved with anyone, not even someone as attractive as Freddie.

They lapsed into friendly silence. She kept her eyes firmly on the road and he was equally quiet, which was unusual for him. 'Can you tell me why this sudden visit to Hawkinge?'

'I shouldn't, but it will be on the news tonight. That bastard Hitler has invaded Guernsey in the Channel Islands, so it could well be about that.'

'That's worrying news – do you think England will be next?' The Channel Islands were part of Britain and the idea that they were now occupied made an invasion in England seem more real.

'It's a lot further and across the Channel to get here. The boys in blue are ready to stop the Germans. We might be fewer in number but are more determined than the Luftwaffe. We've got more to lose.'

They were held up briefly behind the local bus but the driver, recognising theirs was a staff car, kindly pulled over and let her drive past. As always when entering a base, she slowed down ready to produce her identity papers. The guard glanced in the window and waved her on with a salute.

'I'll drop you at the admin building, shall I? I'll park and then wait in the NAAFI.'

'Do that. I don't know how long I'll be.' His expression was distracted, and he barely acknowledged her as he got out of the car and strode away.

Di expertly reversed the car and then parked it somewhere it wouldn't be in the way. She remained, leaning on the bonnet, enjoying the sunshine whilst watching aircraft landing and taking off. These weren't squadrons being scrambled but, she thought, reconnaissance flights in some cases and transport delivering goods and pilots.

She'd no desire to fly, although she'd heard that a handful of women had been recruited to join the Air Transport Axillary – better known as the ATA – and were now flying Tiger Moths. She wondered if they'd ever be considered suitable to deliver operational aircraft.

Her ambition was to become an officer and she was hoping that once the full contingent of WAAF were installed in the new accommodation at Manston, she'd be promoted. First, she needed to become a corporal like her best friend Millie, and then work her way up the ranks.

People had said last year when the war started that it would be all over by Christmas, but she was confident that she'd ample opportunity to further her career. One thing she wasn't going to do was get married or even seriously involved with any chap.

It was all very well for the men, as they didn't run the risk of getting pregnant and being dismissed from the service. Was Millie already in an interesting condition? Since her friend had returned from her brief honeymoon last week, they'd scarcely had time to talk, but if looks were anything to go by, marriage definitely suited Millie.

Freddie was rather keen to become her official boyfriend. For a fighter pilot, life moved fast and was probably going to be much shorter than it should be. Therefore, it seemed reasonable he would want to hurry things along, whereas she wanted to take things at a snail's pace.

Her intention when she'd signed up had been to make her career in the WAAF, become an officer eventually, and having a boyfriend didn't really fit in with this plan.

Freddie joined the other officers and could scarcely see across the room through the haze of cigarette smoke. He preferred a pipe and always had his trusty meerschaum and tin of tobacco in the inside pocket of his uniform jacket.

'What ho, old bean,' he greeted a chap he knew quite well. 'Any inkling what this scrum is for? Channel Islands?'

'Freddie, good to see you,' Flight Lieutenant Frank Rhodes replied cheerfully. 'I know as much as you do, which is damn all. Very likely to be the invasion of Guernsey, but you never know. It could be something else entirely. It's all going to kick off any moment, that's one thing I'm certain of.'

There was a huddle of senior bods around the table at the front of the room. Freddie recognised one of them as the spy – the intelligence officer – who debriefed the returning flyers at Manston.

The room was called to order and after a few minutes, an air commodore – Freddie didn't catch his name – told them what was going on in the Channel Islands. He was shocked to discover the

War Office had abandoned the islands as they were considered of no strategical importance.

'The Germans didn't know we'd demilitarised and arrived to find a compliant population and no kites to capture. Unfortunately, they bombed half a dozen lorries collecting tomatoes, believing them to be troop carriers, and a few civilians were killed.' The senior officer looked at his notes before continuing. 'I can assure you, gentlemen, the Channel Islands will be the only British soil those German bastards will occupy.'

Freddie exchanged a glance with Frank. He wasn't sure why this meeting had been called, as it obviously wasn't to do with rescuing anyone from Jersey, Guernsey or the other islands he couldn't remember the names of.

'Your job for the next few days will be to protect convoys of shipping travelling down the Dover Strait. The Blenheims will drop bombs on any subs and you chaps will engage the Luftwaffe fighters.'

Some wag behind him said quite audibly that they'd already been doing this, so coming here this morning was a waste of everybody's time. There was a general murmur of agreement.

The senior chap ignored this unwanted interruption and carried on. 'We will continue to fly reconnaissance along the coast as well as escorting the merchant ships. All leave is cancelled. The balloon's about to go up, gentlemen, the Prime Minister is relying on you to protect the country from invasion. The RAF, according to Mr Churchill, having fought the Battle of France, will now be fighting the Battle of Britain.'

There was a spontaneous round of applause, cheers and stamping of feet. This was the sort of rousing talk they needed to hear. The next few weeks, months possibly, were going to be difficult, and there would no doubt be horrendous losses. He looked around at the familiar faces, wondering how many of them would still be there when all this was over.

When the noise had subsided, the air commodore just had a few more words of encouragement. He asked them to ensure that all their own bods were aware of what was coming and were ready to do their bit without flinching.

The meeting broke up and the majority of the chaps headed for the Officers' Mess, but Freddie went in search of Di. Spending time with her was preferable to swilling warm beer in the mess.

As the weather was pleasant, there were tables and chairs set out on the grass outside the NAAFI and he eventually found her sitting at one of these, engrossed in a novel of some sort.

'I thought you'd abandoned me, Di, when I couldn't see you inside. What can I get you, as this is my treat?'

She smiled and put her book down with some reluctance. 'I took the liberty of ordering for us, and the nice girl behind the counter will have it ready for you. Two rounds of cheese and pickle sandwiches, tea and an iced bun each for dessert.'

'Actual cheese?'

'Yes, I can't tell you how excited I was to discover we didn't have to have spam and piccalilli.'

He was back with the tray in minutes and was somewhat put out to find Di with her nose in the book again. He put the food down with unnecessary force, making the crockery and cutlery jump.

She looked up with a guilty grin. 'Sorry, I borrowed this from one of the girls and I've got to give it back this afternoon. It's an American book about a private investigator called Philip Marlowe. It's excellent – I can highly recommend it.'

She held up the cover so he could read the name of the author. 'Raymond Chandler – never heard of him, but I'll take your word for it and see if I can obtain a copy for myself.'

They were halfway through their sandwiches when the Tannoy screamed. A squadron was being scrambled and this was reminder enough that they shouldn't be wasting time here when they might well be needed at Manston.

'Let's finish up and get going, Di, I feel a bit guilty. If they've gone up, then no doubt my squadron will be next. How quickly can you get us back to base?'

2

Joanna nodded and smiled as she made her way to the middle of the bus, where there were sufficient seats for the five of them. Naturally, she sat next to Elizabeth, as usual wanted to be by the window. The twins sat together and Jean sat next to a stout, sour-faced housewife who remained firmly in situ, leaving barely enough room for a child to sit.

'Please move your bag and yourself so I can sit down,' Jean said loudly. Several heads turned and being subjected to this scrutiny was enough to make the miserable woman shift across.

Elizabeth nodded her approval. 'Have you noticed the change in Jean since she took over the dressmaking and mending for the household?'

'I have. In fact, despite the emptiness of the house at the moment, there's a happy atmosphere. Even Betty seems to have a bit of a spring in her step nowadays.'

'That will be because she's resumed marital relations with her husband.'

If her mother-in-law had announced she was a devil worshipper, Joanna couldn't have been more shocked. 'Shush – you mustn't say things like that in public. I can't imagine how you obtained this information, as I didn't know you were on close terms with Betty.'

Elizabeth was unbothered by this gentle reprimand. Being a wealthy aristocrat in her seventies meant she could more or less ignore the usual rules and get away with it.

'She discussed it with Jean, who then told me.'

Now Joanna was bewildered. 'Why would Betty want to discuss something so intimate with a middle-aged spinster like Jean?'

'Oh, Jean was married once, a long time ago, and still uses her maiden name. I've no idea what happened to her husband and have never liked to enquire.'

'How extraordinary – to me, she's the epitome of an unmarried lady. But it's none of our business, and I suggest we change the subject to something less contentious. There are only a few single seats left so it will be standing room only for many of those waiting to board when we reach the village.'

Liza had struck up a lively conversation with a girl of a similar age who was sitting on the other side of the central aisle. The only time the twins got to mix with young people their own age was before and after church. There was a social at the village hall on Saturday evening, and Joanna decided that they would all attend.

She twisted in her seat and spoke to Joe. 'Do you think you could drive the Bentley?'

His eyes lit up. 'I reckon so, my lady. I'm a dab hand with the tractor and I can't see it's a lot different.'

'It hasn't been used for a few months, so you'd better see if it still runs. I know we've still got plenty of petrol in the cans stored behind the barn.'

Obviously, his sister had overheard this exchange and immediately wanted to know why her brother would need to drive the Bentley.

'I want us all to go to the event at the village hall this Saturday. It will be far more convenient to have our own vehicle rather than be obliged to use public transport.'

'Cor, that's the ticket. I were... I was going to ask if Joe and I could go but I reckon it'll be better if all of us do.'

Joanna was a little uncomfortable holding a conversation so publicly and was about to turn back when Liza continued.

'It's ever so busy on the bus today because it's market day in Ramsgate. Good thing I've bought two baskets.'

'Brought, Liza, not bought,' Elizabeth pointed out.

The girl laughed and resumed her chat with her new acquaintance. The omnibus lurched and bumped to a standstill opposite the church and, sure enough, there were more than a dozen housewives waiting to clamber on.

Joanna was inordinately proud that the twins immediately offered their seats, as did the girl on the opposite side of the aisle. The three of them then shuffled to the rear of the vehicle so she was no longer able to see them.

Elizabeth chuckled. 'Much better for the youngsters to talk amongst themselves. How far is it from Stodham to Ramsgate?'

'No more than five miles. We should be there in twenty minutes or so.'

Even with the windows slid back, it was unpleasantly stuffy and decidedly smelly by the time the bus rattled to a standstill in the station forecourt.

'Good heavens, do we alight here?' Elizabeth asked, not sounding too happy about the prospect of walking down the steep hill towards the promenade.

'Not everybody is getting off, so I'm assuming the bus does take us to the shops.'

The lady sitting in front overheard and answered with a cheerful smile. 'The bus goes down Hatham Street, my lady, and then turns left onto the High Street. You can get off anywhere along there and it will lead you into the shops. Or you can stay on and get off by the Royal Hotel. They do ever such a nice lunch there.'

'Thank you, that's very helpful.'

Joanna realised she should have known this person's name but it was too late to ask, as the bus conductor rang the bell and they were moving off again. More than half the travellers had disembarked, which meant the atmosphere was slightly more fragrant. It would be a relief to get out and stroll along the seafront and breathe in some fresh air.

The last time she'd been here was to help when the soldiers had come back from Dunkirk – it seemed like a lifetime ago, as so much had changed, but in reality it was only a few weeks.

After the memorial service for Joanna's husband and the men from the village, Elizabeth had announced she was no longer wearing black and in support of her mother-in-law, Joanna had decided she too would abandon widow's weeds. She wasn't flamboyantly dressed, far from it, but was smartly attired in a grey linen suit with a pencil skirt and nipped in waist. Her hat comprised a few dyed grey feathers attached to a dark grey base and held in place by two large pins.

She'd had the forethought to wear kitten-heeled court shoes so she could walk comfortably for miles, although she doubted that Elizabeth would wish to do more than a mile at the most.

She was obliged to assist Elizabeth down the steps – something she thought the bus conductor should have done, instead of jumping down and lolling against the side of the vehicle smoking a Woodbine.

'Good heavens, my dear,' Elizabeth said, 'surely that's the newly elevated Lord Harcourt striding towards us.'

* * *

Di was an expert driver and covered the twenty miles in record time. She breathed a sigh of relief when she saw the resident squadrons were still parked in readiness on the aprons surrounding the runway.

'Shall I take you to dispersal or do you have to report to admin first?'

'Dispersal, please. Thank god they didn't have to go up without me.'

She screeched to a halt beside the small group of huts, drawing the attention of the numerous young pilots stretched out on the grass, Mae Wests on, waiting for the call. Freddie was out of the car without a backward glance and strode across to join his men.

If MT – motor transport – girls were allowed to wear overalls when working on the base, then why did the pilots have to wear a jacket and tie? As far as she could see, none of them had on their thick flying boots or sheepskin jackets today and she'd noticed at least one of them was actually wearing shiny black polished shoes.

Surely it would still be freezing flying at 20,000 feet? They had no heating in the kites and had to wear oxygen masks to be able to breathe. Perhaps they snatched up their warmer garments – their flying suits – when the order came.

The man answering the telephone shouted, 'Squadron scramble!' and then rushed out to ring the bell hanging outside so that the ground crew would know to have the fighters started and ready to leave the minute the pilots bundled into their cockpits.

Freddie had told her they expected to be airborne within three minutes of getting the signal. That hardly gave them time to step into their thick flying suits. Personally, she'd rather be hot whilst waiting than freezing cold whilst fighting for her life in the sky.

It didn't do to dwell on these things, and Di roared back down the runway to the motor pool. After parking the car in its designated place, she signed the book to show she'd brought it back unharmed, and then hurriedly changed into her work clothes. Climbing in and out of a three-ton lorry just wasn't possible in her normal uniform.

Millie was speaking to Sarge when Di reported for duty. 'Goodness, you're back early.'

'They were scrambled at Hawkinge, and Freddie wanted to return in case his boys went up too.'

'Two sirens have gone off whilst you've been away – we all dived into the nearest trench, but they were both false alarms,' Millie said.

'I think everyone's on edge, expecting the balloon to go up at any moment or for Hitler to begin the invasion. I must admit that before I set out, I always do a mental check as to where the nearest shelter or ditch is situated, just in case.'

Sarge nodded. 'You're right to be cautious, love, if they strafe Manston, anyone caught out in the open will go for a Burton. This place is going to be dangerous when things kick off.'

'I overheard some bigwigs talking earlier today,' Di said. 'It seems that Manston is expected to be the first base that will be bombed. It's on the flight path from France to London. The Luftwaffe have to wipe out the RAF before the Germans can invade.'

'I reckon Ramsgate will cop a lot as well. It's a good thing they've got the old railway tunnels to use as shelters, as they're going to need them.'

Not wanting to discuss such a depressing subject any further, Di collected her work slip and saw that she and Millie were to take several cases of spare parts to the other end of the base, where the fighters that could be mended on base were repaired.

The boxes they wanted were piled up outside and they rushed off to begin loading them onto the lorry.

'To turn the subject to something jollier,' Millie said. 'There's some sort of party in Stodham Village Hall on Saturday. Ted and I are going if we can – do you think that you and Freddie might come?'

She was about to say a categorical no, tell her friend that she didn't want to be seen with anyone, and especially not an officer, but said something else entirely. An evening at a village social would be rather jolly and she'd rather be escorted by someone than go on her own and be pestered by strangers.

'Yes, if he wants to take me, then I'll be happy to come. Let's pray they get some time off, that the Germans haven't started bombing us by then.'

Millie's smile was radiant. 'You'll be in charge of the girls on base tonight, as Ted and I are staying in a B&B – we've both got a twelve-hour pass.'

'It must be so hard for you, being married but living apart.'

'Not as difficult for me as it is for the women with husbands posted away. Ted thinks they won't be going anywhere for the moment, which is a relief.'

Di tossed the last box into the back of the waiting lorry and together they pulled up the tailgate and fastened it.

'Are you driving?'

Millie nodded. 'If you don't mind, then I will. Keeping busy is the answer at the moment, otherwise every minute will drag until I'm off duty at eight tonight.'

They didn't have to unload, as two aircrew were waiting to do that. The parts were needed urgently, and Di wondered why they hadn't been delivered sooner.

'There must have been a driver free to bring these over, Millie, so why did they have to wait for us?'

'I haven't the foggiest. The four of us have been busy since seven o'clock this morning and the men still available in the motor pool have been driving the bowsers. There's also been a fire drill. I expect they were involved in that, as so far we haven't been asked to drive the fire tender.'

When her shift eventually finished, Di returned to the WAAF accommodation, eager to check that the girls in her charge for tonight had no problems that she needed to deal with. They'd been put as far away from the men as was possible – probably a good idea, after what had happened a few weeks ago.

If the two girls who'd been working as prostitutes hadn't been caught, and their pimps hadn't threatened her, then Di wouldn't now be almost walking out with Freddie. And as much as she liked Freddie, the young pilots risked their lives every time they flew. There'd already been several losses at Manston, and it would only get worse. Being involved with someone in such a dangerous occu-pation could well lead to heartbreak – hopefully not for her or Millie – but certainly for the wives and girlfriends of other flyers.

Was she being foolish to keep seeing Freddie?

* * *

Freddie didn't make a general announcement about what he'd been told at the meeting but wandered about from group to group and spoke to his fellow flyers individually. He didn't dwell on the likeli-hood that many of them wouldn't make it through these next few weeks – nobody needed reminding of that grim fact.

They weren't scrambled and he was able to settle down beside Ted Thorrington, who'd become a close friend over the past weeks. Despite being the youngest member of the squadron, the least experienced initially, he was by far the best pilot. When he'd asked to transfer from Hurries to Spits, Freddie hadn't hesitated. Good pilots were like gold dust.

'Looks like you're going to get away as planned, old boy, nothing much happening here at the moment.' Freddie had his own deckchair – a gift from Ted when he'd joined the squadron. No doubt some poor sod somewhere else was bemoaning the loss of his precious seat.

'Are you coming to the village hall on Saturday?' Ted said. 'We're not rostered on at the moment.'

'If I can persuade Di to accompany me, then yes, I'll go. Has Millie told you anything about Di and me?'

'If she had, I wouldn't tell you. Is she dragging her feet?'

'She is. One minute I think she feels the same way I do, the next I'm convinced she's not interested.'

'No point in asking me about women, as you've got far more experience of the fair sex than I have. I'd never even kissed a girl until I met Millie and we've been learning about this married malarkey together.'

Freddie almost fell out of his deckchair. 'Good god! Obviously a very quick learner – you're my best pilot and the only chap that's actually married.'

'So I'll be promoted to flight lieutenant any day soon?' Ted grinned and looked hopefully at his empty mug as if expecting it to miraculously refill itself.

'I'm sure there's a brew in the dispersal hut. Bring one back for me, there's a good fellow.'

Ted levered himself out of the deckchair and saluted, forgetting he had his tin mug in his hand. Freddie was still laughing when an MT lorry lumbered to a halt on the grass a few yards from where he was sitting.

Di jumped down from the passenger side and waved. Millie appeared beside her and the two of them ran across, laughing, waving and calling out greetings to the other chaps, most of whom they knew quite well, having driven them about the place for the past few months. He heaved himself out of the deckchair and was standing to greet her when she arrived.

'We can't stop long. Millie spotted Ted and decided she had to speak to him.'

'He's gone to find me a cuppa. He won't be long. Have you heard about the jollity on Saturday? I wondered if you'd like to come with me if I'm able to get away.'

'I'd love to. It's hard to believe that at any moment the Germans might appear on the horizon and everything will change.'

'Hopefully not before Saturday – the Met chappie said there's bad weather coming in tonight, which is going to make the Channel too rough for Hitler to bring the barges across.'

Di was well aware that before any invasion took place, the Luftwaffe would attempt to destroy the RAF bases and as many kites as they could. However, it was better for morale if they didn't mention this.

Ted returned with his lovely wife at his side and handed Freddie a brimming mug. 'Here you are, Skip, a bit stewed but welcome nevertheless.'

'Thanks, having a minion to fetch and carry for me is one of the few perks of being a CO. Millie, when do you finish?'

'I'm on duty until eight, but I don't have anything particular to do until then. I wish I did.'

'Push off now, both of you. I'm your senior officer and give you permission. Stay on the base just in case, I'm sure you can find yourself a quiet corner.'

Neither of them argued. Ted had a dilapidated bicycle leaning drunkenly against the hut and he snatched it up and Millie scrambled onto the crossbar. They were gone before Freddie had taken a couple of slurps from his tea.

Di was watching their departure anxiously. 'I honestly think they're both more likely to come to a bad end riding that thing than doing anything else on this base.' She turned and her smile made him slop the hot tea over his hand.

'That was a kind thing you did, Freddie. I'm sure you could get into hot water if anybody reported them.'

'I've got broad shoulders and friends in high places. I'll talk myself out of any repercussions, don't worry about me.'

She pointed at the second mug of tea. 'If that's going spare, can I have it?'

'I should sit down first, or you're likely to end up with most of it in your lap.' He scowled at the inoffensive seat. 'That deckchair has a mind of its own and if anyone apart from Ted attempts to sit on it, it quite often collapses.'

She laughed and sat down with some hesitancy. Freddie handed over the tea and couldn't keep his amusement hidden. They both laughed. Although she couldn't stay long, he believed things might have changed between them. He hoped so.

3

Joanna's eyes widened. It was indeed Peter Harcourt and he appeared to be delighted to see them. She wasn't so sure, as despite his charm, wit and obvious good looks, she didn't quite trust him.

'Good morning, my ladies, what a delightful surprise to meet you here.'

Joanna was still trying to gather her wits and think of something to say that wouldn't reveal her unease when Elizabeth stepped in.

'Good morning, my lord. Might I enquire what you're doing in Ramsgate when you have important work to do in London?'

He looked somewhat taken aback at her direct approach but rallied marvellously. 'I do get the occasional free day, ma'am. And I had business matters to attend to.'

'What business could you possibly have in Ramsgate? You didn't even know the place existed until my son died and you inherited the title!'

Joanna decided she'd better step in and try and smooth the awkward situation over. 'It's none of our business, Elizabeth, as well you know. We're in search of coffee and hopefully cake – would you care to join us?'

She turned and spoke quietly to Liza, Joe and Jean, who were listening avidly to this exchange. 'Why don't you explore the market and then join us at the hotel on the parade? I think you have sufficient for your needs.'

'We do, ta,' Liza said happily. 'TTFN.'

Elizabeth had listened to this exchange. 'What on earth is the girl talking about?'

'Ta ta for now – I rather like it.' Joanna smiled in what she hoped was a friendly manner at the unwanted visitor. 'Well, Peter, are you coming or are you too busy attending to your business?'

For a second, his eyes were hard, calculating, and then he was charming and smiling once more. 'I'd be delighted to come with you, Joanna. I must admit, I'm surprised to see you here, as I didn't know that you frequented Ramsgate.'

Joanna felt Elizabeth stiffen and knew her mother-in-law was going to say something wildly inappropriate but, for some explicable reason, she didn't intervene and waited with interest to see what was going to be said.

'Not nearly as surprised as we are, my lord, to see you prowling about a town in which the only business you could possibly have is poking your nose into our affairs.'

To her astonishment, he laughed and didn't take offence. 'Touché, my lady. I prefer to have this discussion in the comfort of the hotel. Shall we leave this until we're there?'

Elizabeth snorted but didn't argue. 'Joanna, my dear, would you kindly hold my arm, as I'm not sure I'm quite steady on my feet this morning?'

'Of course, the last thing we want is for you to suffer an accident.'

This meant that Peter had to walk behind them, as they couldn't possibly take up the entire pavement. Her mother-in-law glanced up and winked, and Joanna had difficulty not laughing out loud.

The doorman bowed them in like royalty. She supposed they were the nearest to aristocracy Ramsgate would see – two ladies and a lord in one go was probably the most exciting thing that had happened at the hotel for decades.

They were ushered to a small private coffee lounge with large windows facing the sea. There were only two tables and neither of them were occupied.

'What can we get you and your guests, my lord?'

Peter was obviously staying here, as otherwise the doorman wouldn't have known who he was, and this explained the obsequious welcome they'd received. Joanna doubted the doorman would remember her, as she'd only visited a couple of times with David and that had been years ago.

'We would like coffee and whatever pastries are available.'

'Yes, sir.' He pulled out the chairs so they could be seated and then vanished silently as all good servants should.

'So, my lord, you're staying here. Kindly explain yourself.'

Peter was no longer smiling, and he stared at Elizabeth with dislike. 'My lady, forgive me for being blunt, but it's none of your damn business what I do or where I stay.'

Instead of being offended, Elizabeth smiled. 'Good for you, young man, I was just testing your mettle. It doesn't do to have the head of the family a wishy-washy sort of fellow. I'm sorry for finding this amusing, Peter, but your reaction was wonderful. Honestly, neither of us have any intention of enquiring any further as to your reasons for being in Ramsgate.' Elizabeth smiled. 'I've no need to ask questions as I already know what you're doing here. You've been to the bank that holds the debt.'

Again, there was that flash of something hard in his expression, but it passed so swiftly Joanna thought she might have imagined it.

'I was indeed at the bank.' The rattle of a trolley heralded the arrival of their order. 'Excellent, our refreshments are here.'

After that, they talked about the situation in the Channel Islands, the possibility of an imminent invasion and the risk to Goodwill House if bombs meant for Manston went astray.

Half an hour later, Peter politely excused himself and left. Joanna waited until she was sure he was out of earshot before voicing her doubts about the new Lord Harcourt to her mother-in-law.

* * *

Di regretted her impulsive decision to attend the weekend social event in the village with Freddie. Having already been the subject of unpleasant gossip a few weeks ago when she'd been attacked on the way back to Goodwill House, she was reluctant to make herself a talking point again.

She was a lowly LACW – not even a corporal like Millie, but one rank behind – and being seen on the arm of a squadron leader was bound to raise eyebrows and possibly get them both into hot water.

Her career progress was more important than furthering her relationship with Freddie and blotting her copybook like this might well make her ineligible for officer training when that became available. Freddie might get a ticking off from his senior officer, but he was unlikely to be moved or demoted, whereas this could well happen to her.

Di bit her lip. Would it be worse to stand him up or go with him and risk the repercussions that would inevitably follow? This was a decision she'd make nearer the time. It was quite possible his squadron would be on permanent readiness by then.

There were three stages of this. The first was when the pilots would be expected to be in their kites and in the air within three minutes. In the second, they had fifteen minutes and in the third, there was thirty minutes' grace before they had to be strapped in and ready to take off. Some flyers at the first stage often sat in their cockpits so they could be in the air in time.

Dwelling on what was coming would only lower her spirits and Mr Churchill wanted everybody to think positively, to believe implicitly that however bad things seemed, eventually Great Britain would win the war. She agreed with him, as being miserable wouldn't help anyone.

Di and Millie had been best friends since training, but things had changed since Millie had married. Di didn't make friends easily and doubted she'd ever be as close to another girl as she was to her best friend.

She would attend the social. It would be a mixture of dancing, silly party games and cardplaying. No alcohol, just tea and biscuits, but there were three pubs in the village and many of the attendees nipped out to get a drink several times during the event.

And this one would quite possibly be the last one for some time if the bombing started, after that holding such an event might be too risky.

She would spend the evening in Freddie's company and then make a radical decision. If, after being with him for several hours, she believed that he might become someone special in her life, then she'd remain at Manston and take the flak that such a relationship would attract.

If, however, her feelings were lukewarm, then she would put in for a transfer and remove herself from temptation. She would request a posting to another operational base so nobody could say she was running away.

* * *

With Millie away overnight, Di was too busy to think about Saturday night or the idea that she might be putting in for a transfer. No flyers had lost their lives, no kites had been shot down, but one inexperienced flyer had misjudged his landing and crashed his Hurricane. It was fortunate for the young man concerned that the damage had been minimal and the aircraft could be repaired on the base.

Millie had managed to persuade Sarge to allow them to use the small Austin Seven that Saturday evening. This meant the four of them could travel in comfort. Everybody not on duty was going to walk down to the village, as it was only two miles and on a warm summer's evening this wasn't a hardship.

Millie was driving and Ted sat next to her in the front, which meant that Di was sitting far too close to Freddie on the narrow rear seat.

There were two other cars already parked in front of the hall and a constant stream of villagers hurrying towards the doors.

'They usually hold these sorts of shindigs in the afternoon because of the blackout,' Ted said helpfully. 'With double summer time, it doesn't get dark until after eleven, and this will be finished long before them.'

'It does sound rather jolly with the music coming out through the open windows and everybody in their pretty summer dresses,' Di said.

'Not everybody. I don't think Ted and I would suit a floral frock.'

Ted chuckled as he stepped in close and put his arm possessively around Millie's waist. 'Speak for yourself, Skip. I think I'd look tickety-boo in one.'

'Don't be so pedantic, both of you,' Di said, pretending to be cross. 'WAAFs are obviously in uniform too. Nights like this, I wish I could wear something floaty and cool and not this heavy blue serge.'

'I'm just glad I don't have to think about what I'm going to put on – we've absolutely no choice.' Millie smiled. 'That's not quite true, as we could always turn up in our overalls.'

'God forbid!' Ted said. 'At least in your regular uniform I can see your legs.'

They were about to go in when the Bentley from Goodwill House arrived, driven by Joe of all people. Di turned back in order to speak to Joanna and the others, but Millie had already disappeared inside.

She rushed over and opened the rear passenger door. 'My lady, it's so good to see you here.'

'Di, you look well. I've brought the twins, as it's high time they made friends their own age. I couldn't persuade Elizabeth to accompany us, but Jean has come.'

After exchanging greetings, the five of them headed for the jollity inside. Millie and Ted were dancing a lively polka with dozens of other couples in the space in the centre of the hall, but Di could see no sign of her escort. If she and Freddie were attending the event together, shouldn't he be at her side?

* * *

Freddie only realised Di wasn't with him as he joined the queue to pay his entrance fee. He went immediately to see where she was and decided not to intrude on her reunion with her former landlady.

When he reached the two ladies sitting behind a trestle table collecting the entrance fee from the eager partygoers, he dropped two coins into the saucer with a smile.

'Please take for two, my girlfriend will be in in a minute.'

'You'll find, Squadron Leader, that several of your fellow airmen have left their jackets in that room over there. It's a bit of a crush tonight and rather hot.'

'Thank you, I might well do that.' Freddie moved out of the way so the villagers behind him could pay their dues and then stood by the door waiting for Di. Had he been premature in calling her his girlfriend? He hoped not but still wasn't entirely sure if she was ready to make their friendship official.

The sound of raised male voices coming from the cloakroom attracted his attention. He was the most senior officer present, so it was down to him to step in if the fracas was being caused by chaps from the base.

He pushed open the door with more force than was necessary, knowing the slam of the wood against the wall would interrupt whatever argument was taking place. It did the trick.

'Blimey, mate, come in, why don't you?' The speaker was a youth of no more than sixteen.

'Sorry, don't know my own strength.' Freddie glanced around the cloakroom as if looking for something or someone. 'As you were, chaps.'

He paused outside the door for a few moments to be sure whatever the two lads had been fighting about was now forgotten. Satisfied he wouldn't be needed to separate them after all, he returned to the fray.

Di was looking for him. 'Sorry, old bean, thought two of my blokes might be having a fight and just had to check. Always on duty, I'm afraid.'

She smiled. 'I take it you weren't needed.'

'No, two youngsters no doubt arguing about a girl but when I barged in, they forgot their differences in order to swear at me.'

'Do you mind if we go somewhere else and don't stay here? I'd much prefer to have a quiet drink in one of the pubs,' Di said.

'Are you sure you don't want to dance?'

'Absolutely certain.'

There were still people waiting to come in, so their absence wouldn't be noted. Once they were outside, she explained why she wanted to leave.

'You were the only senior officer present and if we'd stayed, you would have been on duty all evening. Much better to let them enjoy themselves. Why aren't there any other people of your rank?'

'For exactly the reason you've just stated. I was in two minds about agreeing to come, but if it meant spending time with you, then I was happy to do so.'

'I've not been in any of these pubs – shall we go into the Greyhound? It looks quite pleasant.'

There were a few ancient chaps playing dominoes in the public bar, but the saloon bar was empty as was only to be expected.

'What's your poison?'

'A lemonade or ginger beer – I only drink champagne and only at weddings.' Di grinned. 'As I've not been to any weddings, I've not actually even tasted champagne.'

The landlady was a cheerful soul and suggested they might like to sit in the garden at the rear of the building. 'It's a shame to be inside on a nice night like this. There's a couple of benches and a table and no one else out there because every blooming person's at the village hall tonight.'

Freddie carried his pint and Di took her glass of lemonade as they made their way outside.

'The bench with the honeysuckle behind it would be perfect. Listen, we can hear the birds singing and even the bees humming. We can pretend there's not a war on for a little while.'

The bench wasn't that clean and Freddie was about to spread out his handkerchief for her to sit on, but she ignored the dirt and sat down.

'We can't stay here all evening. Millie will wonder where we've gone and we'll need a lift back at the end.'

He nodded. 'An hour? I doubt they're going to want to return to the base before that.' He wanted to suggest longer but didn't want to seem presumptuous.

'To be honest, I'm surprised Ted and Millie wanted to come at all as they get so little time together,' Di said.

'Ted's the only married bod in my squadron, though most of them have got girlfriends or fiancées somewhere or other.'

'As you've mentioned the subject of girlfriends, I'm still not sure we should be more than friends. I'm determined to be an officer one day and I don't want any negative comments on my record.'

'I honestly don't think anybody gives a damn about our private lives. As long as I'm doing my job, taking care of my men and so forth, Win Co isn't going to interfere.' But Di didn't look convinced. 'Also, at the moment, your senior officer's Millie and she's hardly going to write you up for something she did herself.'

This was true but it didn't alter the fact that any kind of relationship with him wasn't something she'd planned or was even sure she wanted. Was her career in the WAAF more important than getting to know him?

Finally, Di came to a decision and sat back, looking happier and more relaxed. 'How silly of me – until we have our own queen bee and actual officers, I'm in the clear. If you're quite sure nobody's going to make a fuss, then I'd like to give it a go.'

Freddie carefully put down his beer, removed the lemonade from her hand and closed the distance between them. Her eyes widened but he didn't give her time to object. He reached out, cupped her face with his hand, tilted her chin and kissed her gently.

'I hope I haven't overstepped the mark, dear girl, but I believe as your official boyfriend it's in order for me to kiss you occasionally.'

'I believe that's correct, although I know nothing about the etiquette involved. I've deliberately avoided any sort of romantic entanglement.' Her smile made him want to kiss her again and more thoroughly this time. 'If I'm honest, and I usually am, I was at boarding school until I was eighteen and then promptly enlisted in the WAAF, so I've not really had any time to get involved.'

'Good god, you've been surrounded by eager airmen for the past year. I don't understand why a girl as lovely as you has remained unattached until now.'

'Don't look so smug, Squadron Leader, you just happened to be in the right place at the right time! I could have settled upon any one of a dozen other equally attractive officers.'

They both knew this wasn't true. Until she'd met him, her feelings hadn't been engaged. Instead of moving away, putting a respectable distance between them, he slid his arm around her waist and drew her close. She made no objection. In fact, she rested her head on his shoulder for a few moments.

'Pass me my lemonade, Freddie, seems a pity to let it go flat.'

Reluctantly he leaned down and picked the glass up and then retrieved his own beer. They sipped their drinks, both lost in thought.

'How's this going to work, Freddie?'

'I haven't the foggiest. On the plus side, you're living on the base now and even if I'm permanently tied to my kite, you can come and see me when you get any free time.'

'If Millie and Ted can manage, then we can too. The new NAAFI building should be open any day so we can meet up there, can't we?'

They were interrupted by the sudden arrival of the landlady. 'Here, Squadron Leader, you'd better get back to the village hall smartish. Your lads are knocking seven bells out of some soldiers.'

4

_____

Joanna had been enjoying the evening, not dancing herself, but watching the twins and the other young people skipping about the floor with enthusiasm. Jean had gravitated towards a trio of similar ladies and was sitting with them, chatting away happily.

'My lady, I'm delighted to see you here, but I'm rather surprised, as I didn't think a village event was to your taste.' The local doctor had drifted up beside her.

'Good evening, Dr Willoughby, I'm equally surprised to find you here. I thought you far too busy to attend.'

A couple gyrated towards her and only his swift reaction prevented her from being tumbled to the boards. 'Goodness me, thank you. I'm going to find a seat somewhere safe.'

She looked around hopefully, but every seat was occupied. She rather thought that the entire village must be here tonight.

'Shall we go outside? I seem to recall that there are a couple of benches under the windows. We can listen to the music from there without being sent flying.' He nodded towards the dancefloor. 'Unless, of course, you would care to dance with me?'

She gave his request some thought. It wouldn't do to be seen to be enjoying the company of a single gentleman so soon after the demise of her husband. However, a casual chat wouldn't be frowned on. 'I think not. I do enjoy a waltz or a foxtrot but am not fond of the polka or Gay Gordons.'

There were indeed two benches outside, although they looked somewhat rickety. 'I suggest that you try one out for us, Dr Willoughby, as I've no wish to end up on my derrière in the dirt.'

His smile was really quite attractive, and he obediently bounced up and down on the nearest bench. She was relieved it remained intact, as he'd been somewhat more vigorous than she thought sensible.

Joanna smoothed her skirt under her bottom and sat down carefully. He joined her and the plank of wood creaked somewhat ominously but remained in one piece. They had talked about the weather, the war, and a worrying outbreak of measles in the village when they were interrupted by the arrival of a group of noisy and somewhat inebriated soldiers.

'Oh dear, where have they come from? Their barracks, I believe, are in Ramsgate.'

He frowned. 'Never a good idea to have soldiers and RAF at the same do, especially if there's alcohol involved.'

'As this event is teetotal, at least the boys in blue will be sober. I rather think that these young men, from their language and the noise they're making, have already visited the pub.'

'Let's hope you're right about the RAF, my lady. I've been here since the beginning and, so far, I haven't seen any of them nip across to the Greyhound.'

The raucous group of soldiers barged into the village hall. She could hear them loudly demanding to be admitted. The noise level began to rise.

The doctor was on his feet. 'The social is at capacity – it

wouldn't be safe to allow anyone else in and particularly not that belligerent group.' He politely offered his hand to assist her.

'Thank you, but I'm not decrepit just yet. I'm perfectly capable of getting up from a bench without help.' She smiled. 'Unless, of course, you are mistaking me for the other Lady Harcourt.'

'I should think not. Perhaps you should remain out here, my lady, it might be a tad lively in there.'

She was about to argue when the sound of breaking furniture, crashing and shouts of rage made her decide she would be better off outside. The doctor was about to go up the steps that led to the double door when a lowly airman erupted from the hall.

'We need Freddie – he can sort it out. Ted's doing his best, but one officer's not enough. Do you know where he is?'

'I should try the pub over the road if he's not in the hall,' Dr Willoughby told him, and the young man raced across and into the Greyhound.

Fortunately, there was a fire exit at the other end of the hall, which someone had sensibly opened, and people were now pouring out – some annoyed, some upset, but all of them wanting to get back to the fun at the earliest possible opportunity.

Joanna scanned the milling crowd for the twins and Jean and after a few moments saw all three of them. They hurried towards her.

'I've never seen the like, my lady, them buggers in brown barged in without a by-your-leave and then the RAF took exception and now they're smashing up the place,' Liza said, forgetting her diction and her manners in her excitement.

'I think someone has gone to fetch the village policeman – not that I think he'll be able to do anything. He's past his prime and is so fat I'm surprised his bicycle doesn't collapse under his weight,' Jean said.

Joe nodded. Neither of them seemed particularly worried by the fracas continuing to grow in volume in the hall. 'It's you they're going to need, Doc, so I hope you've got your bag handy.'

* * *

Di was left to juggle the two still-full glasses as Freddie followed the young airman out of the garden at the double. She was halfway across the road when it occurred to her that she might be accused of stealing the glasses – once they were empty, she'd make sure she took them back, with an apology.

The thuds and shouts coming from the hall echoed down the street. It hardly seemed fair for Freddie and Ted to sort this out. What they needed were the MPs – the military police – to take care of the soldiers and the RAFP to be called to deal with the airmen.

There was a red telephone box a hundred yards from the village hall. Di shoved the brimming glasses into the hands of the nearest villagers and then ran to it. She heaved open the door and snatched up the receiver. She had her pennies ready and knew the number for the base by heart.

Gill Andrews was on duty in the office and Di quickly explained the circumstances. 'Get our boys mobilised immediately and get in touch with whoever's in charge of the artillery surrounding the base.'

'What a turnup for the books – you don't expect a punch-up when you go out for the evening. At least, not down here you don't,' Gill said cheerfully.

When Di pressed button B, a penny dropped down into the little metal cup so she'd obviously not used up all the money she'd inserted at the beginning of the conversation. She dashed back to the village hall, praying that nobody involved in the fight would be seriously hurt, especially Freddie and Ted.

There were no airmen outside with the villagers, but Millie was standing to one side with the WAAFs who'd come to Stodham hoping for a nice night out. She was pretty sure that at least five of the girls were walking out with airmen, which was only to be expected when they were living on the same base.

'Millie, what's going on inside? I sent for the MPs and RAFPs and they should be here pretty rapidly.'

'The brown jobs came in looking for trouble. The ladies on the door refused them entry but they just charged in and started throwing their weight about. Naturally, our boys objected, and the brawl was inevitable.'

'It sounds as though they're smashing up the furniture.'

'I think it's more that they're falling into it. When I ushered our girls out, there were a few black eyes, cut lips, but nothing more serious.'

'That's a relief. Did I do the right thing calling for reinforcements? I should really have asked you, as you're more senior than I am.'

'No, Di, I was about to do the same. Let's hope they get here soon so the miscreants can be arrested, the mess cleared up and the event can continue.' Millie was flinching every time there was a bang or a crash in the hall. The language was appalling, but no worse than they'd heard before.

Every so often, there was a sickening thump, groans and cries of pain. Whatever Millie said, someone was getting hurt in there.

'Is that Dr Willoughby going in with his medical bag?' Di asked.

'It is. I think we'd better go in search of a first-aid kit and offer our services too. We've both got a basic first-aid certificate, haven't we?'

They were about to head for the doors when there was the screech of brakes and two cars pulled up. The doors opened and five RAF policeman leapt out of each vehicle. There was no need for them to ask where the fight was – they could hear it for themselves.

Within moments of them going in, the noise abated and when the MPs arrived in an equal hurry, it was more or less over.

The partygoers had been milling about outside, but now the excitement was over, a number of both men and women sloped off to the pub. Di then remembered she'd got two glasses to find and return.

'They haven't sent a lorry for any of the men they arrested, so I suppose they'll have to march them back. I hope nobody was seriously injured and that the hall can be sorted out, but somehow I doubt it,' Millie said.

'I don't suppose Freddie or Ted will be able to join us for a while, so I'm going in search of the glasses I stole from over the road. I don't suppose you've seen them?'

'There are two on the bench under the window – they could be the ones you're looking for.'

'Jolly good, I'll return them before they get broken. If Freddie's looking for me, tell him I'll be back in a minute.' She smiled at her friend. 'We're now officially going out together. He kissed me, and I must say it was rather nice.'

Millie hugged her. 'I'm so glad that you've decided to give it a go. Ted and I think you're perfect for each other. Mind you, I don't recommend rushing into things the way we did, as it's created all sorts of problems.'

'We'll talk tonight.' What was Millie referring to? Surely she wasn't regretting her marriage so soon? Di shook her head – no, they were both so happy. It must be something else. She dashed across and grabbed the glasses, amused to find they were both empty. She wasn't sure she would have finished somebody else's drink – but there was a war on, and *waste not, want not* was on posters all over the place.

She peered through the open window and was both shocked and relieved by what she saw. There didn't seem to be a chair or trestle table left standing but there were no RAF men or soldiers unconscious on the floor. Obviously, the social would have to be abandoned.

The doctor was busy patching up one or two of the men and Ted and Freddie were talking to the RAFP, no doubt explaining how the fight had started. The airmen involved, apart from looking a bit dishevelled and in some cases bruised and battered, were chatting nonchalantly at one end of the room.

However, all eight soldiers were obviously under arrest, and they were slumped on the floor, looking dejected. Di hoped they wouldn't be severely punished, but army discipline was a lot tighter than that of the RAF.

The noise from the public bar indicated it was now full but there weren't many in the saloon and she was able to put the glasses on the nearest table and slip out without being seen. The landlady would be happy about how things turned out, so it wasn't all bad news.

Word had spread through the waiting revellers that the event was now cancelled and they began drifting away. Those with children were presumably going home, but the others were heading for one of the three public houses in the village.

Millie was waiting for her. 'I'm going to walk back with the girls, so will you wait and drive Ted and Freddie when they're ready to go?'

'Let me walk the girls home, you should spend every available minute with your husband.'

'Thank you, but it's my duty to lead from the front – literally, in this case. You'll be doing your bit by driving the officers home.'

* * *

Freddie made sure that none of his men would be put on a charge for what had happened. Ted had made it very clear they were only protecting the other guests from the rampaging, drunken brown jobs.

'Bloody nuisance, having our evening ruined like this. I was enjoying a quiet drink with Di when this kicked off.'

Ted was looking out of the window and scowled. 'Millie's taking the girls back on foot. I assume Di's going to drive us to the base. Look, can I leave you to finish off here and then I can at least walk with my wife, even if I can't do anything else tonight?'

'Go, old bean, there's not much more to do here and as senior officer, it's my job to do it.'

A further tedious twenty minutes later, the soldiers had been marched away in disgrace.

'There's no need for you to hang about,' Freddie told the NCO in charge of the RAFP, and the young man saluted and led his men away.

'Right, get on with it you lot,' he ordered the airmen, 'and think yourselves lucky you're not on a charge. I'll be back in a minute.' His men had to do what they could to repair the hall as their punishment.

He met the two ladies who'd been taking the coins at the door earlier tonight hovering anxiously outside. 'I apologise for the part my men had in ruining your social. It looks worse than it is, but they're in there putting things right now.'

'Thank you, Squadron Leader, it wasn't your boys' fault. My Bill's a carpenter and has gone to fetch his tool bag so he can fix anything that's repairable. His eyesight's not A1 so they don't want him in any of the services.'

'That's good, ma'am, with an expert on hand, we should get things tickety-boo in no time. Excuse me for a moment, I just need to speak to my girlfriend.' Just saying these words made Freddie happy.

He didn't have to look far for her, as Di was on her way in. 'I could see our boys busy tidying up and Ted just dashed off after Millie and the girls. As you've obviously got to stay here, I thought I could help. There will be cups and saucers and so on to collect and wash up.'

'The sooner we get things sorted, the sooner we can go. Your help will be appreciated.'

In less than an hour, the hall was as it should be. 'Right, men, you're dismissed. March straight back to the base – no detours to the pub. Is that clear?'

There was a chorus of agreement, a sprinkling of salutes and the men set off cheerfully. The ladies thanked Freddie for putting things right, he smiled and nodded at them, and went in search of Di, who'd finished in the kitchen some time ago.

'There you are, Freddie, I was going to suggest that we return to the pub but it's far too busy now. We might as well go back to Manston and see if they've finally opened the NAAFI.'

'I'm sorry it took so long. Not a good idea to leave the locals unhappy with our chaps. I was thinking that maybe the fish and chip shop might still be open.'

'Fish and chips? Now that's exactly what I'd like. I've had supper from there once before and it was delicious. I suppose being so near the coast, the fish is always fresh and there are certainly plenty of potatoes growing around here.'

'No point in taking the car, it's impossible to park outside as the street's so narrow. We'll walk there and then we can sit on a bench and eat.'

One of the ladies was just about to lock the hall door and overheard the conversation. 'Here, I'll give you the key, Squadron

Leader, then you can make yourself a cuppa. Least I can do after all the help you've given us putting things straight.'

'That's so kind of you,' Di said. 'Where do we take it when we've finished?'

'I live in one of the cottages just before you turn into the lane that leads to Manston. Bluebell Cottage – it's got a blue door and the name's ever so clear. No need to hurry, you bring it whenever you want. Put it through the letterbox – you don't need to knock.'

'Why don't you get the fish and chips and I'll make the tea and get some plates ready?' Di said. 'Unless you'd prefer to eat it out of the paper with your fingers?'

'No, let's be civilised this evening. I won't be long. What do you want?'

'Cod and chips, but whatever fish they've got will be fine. I like lots of salt and vinegar.'

As Freddie approached the fish and chip shop, the welcome aroma of hot fat drifted towards them. He pushed his way through into the steamy interior and was pleased there were only two others waiting. One of them was an elderly gent with a flat cap and gaiters who nodded. 'Just in time, young man, Sid's closing any minute.'

Sid, presumably the man in the apron behind the counter, grinned and waved his scoop. 'What can I do you for? I've got plenty of chips but only rock left.'

'Two portions of double chips and rock will be splendid. Thank you. We've been sorting out the chaos at the hall, which is why we're so late.'

'I heard about that. It weren't your boys' fault, mate, from what I've heard.'

Ten minutes later, Freddie emerged with a hot, vinegary newspaper-wrapped parcel under his arm. Sid immediately locked the door behind him and pulled down the blinds. Freddie walked briskly down the street and turned right into the High Street and then back to the village hall.

It was almost ten o'clock – he had to be at the base by eleven – so they didn't have much time to eat their supper, clear up behind them and drop the key at Bluebell Cottage.

Di had set up a small table in the kitchen with cutlery, plates and two mugs of freshly brewed tea.

'That smells scrumptious, Freddie, I can't tell you how ravenous I am suddenly.'

He unwrapped the newspaper and handed her one of the parcels. 'Double chips but just rock – we were the very last customers and he'd run out of everything else.'

'I absolutely don't care. There's extra salt but I couldn't find any vinegar.'

Having asked for cutlery, they both ignored it and devoured the fish and chips using their fingers and eating it straight from the paper. Freddie had never shared a meal like this with a girl before but it seemed right, comfortable, to be doing so with her. When they'd finished, he collected the debris.

'I'll put this in the dustbin outside the back. If we leave the paper in here, the kitchen will reek of stale fat and vinegar.'

Di smiled. 'I wasn't always so domestic but being a WAAF makes one take an interest in such things.'

'Did you have staff to do everything?' He knew very little about her background.

'Heavens, no, just a cook and a housemaid. Oh, and a gardener, of course.'

'Very grand. We had a daily woman, a weekly gardener, but no live-in staff.'

'You have an orderly to take care of you now. I prefer things how they are. What about you?'

Freddie felt a wave of affection for this intelligent and lovely girl. If someone had told him talking about housework with a girl would be so enjoyable, he would have laughed.

By the time he returned, the kitchen was immaculate and Di was waiting with the key in her hand. He knew exactly the cottage they needed as he'd noticed the bright blue door – all the other cottages had a dark colour.

They were waved through the gate to the base without their identity cards being checked – hardly surprising, as they were both well known to the guards. He wished the evening could go on for longer, that they could spend more time together.

'I'm sorry things turned out like this, Di, hopefully next time we go out there'll be less drama and time to chat and get to know each other.'

'I look forward to that. Shall I drop you at the mess?'

'Yes, that'll be splendid.'

When they were stationary, he swivelled in his seat and leaned in – she did the same and this time he prolonged the kiss. He hoped she'd enjoyed it as much as he had.

'Good night, sweetheart, I'll see you sometime tomorrow, I expect.' He jumped out of the car and watched her drive away. Was this the right time to be falling in love? He could go for a Burton and leave her broken-hearted if they got too involved.

Despite his misgiving, he went to his room a happy man.

5

Joanna was rather relieved to be returning to the safety of Goodwill House somewhat earlier than planned.

'I'm sorry the two of you have missed out tonight,' she said to the twins once they'd safely arrived home. She'd thought it best not to talk to Joe whilst he was driving, as he was so inexperienced.

'That's all right, my lady,' Joe replied.

'I think it's high time you stopped addressing me by my title. You call Miss Baxter "Auntie Jean", so I thought you might like to call me "Aunt Joanna". I suggest you continue to call my mother-in-law "my lady".'

'Blimey,' Liza said with a grin as they made their way from the barn, where the Bentley had been parked, to the back door. 'We'd not dare call her anything else. Ta ever so. Aunt Joanna's perfect, ain't it... isn't it, Joe?'

'It certainly is. And don't worry about us missing out, seeing those soldiers sorted out by our boys was the best entertainment yet.'

'Joe, I'd not taken you for a young man who would enjoy any sort of aggression.' This was said with a smile, so he knew it wasn't a real criticism. 'I was thinking that maybe you two might like to go to the cinema once a week. I believe there's an afternoon matinee in Ramsgate you could attend.'

'The pictures? I've never been but I'd like to. I don't care what it is, it'll be like magic, won't it, Joe? We can catch the bus easy enough.'

'Auntie Jean, you'll come with us, won't you? We could have a bite to eat after too,' Joe said.

'I'd be delighted to accompany you both,' Jean said. 'I've not been for years, and when I last went it was silent films. It will be exciting to hear the film stars actually speak.'

Elizabeth would be eager to know why they'd returned early, so Joanna headed for the drawing room and was almost knocked from her feet by the enthusiastic welcome of her dog, Lazzy.

'Get down, silly boy, you're far too big to rush around the house like that.'

'Goodness me, I didn't expect you back for another couple of hours, my dear. Tell me what happened to bring you home so soon.'

The French doors were wide open, letting in the warm evening air. 'I'm afraid our jaunt to the village wasn't a great success, but I'll tell you all about it later. Liza and Joe are now going to call me Aunt Joanna, which is far more exciting.'

'As long as they don't call me Great-Aunt Elizabeth – I'm not yet comfortable with the informality.'

Liza appeared at the door. 'I've put the kettle on – do you want tea or coffee? Joe's making sandwiches as we're a bit peckish after all that excitement.'

'Coffee will be splendid. I'm going to miss it when the last tin's finished,' Joanna said as she sat down. The telephone rang loudly in the hall and with a sigh, she got to her feet and went to answer it. 'Goodwill House, Lady Harcourt speaking.'

'My lady, it's Dr Willoughby. I'm sorry to call you so late, but I thought you'd want to know your housekeeper, Mrs Smith, has contracted the measles. She's rather poorly and obviously won't be at work for a while.'

'That's awful news. I would have thought that she'd had it when she was a child but obviously not. I believe that measles in an adult can be very serious.'

'That's true, my lady, but I'll do everything I can to see her through this illness safely. Please don't visit, as it's very infectious.'

'I won't and I'll not let the twins come either. I don't think that her husband's even able to boil an egg. If there's someone in the village who would be prepared to go in and take care of her, do the cooking and so on, I'll pay whatever's necessary.'

'Thank you, my lady, I was hoping you might offer to help out financially. I know exactly the person to ask and am certain that she's already had measles so will be safe. I'll be in touch with you tomorrow with the details. Good night, and thank you again.'

She heard the line go dead and put down the receiver. The thought that her dearest friend was so poorly was worrying. Betty was a strong, healthy young woman, surely measles couldn't be that serious?

Thank goodness they didn't have any boarders at the moment. She was sure that they could manage; Liza and Jean could do the cooking and so on, and Joan and Val, from the village, would take care of the housework and laundry.

'Who was that, Joanna?'

She hurried back into the drawing room, having decided not to make too much of the bad news as she didn't want to upset Elizabeth, who wasn't very robust herself. 'Betty's unwell with measles. I've offered to pay for a nurse as Bert won't be any use at all. I still have most of the money from selling David's hunters put by, which is fortunate, don't you think? Let's hope that our new solicitor, Mr Broome, can get the legal matters sorted so we know where we are financially. All the revenue from the farms was going to the bank, so once we have that, we should be in a better place. In fact, I don't know that we need to take in lodgers any more.'

'We must continue to do so, Joanna, this house is far too big for just the five of us. And I rather enjoyed having the girls around.'

'If you're sure, then we'll continue.'

'I can only think of one reason why Lieutenant Colonel Harcourt was in Ramsgate,' Elizabeth said, 'and that was because he was poking his nose in our business. I have a nasty suspicion that his charm is superficial and underneath it, he's not a very pleasant gentleman.'

Her mother-in-law had abruptly changed the subject. She tended to do this and Joanna thought this might be age related.

'I agree absolutely,' Joanna said. 'It did occur to me that if he could somehow persuade the bank to sell the loan to him, and then prevent you from paying it, he would then not only have the title but the estates as well.'

This had been something that had been bothering her, but she'd kept these thoughts to herself. She was head of the household now and it was her duty to protect those in her care.

'Mr Broome assured us that he had the bank's written agreement that my investments would settle the debt. I don't see how they can renege on that.' Elizabeth had obviously been thinking about this for some time too.

'If that objectionable man who came to see us – David's solicitor, Mr Culley – was anything to go by I think they'll do whatever they want if it makes them richer,' Joanna said.

'Are you suggesting that the bank, the solicitors and the accountants could be working together? That they might have been swindling the estate in some way?'

'I wasn't, but now you mention it, I think that's quite possibly what has been happening. David kept up the pretence that we were solvent and I know the bank were always happy to cash his cheques and pay his bills until he left for France last year.'

This was the first time Joanna had voiced her fears and it was good to be able to share her doubts with someone who understood.

'You must ring Mr Broome in the morning, my dear, and ascertain exactly what's going on. Tell him that we saw Harcourt in Ramsgate and see what he says about this.'

Di dropped the car off in its designated place, retrieved her bicycle from where it was hidden behind the hangar that was used by the motor pool, and pedalled slowly across the base, automatically counting the kites that stood ready to be scrambled.

There was the continuous sound of aerial combat in the Channel, the thump thump of the ack ack guns from somewhere around Dover, or perhaps further along at Hastings. Bentley Priory just outside London – from where the bigwigs controlled this sector of the RAF – tried to give each base a few days' respite where possible.

Manston had been in the thick of it during Dunkirk and afterwards – they had lost several pilots and a dozen aircraft – but since then, nobody had failed to return.

Di still wasn't sure that becoming involved with Freddie would be good for either of them, as it might well end in heartbreak. Was this enough to stop something that seemed to make them both so happy?

She justified her growing feelings for him by telling herself that it was her duty to do everything she could to keep a brave young man like him focused on his work. If having her as a girlfriend would help him be a better pilot, then wasn't she helping the war effort? She smiled at her nonsense. She wanted to be his girlfriend because she really liked him, not for any other noble reason.

There were four WAAF drivers working at the MT – Millie and herself, plus the new girls who'd arrived when the previous two had been arrested for working as prostitutes on the base. No one was on duty tonight, but she expected that would change when the balloon went up.

The huddle of huts and brick-built buildings erected for the WAAF was situated as far away from the accommodation for the men as was physically possible. This meant that without a bicycle, or the use of one of the cars or lorries from the MT pool, they'd have to walk miles to get anywhere.

It was an easier ride along the runway but a much longer one so, like the others usually did, she chose to go across the grass and travel diagonally to her housing. This wasn't something to do when it was dark but was perfectly safe at dusk.

She almost flew over the handlebars when the front wheel dropped into a pothole, but she just managed to stay upright. Her near disaster had been witnessed by two of the girls, who greeted her with laughter.

'Enjoy your trip, Di? You almost came a cropper,' one of them said she as she puffed on her cigarette.

'You two should be in bed, not out here smoking in your nighties.'

'Smoking ain't allowed inside so we've got no option. Anyway, we needed the bog so had to come out.'

There were two Nissen huts and each had room for thirty girls, but so far there were only a dozen on base. Millie had said the full contingent would be arriving at the end of the month. Hopefully, the ablutions block would be finished by then, as at the moment only half of it was functioning.

It wasn't too bad trekking across the bitumen in the summer, but it was going to be absolutely beastly in the winter.

Millie met her as she was going in, her wash bag in one hand

and her towel over her shoulder. 'You're the last, Di, so we can all get some shut eye now. I've told the others lights out in half an hour.' She sniffed appreciatively. 'I can smell chips – you lucky thing – we had to make do with spam and piccalilli sandwiches.'

'Poor you. I'll join you in the ablutions. I've just got to grab my wash bag and towel.'

Di dashed in through the vestibule, in which there were thirty pegs upon which the girls hung their tin hats, haversacks and groundsheets-cum-raincoats every night. There was a potbellied metal stove against the far wall, which hopefully would keep the clothing from freezing solid in the winter.

Millie, as a corporal, had her own private space. It had exactly the same metal bedstead and locker as the rest of them, but there were flimsy walls around it to give her some privacy. Di had the adjacent bed and was looking forward to the time when she too would be an NCO and be able to occupy the other private space opposite the one Millie had. This was vacant at the moment, like the majority of the beds.

She snatched up what she needed and ran across to join her friend. Their voices echoed in the chilly, empty block.

'I don't know how you can bear to say goodnight to Ted when you should be sleeping beside him every night.'

Millie had been cleaning her teeth; she rinsed her mouth, dried her toothbrush and replaced it carefully in her wash bag before answering.

'Actually, I have a nasty suspicion that might all be going to change very soon. I'm as regular as clockwork and am now two weeks late.'

'Golly, you think you might be pregnant? You'll have to leave. You were determined to be an officer and now you're just going to be a housewife and mother.' This news would be devasting for

Millie and Ted, as the last thing anyone would want right now was to have baby in the middle of a war.

'Thanks for reminding me what I'm giving up. But Ted and I have already talked about it and he's looking for somewhere we can rent. There's an empty cottage in the row right outside the base and we're hoping to get that. I'll join the WVS, the WI...'

'I think pregnant women are going to be evacuated,' said Di. 'If it wasn't for the outbreak of measles, the school, teachers and children would already have gone. I think they're going somewhere in Norfolk but I'm not exactly sure.'

'I hadn't thought of that. It's up to me if I go and if Ted's risking his life every day, then the least I can do is stay where I am. Then he can see me if he gets an hour or so free.'

'This time next year, you might be a mother.'

'I might be a widow too. But at least if anything happens to Ted then I'll have something – someone – to remember him by. A son or daughter will be a small compensation.'

'This is a depressing conversation. Not every single pilot will die. Why shouldn't he and Freddie be two of the lucky ones?'

Freddie could be one of those who died, and this wasn't a happy thought. Di was conflicted by this news. How would she feel in Millie's shoes? War was changing her views on everything and maybe her determination to concentrate on becoming a career officer wasn't quite so important now.

* * *

Freddie had his own room now he was a senior officer and rather missed the comradeship of sharing. Ted, as a flying officer, only one up from the lowest officer rank, was billeted in a different part of the building.

'I say, Freddie, have you heard the latest?' The speaker was

Flight Lieutenant Johnny Robinson, known as Robbie. He was not in Freddie's squadron as he flew a Hurry.

'Until I know what the news is, I've no idea if I've heard it.'

'Oh, very droll. Win Co has said we can have a bit of a party – the NCOs and other ranks are going to hold one too – Monday night. Officers' Mess for us. We can invite a lady friend – do you have one?'

'I do, as it happens. I take it these events are for RAF personnel only?'

'Roger that, Freddie. Manston has been removed from operational duty for two days to allow things to be put in tip-top condition. Too many bullet holes in many of the kites, don't you know.'

'And to give us a breather, obviously. Thanks for the gen, Robbie. Are the married chaps going to get a twenty-four-hour pass?'

'Haven't the foggiest, but it makes sense. Ted Thorrington will be a happy man tonight.'

Freddie made his way to the junior officers' accommodation and was in luck – Ted was just coming in from the door that led to the mess.

'Have you heard? Only one squadron of Blenheims and one of Hurries are remaining on duty and the rest of us are being stood down until dawn on Tuesday.'

'That's bloody good news. I've just heard Millie and I have got that cottage and it's reasonably well furnished too. With luck, I can get the key first thing and we'll have time to get settled before it all kicks off.'

'I'm happy for you and Millie,' Freddie said. 'Having your own place will make things a bit easier for you. The other thing, old bean, is that there's going to be a party of sorts on Monday night. I'll be bringing Di and I expect Millie will want to come along if only for a couple of hours. Especially as tonight was a shambles.'

Freddie said goodnight to his friend and returned to his own billet, where his orderly had put out a clean shirt and collar, underwear and socks ready for the morning.

He was vaguely uncomfortable at being waited on, even knowing it was his right as a senior officer. He was awash with tea so didn't wander down to the small kitchen at the end of the corridor to make himself a brew.

Freddie opened the window in his bedroom wide and leaned on the sill, listening. It was eerily quiet, not even the sound of voices drifting across the runway from the hangars on the far side.

Then his ears tuned into more distant sounds. There were dogfights going on in the Channel, the guns from both sides were firing. He couldn't see the searchlights that would be criss-crossing the sky from where he was.

Noise carried further in the darkness. He thought the convoy the RAF were protecting must be well past Dover or he'd hear the guns and the kites more clearly. He wasn't going to think about what might happen in the near future, as by some miracle, he and his men had just been given more than two days on the ground. He was going to make the most of it.

He could get to know Di better and hopefully convince her that they could make a go of it.

* * *

The next morning, there was a different atmosphere on the base – everyone Freddie passed was smiling. There were no buses on a Sunday but he was quite certain that tomorrow the nine-thirty to Stodham and Ramsgate would be packed with those airmen who were lucky enough to be off duty making the most of their free time.

He was hailed by Di, riding furiously towards him. 'I was

thinking we could go to the local church for matins. I'm just going to get a pass so I can leave the base for the morning.'

'That sounds like a good idea. Listening to our padre droning on every Sunday is something I'm happy to avoid.'

He could hardly embrace her, but he hoped his smile was enough to tell her how pleased he was to see her. An NCO, sitting behind a desk in an office, had been given a pile of slips already signed by the adjutant and was just adding the name of the applicant, stamping it, and handing them over to whoever asked.

Ten minutes later, after Di had hidden her bicycle – some blighter would take it if she left it visible – they were walking out of the base and heading for the village.

'I'm not a regular churchgoer, Di, I just pay lip service as many of us do. That said, I heard there's a new vicar taken over recently and the chaps that have attended the church were impressed.'

'Millie and I went to the memorial service for Lord Harcourt and the other four men who lost their lives at Dunkirk. The service was excellent and his sermon commendably brief.'

They walked briskly but still were able to chat. The more time he spent in her company, the happier he was. They arrived at the church in just over half an hour, joining a steady stream of villagers in their Sunday best heading in the same direction. The two Lady Harcourts and their household were already seated in their privileged position at the front of the church.

'There's room over there, under the window, Freddie.' Di led the way and he followed.

The book of common prayer and the hymn book were on the narrow shelf in front of the pew. Di immediately knelt and bowed her head. Everyone was doing the same, so Freddie had no option but to copy their actions. Like many of his fellow flyers, he attended church parade because it was obligatory, as it was hard to believe in the Almighty when there was so much misery, death and destruction surrounding them.

Whilst he was on his knees, he thought it wouldn't hurt to send up a quick prayer in case there was someone listening.

'God, I don't know how long it'll be before I have the honour to join you in your celestial home, but I want to thank you for bringing this lovely girl into my life. Amen.'

6

Joanna was somewhat reassured by the solicitors saying that the document between the bank and Elizabeth was legal and had been ratified in every way it should have been. This didn't stop her worrying about how things might change if what she suspected was the truth – that the new Lord Harcourt was plotting against them.

She was surprised, but pleased, to see Di and her charming officer friend in church that morning. The sermon had been short and excellent. The new vicar, Mr Evans, was a welcome addition to Stodham.

Miss Forsyth wasn't as lovely as her friend, Millie, but could still be counted attractive. With her dark hair swept up in a fashionable roll around her face, her beautiful blue eyes complemented by the colour of her uniform, she was certainly attracting attention. She was taller than most girls and although not slender, she certainly wasn't overweight.

Squadron Leader Hanover was only half a head taller than her but had broad shoulders, a commendably straight back and pleasant if not striking features. When he smiled, it was a different matter altogether, as even someone as ancient as herself found him almost irresistible.

Joanna smiled to herself, knowing that a recently widowed woman should not be thinking such things.

'Joanna, I've spoken to you twice and you've not answered. Whatever are you daydreaming about this time?' Elizabeth, who was holding her arm, gave it a sharp tug.

'I beg your pardon; I was just thinking that Di and her young man make an attractive couple. I think it might be the uniform, as those in khaki don't seem nearly as good-looking.'

'Blue is certainly a better colour. I think the RAF far too relaxed in their attitude to discipline. One can be quite sure none of the nonsense that has taken place on that base would ever have taken place in an army camp.' This rambling comment, which had little to do with the subject, was a worrying and more frequent occurrence. She would speak to Dr Willoughby about it next time she bumped into him. Also Elizabeth had apparently already forgotten about the chaos the soldiers, and not the airmen, caused in the village yesterday.

The twins rushed over to speak to Di and her young man and Jean followed them. Joanna escorted her mother-in-law to join them.

'Freddie says he'll put in a good word for me when I'm old enough to join the RAF. I might not have the education to be a pilot but I can be a gunner in a bomber,' Joe said excitedly.

Joanna spoke without thinking. 'Joe, please don't talk about something that might never happen. You and Liza will be fifteen in September so you couldn't join up even if you wanted to until 1943. The war will be over by then.'

Elizabeth snorted inelegantly. 'It might well be, my dear, but let's pray it's not the Germans that win, as then we'll be overrun with Nazis in jackboots.'

'The Americans wouldn't stand by and let us be invaded—'

'Would they not? From what I've heard, the barges that Hitler will use to bring the tanks here are being made ready as we speak, and I don't see any sign of the Americans arriving, do you, Joanna?'

This was a highly unsuitable conversation to be having, as it was tantamount to treason to talk about the possibility of Great Britain losing the war, however badly things might be going.

Joe dashed off to un-hitch Starlight, the grey mare that had once been Joanna's daughter's horse, but who now pulled the trap in which Elizabeth travelled when going to church.

Once her mother-in-law was safely settled next to Joe in the trap, Joanna looked around for Liza. Jean beckoned her over.

'I told her she could go into the village with her new friends for a while. I hope that was all right, my lady.'

'Of course, I want them both to have friends their own age, as long as they're suitable. I'll get Joe to return to the village and fetch her later.'

It was pleasant strolling back to Goodwill House. The roads were empty because there wasn't much petrol to be had. Rationing for this had come in at the start of the war, and even though there were coupons available to buy sufficient gallons to travel two hundred miles in a month, there wasn't any to be had for ordinary civilians.

Naturally, doctors, delivery drivers, public transport and so on had no difficulty obtaining fuel, but for everybody else, it was almost impossible to get. Joanna wondered if she should give away the dozens of metal cans filled with petrol that were stored in an outhouse behind the barn. David had commandeered the contents from somewhere before he'd dashed off to France to die.

'I've not heard any planes go past today. If you listen carefully, then you can hear the sound of gunfire and possibly dogfights somewhere miles away, but Manston has been quiet,' Joanna said.

'Di told us that the base is non-operational until Tuesday morning. I think they're preparing for something big,' Jean replied.

'I do hope not, but I expect you're right. We mustn't actually go in, but I'm going to call by and see how Betty's doing. Measles is even more dangerous for adults than for children. I'm really worried about her.'

'Val told me that half the children in the village have got it. They've been put in quarantine and the rest of the school and the teachers will be leaving for Norfolk at the end of the week. Those who are unwell will join them later.'

'I wish they'd gone several weeks ago,' Joanna said. 'I suggested it to the mothers several times at the WVS meetings but a lot of them were reluctant. The village will seem strange without children running about and playing ball in the street.'

Jean looked sceptical. Joanna realised that she'd spoken as if she was a villager when, in fact, she couldn't remember the last time she'd seen any children playing anywhere as she rarely went into the village nowadays.

Years ago, she'd been an ordinary village girl, educated at the local grammar school, with no aspirations apart from finding herself a husband. It was hardly surprising that when David Harcourt had pounced on her, she hadn't hesitated. What young girl twenty years ago turned down the chance of marrying an actual lord living in a stately home?

* * *

Di spent the remainder of the day with Freddie and despite her initial reservations about getting too involved, she knew it was probably too late. He stirred something inside her, something she didn't know she had, something she'd watched Millie experience without envy. At the time, she'd been relieved she wasn't emotionally entangled with a young man, but having someone of her own, someone who would put her first, far outweighed being single.

They were sitting on the grass in the sun, along with a dozen or more officers, outside the mess.

'I don't think any of your girls, apart from you and Millie, will be coming to the do at the Officers' Mess tomorrow night,' said Freddie. 'However, I'm pretty sure a couple of them will be attending the dance at the Sergeants' Mess – I expect those left over will get an invite to the one for other ranks. Is that going to be a problem, do you think?'

'What you mean? Are you suggesting that those not invited by a sergeant, NCO or an officer will be annoyed?'

'I was just thinking about what happened at the last dance. The men involved with that unpleasant business were sent elsewhere, as were the girls, but... but... what I'm asking is: do you think there are any others in your group who might be tempted to throw their caps over the windmill after having a few sweet sherries or gin and its?'

'Fair question,' said Di. 'I'm glad I can say with absolute certainty none of the girls are like that. Don't worry, it's all ticketyboo.'

'It won't be dark for a couple of hours so shall we walk down to the cottage that Millie and Ted have rented and see how they've settled in?'

'That would be spiffing but we can't go without a housewarming gift.'

'Wait there, I'll go in and see if I can buy a bottle of something.'

'You do that, and I'll go to the NAAFI and see if I can get some buns, cakes or sandwiches.'

As it was nearing closing time, the girls behind the counter were delighted to sell her a miscellany of cakes, sausage rolls and buns that otherwise would be past their best by the morning. Nothing was wasted, so by buying these items, Di was doing tomorrow's customers a favour.

Clutching her greaseproof paper bag of treats, she dashed back to find Freddie equally happy with his purchase.

'I've got a bottle of sherry – it's not the sweet stuff, which is what the ladies seem to prefer – and the chap behind the bar was happy to sell it to me.'

With her goodies under her right arm and her left hand in his, they walked to the cottage. Somehow this felt right, not forced or strange. Millie was at the open window and saw them coming down the path.

'The door's open, just come in. I'm so glad to see you. It'll seem like a real home after we've had visitors.'

Di realised she'd not said anything to Freddie about the likelihood of Millie being pregnant, but then it wasn't anything to do with him, really. Whether Ted was an expectant father or not would make no difference to his performance in the sky – in fact, it would perhaps make him keener to stay safe and not take any risks whilst doing his best to shoot down any German kites that he saw.

Millie had her glorious copper-coloured hair tied up in a turban and was wearing her work overalls. There was no sign of Ted, but she could hear him banging about somewhere upstairs.

'What do you think?' Millie asked. Even if Di had thought it a miserable, pokey little place, she wouldn't have said so.

'I love it. It's so much bigger than it looks from the outside – I can't believe it's so well furnished. Who was living here before you?'

Ted yelled from upstairs. 'Freddie, is that you? Come and give us a hand for a minute, will you?'

Freddie gave the bottle of sherry to Di and then vanished upstairs. She heard him swear and smiled. He'd obviously forgotten to duck as he went through a door.

'Golly, if Freddie's tried to knock himself out and he's several inches shorter than Ted, your husband's going to have to be careful he doesn't brain himself.'

'The doors are perfect for me, but you'll have to duck too,' Millie said. 'This is the only time I've been happy to be short. Are those things you're clutching for us?'

'Sorry, I should have given them to you straight away. A bag of assorted cakes and a bottle of sherry.'

'Just what the doctor ordered. We've not eaten all day. We managed to get tea and milk but because the shops are shut, we can't get anything else until tomorrow.'

'Then let's put the kettle on. You can show me the rest of the cottage whilst it's boiling.'

Millie laughed. 'There's not much else to show you apart from the kitchen and scullery. The landlord said we're lucky that we've got electricity and running water – it seems all these cottages have because of Manston.'

'What about the loo? Indoor or outdoor?'

'Half and half – just off the scullery, but you don't have to actually go outside. No bathroom, but we have a galvanised tin bath we can put in front of the range in the kitchen.'

'Ted can use the ablutions on the base and so can you for the moment. I take it you're still late?'

'I am, and although I haven't actually been sick, I've felt nauseous first thing. Please don't say anything to Freddie – if he knows then he'll have to tell the adjutant and I'll have to resign. I'm intending to keep working until I begin to show.'

'I don't think that's wise, old girl. It's not just you you've got to think about now. The base could be bombed at any moment and I'm sure Ted won't want you in any danger.'

'I'll make a decision when I'm absolutely certain that I am pregnant. If I miss my next monthly, I promise I'll resign.'

'Fair enough. I can hear the kettle whistling. Shall I make the tea?' What would she do in Millie's position? Probably the same thing, and she would support her best friend with whatever decision she made.

The back door was open, letting in the summer sun, and Di saw a table and bench in the pretty cottage garden.

'Why don't we take it outside? Freddie and I will be quite happy to sit on the grass.'

'No need to do that. We can take out a couple of these chairs – you make the tea and put out the food and I'll fetch the men.'

There was more than enough for the four of them and most of it was not even stale. They had a second pot of tea, but the sherry remained unopened.

'It's getting dark, Di, we'd better get back to the base.'

'Come for lunch tomorrow,' Millie said. 'I'm going into the village on my trusty bicycle to shop.'

'I doubt that you'll get very much without a ration book,' Di said gloomily.

'It's market day and there's no rationing on the stalls. I'm hoping I'll be able to get the basics anyway.'

'Thank you so much for feeding us tonight,' Ted said with his trademark charming smile.

'I'll have a chat with the chef in the mess, old boy, see what I can get to swell the coffers. Which reminds me, you need to speak to the adjutant and tell him that you're both living off base and then you'll get your ration books returned,' Freddie said.

'We'll do that tomorrow. We'll walk back with you after lunch and make everything official.' Millie nodded at her and Di thought she understood the message. Her friend had discussed things with Ted and decided to tell the powers that be that she thought she might be in an interesting condition.

Freddie put his arm round her and she rather enjoyed the weight across her shoulders. They strolled along the lane, and she could hear voices and see shapes in the gloom ahead of them. They weren't the only ones hurrying to be in before curfew.

'I really enjoyed today, Freddie, and almost envy Ted and Millie in their little cottage.'

'Good god, I don't think we're ready for that sort of commitment just yet, do you?'

She was shocked by his vehemence, as up until that point, she'd believed he was halfway to falling in love with her.

She shrugged off his arm and moved away. 'I see. I thought we were starting a serious relationship. I'm not interested in anything casual, so it's better that this stops now.'

'I'm sorry, I didn't mean to upset you. Ted told me something tonight.'

'Millie told me. Is that why you're so against us getting closer?'

'It is. I don't want to get married, to bring children into this world, when we could be under Nazi rule in a few months if things go badly.'

He closed the distance between them but made no move to touch her. He was leaving it to her. She hadn't meant to put her arms around his neck, but somehow they were there.

'I understand and agree absolutely. That doesn't mean we can't continue to go out with each other, but we just won't even discuss the future until things are more settled.'

This time his kiss was different, demanding initially and then tender and loving. She was sorry when eventually they drew apart.

Freddie smoothed back her ruffled hair and kissed her again – a mere touch of his lips on hers but it still sent tingles of excitement racing around her already overheated body.

'I think I'm falling in love with you, sweetheart, and think you might feel the same way, too, but we've got to put our feelings aside until this bloody war's over. There's nothing I'd like better than to marry you, have the right to share your bed, but that's not going to happen until things improve on the home front.'

Di tilted her head and stared at him. His features were indistinct, but she rather thought they were imprinted on her memory now. Had her feelings really changed so suddenly or was it the shock of Millie's unexpected pregnancy? She was silent for a minute, thinking how to respond.

'If that was a very unromantic and roundabout way of proposing, Squadron Leader Hanover, then my answer will almost certainly be yes. I will marry you when the time's right, but I won't sleep with you because the risk of having a baby is too high.'

His deep baritone laugh boomed across the base and she was certain anyone within a hundred yards would have heard him. 'I rather think that we've just got unofficially engaged, my love. We've only been out together a couple of times, so how did that happen? I thought we were the sensible duo, not like Ted and Millie.'

* * *

Freddie was laughing, not taking it seriously, but he had this horrible feeling that maybe she was. How the hell did that happen? Di was a lovely girl. He was in love with her – at least he thought he was – but was now really the time to be talking about marriage?

He'd better put her straight, as the last thing he wanted was to cause her upset and embarrassment in the future.

'Di, I meant it when I said now was not the time for a serious relationship for either of us. I do want to marry you, but not until the end of the war, and I certainly don't want you to feel tied down by a so-called unofficial engagement.'

Her laugh was genuine and the weight on his chest lifted. 'I know that, I'm not a complete ninny. I do want to go out with you, as I enjoy your company, but you're quite right to say that there's no point in getting serious. Isn't your squadron likely to be posted somewhere else in the country?'

'I heard the other day that Manston's now our home – at least for the moment. God knows what will happen later on.'

'That explains why Ted has moved off base. I did wonder, as Millie told me they couldn't do that because his squadron was only here temporarily.'

'They're both so young to be married and expecting a baby as well. I think Ted told me he's not quite twenty.'

'As we are on the subject of age, Freddie, I'm twenty – how old are you?'

'I'm twenty-four and will be twenty-five in December. I've been in the RAF for six years already, which makes me one of the most experienced pilots and it also explains why I've been promoted so rapidly.'

It was now quite dark and Di still had to make her way to the far side of the base. He was about to offer to escort her when she anticipated his suggestion.

'My cycle's hidden in the bushes behind the officers' accommodation. I'll be back at my billet in no time as I can cycle across the runway without fear of being squashed by anything.'

He walked her around to collect her wheels; before she mounted, he pulled her into his arms and kissed her with more passion than he'd intended.

'Golly, that was rather exciting. I finally understand why girls sometimes do things they shouldn't. Good night, Freddie, no doubt I'll see you at the dance tomorrow, if not before.'

Then she was pedalling furiously into the night without a backward glance. They weren't actually engaged, she hadn't been upset when he'd made it clear it had been a joke. He wasn't quite sure if he was relieved or disappointed by her reaction.

He wasn't a chap given to introspection or deep thought and now wasn't the time to indulge himself in such a pastime. His duty was to his men, his country, and any emotional entanglements must be put firmly to one side.

7

Joanna walked up the path to the cottage in which Betty lived with her husband, Bert, with a sick feeling in her stomach. She should have brought a gift of some sort for the invalid, but it was too late to worry about that. Jean waited at the gate.

She knocked and then stood back, knowing that it would be sensible not to get too close to anybody in the cottage. There was the sound of hurrying footsteps and then the door opened, not fully, but enough for whoever was behind it to speak and be heard.

'My lady, you shouldn't be here. Mr Smith has gone down with the measles too and both he and Mrs Smith are very poorly indeed. I'm living in and taking care of them, as I had the disease when I was a child.'

'I'm so sorry to hear that. It's Edith Jones, isn't it?'

'Yes, it is, my lady. Dr Willoughby has promised he'll let you know how things are going here. There's six kiddies got it but only two of them are bad. The Smiths are the only adults in the village to have it and it's ever so unlucky.'

'It certainly is. If you need anything, anything at all, don't hesitate to ask. Betty is not just my housekeeper, she's also a dear friend.'

'Folk are being very helpful, the larder's full and I've got everything I need, ta very much.'

The door closed, leaving Joanna standing on the doorstep. She blinked back tears. She hadn't cried when her husband had died and yet she was desperately sad about Betty being so ill. Small wonder the vicar had mentioned them by name in his prayers at church this morning.   ·

'I've had measles, my lady, I can visit without danger. I don't think Edith can look after both of them if they're that ill,' Jean said.

'Let me telephone the doctor and ask his opinion. If he agrees that a second nurse would be valuable, then if you're prepared to take on that role, I'd be extremely grateful.'

'Betty and I have become good friends and I'd do anything for her.'

A dreadful thought occurred to Joanna as she hurried home. Had the twins caught the measles when they were little? She hadn't thought to ask and now Liza was gadding about in the village with heaven knows who.

She rushed around to the stable yard, where Joe was unharnessing the mare. 'Joe, have you and your sister had measles?'

He looked up, somewhat startled by her sudden appearance and question. 'I don't actually know. I remember we once both had a high fever, were covered in a red rash and were ill for a week or more. Does that sound like the measles?'

'It does – I thank God for that. When you've finished here, would you mind awfully cycling down to the village and bringing your sister back? I'm not entirely comfortable with her being on her own in the village.'

'I'll be happy to, Aunt Joanna. Liza's a pretty girl and I noticed one or two lads taking more of an interest in her than I'm happy with.'

'In which case, would you be better taking the Bentley? I can't see any of them arguing with a young man driving such a large car.'

'Thank you, but I'll be safer on my bike. If you don't mind, I'd like to get a bit of practice driving it around the park so I know what I'm doing next time. I can't tell you how relieved I was to get us there and back safely the other night.'

'I'm so proud of you and your sister, Joe, and I just pray that this beastly war is over before either of you have to volunteer or get conscripted.'

'I'm going to do my bit, I'm not letting those Nazis march all over my country.'

When he spoke so fiercely, he looked like an adult, not a boy. He would do whatever his conscience prompted him to do, and Joanna knew that her role was just to support him in his decisions.

'On another subject entirely, Joe, we thought that perhaps you and Liza would like to be baptised? Then Elizabeth and I will be your godparents and that will make you really part of the family.'

'I'd like that, but not in front of the congregation, I'd feel a real twerp standing up with everyone watching.'

'Good heavens, it will be a private service. I'll speak to your sister and if she's also happy to proceed, then I'll contact Mr Evans and set things in motion.'

'How's Betty? The house doesn't seem the same without her bustling about.'

Joanna swallowed the lump in her throat. 'I'm going to speak to Dr Willoughby about her now. Jean has offered to assist with the nursing, as Bert has got it as well.'

'I would be happy to help out in the garden if anything needs doing. I know Mr Smith takes a pride in his vegetables. I've learned a lot from old Jimmy and his brother, who look after your grounds.'

'I'm sure Bert will appreciate you going down and keeping things tidy and watered for him.'

Joanna left him to his work and went in, thanking God that he'd sent the twins to her. Joe was right – the house wasn't the same without Betty.

She went straight to the drawing room, intending to talk to Elizabeth, but Jean waylaid her. 'I've spoken to Lady Harcourt and she's happy for me to go. I don't need the doctor's permission.'

'You're quite correct. You have our blessing and our thanks. Betty's an integral part of this household and we all want her to get well as soon as possible.'

'Right then, my lady, I'll pack a few things in a bag and get off immediately.'

'Oh, Joe's going to come down to do whatever's necessary in the garden, so that's one thing the Smiths don't have to worry about.'

'They've got chickens and a pig – if you can spare him, then it would make things easier if he took care of them as well.'

'He can come with you. Can you ride a bicycle?' Jean nodded. 'In which case, you can take mine. It will be easier if you want to come back for anything or go into the village. Joe can come twice a day to do what's necessary.'

Joanna was pleased to see Liza was home without Joe having to fetch her. She was just coming out of the drawing room and had overheard their conversation. 'Liza, I'm so glad you got back on your own.'

'I'll tell him, shall I, Aunt Joanna? I would go too but you need me here to do the cooking and such.'

'Come and join us in the drawing room when you've spoken to him. There's something we need to ask you.'

Whilst she waited for Liza and Joe to come, Joanna had time to think about how her life had changed over the past year. Goodwill House had a purpose and so did she. If David was still alive, none of this would have happened, and she thanked God for how things were for her and for all those living in the house.

Di was busy during the morning on Monday, filling in for Millie. She didn't have a moment to herself to go in search of Freddie and just had to hope that when she pedalled across the base, she'd be able to find him so they could walk down for lunch at the cottage.

She rather thought she was going to enjoy being his girlfriend but had no intention of spending every free minute in his company. An occasional date, a kiss or two, but nothing serious would be tickety-boo. She was pretty sure that if they were both still alive at the end of this dreadful war, then they would marry, but for the moment, it was easier to keep it simple and pretend they weren't already seriously involved.

'I thought we were off duty today, Di, so why do we have to do any of this domestic work?' Phyllis said sourly. She was one of the older members of the group and sometimes forgot that she wasn't in charge.

'We're not actually working, but we still have to do chores. The catering staff have to cook for us and we have to make sure our billet's immaculate. That means getting on with what you've been told to do and not moaning.'

Pamela, who was the same age as Phyllis and just as grumpy, chimed in. 'I don't know how you have the nerve to tell us what to do when you're breaking all the rules by walking out with an officer.'

'I can issue orders because I'm a leading aircraft woman and you're not. If you don't want to be put on a charge, I suggest you shut up and get on.'

She was sure that a real officer wouldn't need to harangue those under her, but despite the fact that she had the propellers on her sleeve indicating she was a junior NCO, this didn't seem to carry much weight with these two. But Pamela had a point, officers and other ranks weren't supposed to fraternise.

The rest of the girls had almost completed polishing the lino around their beds, the biscuits which masqueraded as mattresses, bedding and so on were neatly stacked, and none of them had made a single complaint.

Sally, one of the new drivers, came across to speak to Di. 'Don't take any notice of those two, they didn't get an invite to the dance tonight and they'll be the only two not going.'

'That's unfortunate, but there's nothing I can do about that. If they were only more cheerful and didn't complain all the time, then I'm sure someone would have asked them.'

They were talking quietly so there was no danger of either Pamela or Phyllis overhearing. She was about to get on with her own chores when Sally continued.

'*Are* you stepping out with an officer? Is it that smashing squadron leader you were with the other day?'

'It is. It's nothing serious, but I suppose we shouldn't really be seeing each other at all.'

'Go on, you deserve to have some fun. We all do. I'd give my eye teeth to be in your shoes. He's a real catch.'

There was little point repeating the lie that she and Freddie were just friends, as Sally had returned to her space next to the other new driver, Amy. If Sally knew then so did Amy and soon it would be all over the base.

Di smiled ruefully. It was too late to worry as it was certainly already common knowledge. Nothing remained a secret for very long on Manston. With well over a thousand air force personnel living and working on the base, it was hardly surprising gossip was rife.

There was admin work to complete in the office positioned in the large vestibule outside the sleeping accommodation; Di had volunteered to do all of it so Millie could remain with Ted.

The girls drifted off once they'd finished their domestic duties and Di kept an eye on the time so she wouldn't be late. After placing the filled-in forms in a cardboard folder, she was ready to depart.

It wasn't quite as easy to cycle with the folder under her arm, but she hadn't wanted to bring her cumbersome haversack. She'd also left her tin hat on the peg, but she did have her gas mask, as to be seen without that was tantamount to a hanging offence.

After propping her bike against the wall, she dashed into the admin building and put the folder in the required in-tray. From the noise coming through the open windows of the Officers' Mess, it sounded as though it was full of inebriated young men. Tonight was going to be lively, to say the least, if they were already drinking at lunchtime.

'There you are, Di, I was beginning to think you'd abandoned me and I'd have to go to lunch on my own.' Freddie was standing beside her bicycle with an interesting cardboard box in his arms. He didn't have a gas mask – perhaps officers were exempt.

'Paperwork to complete and hand in, but I'm here now. What's in the box?'

'Ah, you're going to have to wait and see. I hope you're hungry is the only clue I'll give you.' He nodded towards her bike. 'Aren't you going to hide that? Some bugger will nick it if you leave it visible.'

'They shouldn't, because they know it belongs to a member of the MT. Sarge would skin them alive if they took it.'

He grinned and nodded his agreement. 'Did you know that I've got a motorbike? I thought we could go out on it for a jaunt one day.'

'I'm not sure I'd enjoy that. Millie had a ride on the back of it with Ted and told me it was something she never wished to do again.'

'That was with Ted driving – you'll be fine with me.'

She laughed, turning several heads when she did so. 'I believe that you were the person riding that bike and you caused a horse to bolt, almost killed the older Lady Harcourt, and crashed into a fence.'

'Good god, it's not the same bike. That was a total wreck – I've managed to find another one and it's much more powerful and—'

'—And I'm definitely not getting on it. Please tell me what's in the box, I can't bear secrets.' Before he could answer, she recalled the conversation with Sally earlier. 'By the way, the fact that we're going out together is already being talked about. Do you think we should continue?'

'It's none of their damn business. Nobody is going to say anything to me – I'm a senior officer on this base.'

'It's all very well for you to say, Freddie, but I'm in a different position. I could get in a lot of trouble and be posted away from here.'

He looked at her as if she was an imbecile, which didn't help the situation. 'Don't be ridiculous. Millie's the most senior WAAF on the base at the moment and she's hardly going to write you up, is she?'

His dismissive attitude made her really cross. Didn't he understand how important being a WAAF was to her? Everything she knew was here at Manston and she didn't want to leave Millie or her friends at Goodwill House. If she hadn't been so angry, she'd never have said what she did.

'That's true. It hardly seems worth worrying about, as by the time we do get a senior officer, you might not even be here.'

He stopped so abruptly she cannoned into him and the box flew from his hands. By a heroic effort, he managed to grab hold of it before it hit the deck.

'Bloody hell, woman, talk about being blunt.'

For a second, she didn't understand why he'd been so shocked. Then the colour drained from her face. 'I meant that you told me you were likely to be posted away. I didn't mean you could be... that you might have... gone for a Burton.'

* * *

Freddie thought for a horrible moment that she might faint. He dropped the box on the ground and put his arms around her. 'Of course you didn't. I'm a moron. Don't look so upset, darling, I don't know why I thought you capable of saying something so harsh.'

She was trembling and her distress was his fault. Why didn't she answer? Tell him she forgave him?

'Di, I'm so sorry I upset you. Please look at me.'

She was clinging onto the lapels of his jacket as if she didn't have the strength in her limbs to stand upright.

'Shall I give you a piggyback? If I do that, then I can still carry the box.' This ridiculous suggestion had the desired effect. Well, an effect – she kicked him hard on the ankle, making him yelp.

'That serves you right for being a complete ass. Just because you're a bigwig here it doesn't mean that the rules don't apply to me. I'm prepared to continue to go out with you occasionally until the main contingent of WAAFs arrive or until your squadron's posted elsewhere.'

'Fair enough. After my gallant effort saving this box and its contents from damage, I then dropped it anyway.'

'Let's get a move on before we have another row.' She smiled sweetly at him. 'I do hope your ankle isn't too painful, Squadron Leader Hanover.'

He chuckled and harmony was restored. She wasn't like the other girls he'd gone out with, but she was the one he wanted to keep seeing. There'd been a couple of brief liaisons with girls a decent chap wouldn't want to marry, but this was different.

But he had a nasty suspicion he was wrong, that it was wishful thinking, that Di didn't reciprocate his feelings. He was determined to change her mind but thought it would be an uphill slog. He'd never had another girlfriend kick him – so that was a first!

'You might as well tell me what's in the box, as I'm going to see for myself in a minute,' she said as they approached the front garden of the cottage.

'Very well. There's half a dozen meat pasties, an apple crumble, custard, and iced fingers.'

'Golly, let's hope it didn't amalgamate into one soggy mess when you dropped it! The last place we were at, we frequently got dessert mixed in with the dinner. I can tell you that prunes and custard with beef stew isn't very pleasant.'

Spotting the front door already open, Di ran ahead and called out cheerfully, 'Hello, we're here, shall we come through?'

Ted yelled from the garden. 'Yes, Millie's not back from the village yet. She intended to go earlier but I don't suppose she'll be long. I'm just setting up the table I found in the shed.'

His errant wife returned soon after they arrived, bearing largesse in the form of strawberries, freshly dug potatoes and a large lettuce.

'Sorry I wasn't here. Talk amongst yourselves whilst Di and I get things ready. Goodness – did you bring all this?' Millie had seen the contents of the box.

Freddie laughed. 'Well, it wasn't the tooth fairy or Father Christmas, and I don't think there's anyone else here but us.'

'You're a buffoon, Squadron Leader Hanover,' Di said, but she was smiling so obviously didn't mean him to take her comment seriously.

* * *

Two hours sped past, and Freddie was sorry to leave. 'I've got things to do on base, but you stay if you want to, Di. I'll meet you outside the mess at six o'clock.'

Although he'd made the offer, he'd expected her to want to come with him and was disappointed when she just smiled, waved her hand to show she'd heard, and carried on with her conversation with Millie.

Ted walked him out. 'You're on a sticky wicket, my friend, where she's concerned. I don't think she's as convinced as you are.'

'It's sod's law that I fall in love at the most inconvenient time and with a girl who's not as keen as I am to get serious.'

8

Joanna was sitting on the terrace, sipping a very palatable claret that Elizabeth had found in the wine cellar, pleased with how the conversation with Joe and Liza had gone.

'I'll ring the vicar first thing in the morning and see if we can arrange to have the baptism tomorrow afternoon. Both of them can now read well enough to follow the responses. Joe should really have a godfather, as well as two godmothers.'

'Why don't you ask the doctor? He's a fine young man and has already been involved with your family, as it was his assistance that got Sarah a place at the Royal Free to study medicine.' Elizabeth poured herself a second glass but when she offered to do the same for her, Joanna refused.

'That's a good idea. It's too late to ring now, but I'll do it when I contact Mr Evans.'

'Better to do it first. The vicar will want the names of the godparents, won't he?'

'Good point.' Joanna sighed. 'It doesn't seem right to be sitting here enjoying this excellent wine when Betty and Bert are fighting for their lives. One expects to lose friends and family in a war, but for them to be so horribly ill from measles is so unfair.' She pushed away the dreadful thought that Betty might not survive this illness.

'I've not met Mr Smith – is he the same sort of age as Betty?'

'I know that Betty's twenty-five years old and I think that he's five years older. Far too young to die.'

'It certainly is. Don't worry over something you have no control over, my dear, a fruitless exercise. We can add our prayers to those of the village and hope that the Almighty has time to listen. Although he must be very busy at the moment.'

'Joe and Liza are such a comfort to us and I am so very proud of them. To think that a few months ago they arrived here illiterate and rejected by their sole relative, their grandmother.'

Elizabeth nodded. 'You could have added illegitimate to that list, as that's why their grandmother didn't want them. I was thinking, my dear, that perhaps you might think of adopting them? Then they could take the family name and the stigma of their irregular birth would be removed.'

Joanna was surprised that her mother-in-law was the one to suggest what she'd been considering. Having the twins as actual Harcourts, as much her children as Sarah was, was exactly what she wanted. David would be turning in his grave, but she was in charge now and his stifling control no longer influenced her decisions.

'Mr Broome, our solicitor, is visiting on Tuesday,' she said. 'We'll ask him if it would be possible to do so. Perhaps it might be better to leave talking to Mr Evans about the baptism until we've spoken to Mr Broome.'

'I think in the circumstances it might be better not to say anything to anyone until we know whether Betty and Mr Smith are going to recover.'

Joanna thought for a moment before answering. 'Actually, I think now's the perfect time to get things in motion. If the very worst should happen and Betty should die, then the twins will need something positive to think about.'

Nightingales were singing in the woods that bordered the park, there was the occasional bark of a fox, owls hooted to each other, and it was hard to believe that not only was Great Britain poised to repel an invasion by the Germans, but her dearest friend was at this very moment fighting for her life.

'It's strange that Manston's so quiet tonight. It's like the whole world is holding its breath, waiting for the next disaster.'

'Very poetic, my dear, but rather depressing, don't you think?'

'You're quite right, Elizabeth, there's nothing we can do about the war or Betty, but we can do something significant to improve the lives of the children in our care. I just hope that my misgivings about Peter Harcourt are unnecessary, as we really don't need any interference from him.'

* * *

Di delayed her departure from the billet until she was sure that Freddie would be waiting for her. She really didn't want to be accosted by any of the inebriated officers who were, at this very moment, milling about outside the recreation room where the dance was being held.

The sound of their revelry could be heard clearly, even though the WAAF accommodation was a good mile from the building. Phyllis and Pamela had decided to attend the NCO event, despite not having had an actual invitation.

Once everybody had left, Di did a routine inspection and then locked up. The key was hidden in its usual place behind the ablutions block where all the girls knew where to find it. It was quite possible one of them might come home early and she didn't want them to have to sit around outside waiting for her to return with a key. No doubt, once the full contingent was living here, there would always be someone on duty, unlike tonight.

She dismounted from her bicycle some distance from the raucous crowd of airmen, as tonight she wouldn't put it past one of them to take it for a ride around the base. Heaven knows where she'd find it in the morning if they did that.

Freddie's motorcycle was kept under a tarpaulin at the back of the officers' accommodation, so she wheeled her bicycle around the block and carefully hid it next to his. Satisfied it would be there when she wanted it later, she went in search of him and was relieved that he was leaning nonchalantly against the open door, waiting for her.

'I saw you vanish with your bike. Wise move, Di, it'll be safer there tonight. Ted and Millie aren't here yet, so I thought we could walk down and meet them. Safety in numbers and all that.'

'All right, let's do that. It's very noisy in there and I'm not sure I really want to go in.'

'God help us if anything happens between now and tomorrow morning, as I doubt there will be more than a handful of chaps fit to fly.'

'Absolutely – I suppose if Win Co agreed to let everybody get so drunk then he must know something we don't.'

'Giving everybody a forty-eight-hour pass, topped off by this shindig, was a bad move in my opinion. We're back on duty at dawn tomorrow and I can't see many of these revellers even being awake by then.'

This was rather a depressing conversation to be having when they were supposed to be enjoying a light-hearted evening together. 'Why don't you speak to him and get him to do something about it?'

But Freddie wasn't listening, as he'd seen Ted and Millie approaching, hand-in-hand and so obviously in love. Di looked at Freddie and knew in that moment it was possible she might never feel the same way about him. Her eyes didn't light up when she saw him, her pulse didn't race, and she was pretty sure that was what happened when Ted and Millie met. She felt a very strong physical response to him, but that wasn't the same as real love – the love that Millie and Ted shared.

'Hello, you two lovebirds, Freddie and I were just saying we're not sure we actually want to go in as everybody has had too much to drink already,' Di said.

'Not even to dance?' Millie asked.

'Ted, you're by far the tallest, so would you please look through that open window and tell me if it's a good idea to go in.'

He peered in and recoiled, shaking his head, as some wag had thrown half a glass of beer in his face. 'No, not only should we not go in but I think, Freddie, you've got to step in. I know I've not been at Manston for long, but I've never seen anything like it. Even the blokes who rarely drink seem to be plastered tonight.'

Freddie metamorphosed into a grim-faced officer, and the charming young man she'd been with a moment before vanished.

'Look after the ladies, Ted, I'm going to find the Wing Commander and any other senior officers who might be lurking somewhere. This needs to stop and the only way to do it is to close the bar and turf them all out to get some fresh air.'

As Freddie strode towards the admin block, Di was in no doubt that one way or another, the party was about to be cancelled.

'You girls go back to the cottage. Freddie and I will join you when we've got things sorted out here.'

'Darling, don't get involved. Everybody in there is an officer and most of them will be senior to you,' Millie said.

'Freddie's not only my skipper but my best friend. He's going to need as many sober blokes as possible to sort this out.'

Di took her friend's arm. 'Let the men handle it...'

'I'm the most senior WAAF NCO, so I can hardly abandon my

post. Ted, I'm going to wait over there, and you must send out my girls. I'll make sure they get home safely. You need to sleep on the base tonight anyway as you're on duty so early.'

Ted nodded. 'I don't think there are any other WAAF involved with these chaps. Your girls will be at the NCOs' bash. We're going to have to close that down, too, but it won't be for a while. You'd be better off at the cottage, both of you, away from any trouble.'

He didn't wait to hear if either of them agreed with him but hurried after his friend.

'What are you going to do, Millie?'

'I'm not going to the cottage and neither are you. Come on, let's gate crash the other party and remove our girls before the RAFP arrive.'

'Let's hope the police won't be needed tonight.'

Ten minutes later, Di followed her friend into the NCOs' Mess. What a shame such a promising evening was now ruined, but duty and common sense must come before having a good time.

'Golly, it sounds almost as bad in here. If the girls are tiddly then I doubt that you'll be able to persuade them to leave, Millie.'

'When we tell them that the RAFP are on their way, and that it's better if they leave and not risk having their names on a list, they'll be happy to come.'

This might work, as most of the girls were usually no trouble and even after a few glasses of something alcoholic would probably still be prepared to follow a direct order and be aware of the consequences if they didn't.

Freddie was unable to find either of the chaps who outranked him – the Wing Commander and the adjutant both lived off base and both were at home, according to the erk he'd spoken to.

'I'm only to call either of them, sir, in the case of a dire emergency. There are two other squadron leaders – as you know – and I think both of them are in the bar. Can I fetch them for you?'

'Thank you. I'll dig them out myself.' The other two were obviously the ones in charge at the moment.

Ted arrived at his side. 'I know I'm not even a flight lieutenant, but I'm your man. I'm bigger and heavier than most of the blokes here and the fact that I'm not drunk will give me a decided advantage.'

'Good man. What about the girls?'

'I suggested they go to the cottage but rather think that they've gone to collect the WAAFs from the other place. The cottage is locked up and tidy, as neither of us were intending to sleep there tonight.' He rubbed his hand across his eyes. 'God knows when we'll be together again. When Millie resigns, obviously she's going to need somewhere to live and it might as well be there, as she'll have friends around her if we get posted.'

'Is that a euphemism for kicking the bucket?'

Ted grinned. 'Bloody isn't. Come on, let's get this done.'

'We need reinforcements. The other two bods of my rank are in the mess. Let's collect them first.'

'What if they don't agree with you?'

'I don't give a damn what they think,' Freddie said. 'I outrank everybody in the recreation room and they'll bloody well have to do what I tell them. I've already contacted the RAFP and they're on their way over in case they're needed.'

The two men he wanted were sitting with a couple of flight lieutenants, not the worse for drink, thank god. He pushed his way across to them.

'I'm going to close the temporary bar in the recreation room and send everybody home. All the squadrons are back on active duty in seven hours and the men have to be sober by then.'

'Good luck with that, Freddie, I doubt any of them will listen to you. They've been drinking all day.'

'Which is why I'm calling a halt. Are you going to help me or sit on your arses?'

'Well, if you put it like that, old man, we've got no choice but to help you. God – you're going to be the most unpopular bloke in the base after this,' Ronnie Winterton said with a grimace.

'Can't be helped. You know as well as I do, old bean, if the men continue to drink then they'll kill themselves and anyone next to them if they have to scramble tomorrow.'

Ted walked at his right shoulder, the other two of similar rank to him were on his left and the flight lieutenants fell in behind.

When they stepped into the recreation room, Freddie almost gagged. The smell of sweaty bodies, cigarette smoke and stale beer wasn't pleasant. There were dozens of young ladies in amongst the officers and they needed to be got out first.

'Ted and I are going to close the bar. The rest of you stand in front of it.'

He hoped that five senior officers plus his friend would be enough to deter any idiot from disobeying orders. There were four barmen rushing about behind the makeshift counter.

'Right, you lot, no more drinks to be served. Everyone's leaving.'

They exchanged glances but none of them even considered arguing. Once he was certain no inebriated officers could hurdle the bar and help themselves, he and Ted went to join the others.

The roomful of drunken young officers and the dozen or so young women, when faced with an array of determined senior officers, knew better than to argue – the outcome was inevitable.

'Right, men, escort your lady friends from the premises and make sure that they return to their homes safely. Anyone who is foolish enough to continue drinking will be put on a charge. If you don't want to be cleaning latrines for the foreseeable, go outside and get sober.'

Freddie's voice carried wonderfully and despite the continued noise, within a few moments the room was more or less silent and every head was turned in his direction.

One pilot officer was brave enough to speak out. 'Come on, Skip, don't be a killjoy. We could all go for a Burton tomorrow.'

'If you fly drunk then I'd say it's a certainty, sober you've got a chance. Enjoy the rest of your free time, as I doubt you'll get any more in the next few weeks.'

Ted had the nous to move towards the double doors and stand there, arms folded, staring pointedly at the exit. They got the message. There was some binding – but moaning was to be expected in the circumstances.

In less than half an hour, the room was empty apart from the orderlies collecting the glasses and restoring the room to order.

'That was well done, chaps, thank you for your capable assistance,' Freddie said, as if he was the senior officer at the scene.

'Good show, old boy, should have stepped in ourselves as we'd been left in charge. Dereliction of duty on our part. Bloody good job you were on the ball,' one of them said as he prepared to stroll back to his abandoned beer in the mess.

'Hang on, chaps, we've got the NCOs to rout out before you can bugger off.'

'That's a different proposition altogether, my friend. Are you sure you want to poke that particular hornet's nest?'

'We've got no choice. There are a dozen or more Sargeant pilots in there and having drunken ground crew is almost as bad as the flyers being inebriated.'

The four of them exchanged glances and then shrugged and agreed to accompany him. He strode ahead with Ted, leaving them to wander along behind.

'Ted, I hope the girls went to the mess and have been as successful extricating their cohort. I'm trusting that we won't have to go in ourselves. It doesn't do for officers to interfere with other ranks if it can be avoided.'

Thankfully, it wasn't dark, even though it was well past nine o'clock. With luck, the NCOs' party would end as smoothly as the one he'd just left, but somehow he doubted it. He was thankful that Millie and Di had removed their girls safely, as that would make things somewhat easier.

The RAFP had wisely gone to the NCOs' bash and were waiting outside for him to arrive. Again, he took charge and nobody objected. He rather thought he'd blotted his copy book and over-stepped the mark where these other two squadron leaders were concerned. They might make an official complaint to the CO and something would be written on his record saying he wasn't a team player. Making sure his men, and the other chaps, were sober enough to fly tomorrow was more important than his record.

Ted hurried across to speak to Millie, and Freddie watched the girls march away. He was amused and impressed by the fact that they were in perfect step when they could just have strolled off and nobody would have given a damn.

His friend returned at the double. 'Millie spoke to several blokes and they know the score. I'm hoping we won't need to arrest anybody tonight.'

'I'm just going to speak to the police. If they just show them-selves at the door, everybody should troop out without complaint.' He grinned, knowing this was unlikely. 'Thank god there's not a third party at the other ranks' mess.'

'I spotted one of my ground crew and he's gone to tell them that the bar's got to close by ten o'clock.'

'Well done, Ted, I knew I could rely on you. I'm going to put in a recommendation that you're promoted. I want a bod like you as my second-in-command – I don't give a damn about seniority; I know the right man when I see him.'

'Fine, I'm happy to be whatever you need me to be. The RAFP bloke in charge is heading this way. I'll leave you to talk to him.'

Freddie returned the man's salute crisply. 'I'm hopeful this will end peacefully. Damn stupid, letting the men drink themselves to a standstill when we have to be at readiness in a few hours.'

The man agreed and fortunately so did the flyers and ground crew who'd been at the party. No doubt there would be a few fights, a lot of sore heads, but disaster had been averted. Freddie had a nasty suspicion that they were all going to need to be on top from tomorrow.

9

Joanna now helped Elizabeth with her morning routine and had come to rather enjoy this time of enforced intimacy. Not having her own dresser was a new experience for Elizabeth but she'd adjusted wonderfully.

Jean was staying at Betty's cottage and Joe would cycle down as soon as he'd let the chickens, ducks and geese out and fed them. Star was turned out, so he didn't need to do anything for her until he got back. Joanna hoped the news about Betty and her husband would be more encouraging when he returned later.

'No, my dear, I really can't abide another day in grey. It's been six weeks since David died and that is quite long enough. I noticed that the widows and mothers of the others who died weren't wearing black armbands at church yesterday.'

'You're right, Elizabeth, time to move on. I pray that we don't have to go into mourning for anybody else.'

Her mother-in-law ignored her oblique reference to Betty and Bert. 'Jean has made a splendid job of updating my wardrobe. I'm relieved I don't have to wear my skirts at knee level. I think it quite immodest. I'm well aware there's a war on and we need to conserve material, but showing one's knees can hardly be a good thing.'

'I can't see that it makes any difference,' said Joanna. 'There are so few young men around to be stirred at the sight of a lady's knees and I've certainly no objection. We're fortunate that we have a seamstress living here and the wherewithal to have our own clothes made.'

'That's all very well, but new garments have to abide by the regulations which is why I'm going to continue to wear my old clothes.'

'You make them sound like something collected from a church jumble sale when everything you own is exquisitely made and quite obviously haute couture.'

'Your wardrobe is equally expensive, my dear, but I can see why you've chosen to wear the modest garments Jean has made for you. David dressed you only to impress his friends, which is obvious from the gowns you have in your wardrobe. Most of them are totally unsuitable for wearing anywhere but Mayfair.'

Joanna was searching through the many gowns, costumes and frocks in the walk-in closet in Elizabeth's suite of rooms. 'What about this one? It's a delightful shade of blue with beautiful embell-ishments in silver. It's definitely not grey, but not so alarming it would cause offence to those in the village who will expect you to be wearing black for a year.'

She draped it over her arm and turned sideways so Elizabeth could view it.

'Yes, thank you, that's perfect. Do you have something similar you can put on? The solicitor will be here later today and you need to look elegant.'

'Good heavens, why should I need to look elegant for him?'

'Surely you must have noticed how he looks at you? I know it's far too early for you to be considering remarrying, but when you do, I think he might be on the borderline of suitable.'

Joanna wasn't sure how to react to this outrageous suggestion. 'I've no intention of marrying again. I'm enjoying my independence and have no plans to give it up. As for Mr Broome, I think it's more likely he's myopic then looking at me with any degree of interest. Let's talk of something more sensible, shall we?'

On returning to her own rooms, Joanna hastily put back the outfit she'd intended to wear – one of the two grey frocks Jean had made up for her. Instead, she selected a simple costume also in grey but with lavender lapels and cuffs on the jacket. The short-sleeved blouse was made from the same lavender silk and complemented the ensemble perfectly.

As always, she waited in her sitting room until she heard her mother-in-law emerge from her own domain. It wouldn't do to make it obvious that Elizabeth couldn't manage the stairs without assistance any more.

Liza was busy in the kitchen but working silently – usually she sang to herself whilst she prepared breakfast. Not hearing the girl's lovely voice sent a shiver of apprehension down Joanna's spine. She prayed it was just a coincidence and not that things were worse at the cottage in the village.

She was distracted from her worrying thoughts by the arrival of the dog who was now far too large to be considered a puppy, even though he wasn't yet a year old as far as she knew. 'Good morning, Lazzy, I'm delighted to see you too. What's that you've got in your mouth for me?'

'Horrible animal, don't come near me with that. It's the remains of something dead, Joanna, I can smell it from here.'

'No, Elizabeth, it isn't. Come here, silly animal, let me have that sock. It doesn't belong to you.'

Liza appeared from the kitchen. 'Blimey, he's not got one of Joe's socks again, has he? Blooming dog's taken a fancy to them something rotten lately.'

Elizabeth drew breath to correct Liza's diction, but Joanna shook her head. The old lady understood that now was not the time for grammar lessons.

The dog was reluctant to part with his treasure and every time Joanna reached out to take the offending article from his jaws, he danced backwards, wagging his tail and daring her to try again.

After a few moments of coming and going, she admitted defeat. 'Go away, I agree with Elizabeth that you're a horrible dog.' She said this with a smile and he bounced up and nudged her but still managed to evade her grasp and race back into the kitchen.

They were all smiling after his antics and she wondered if he'd done it deliberately, sensing that something wasn't right in the house.

'Do you know when Joe will be back, Liza?'

'No, Aunt Joanna, he never said.' The girl stopped and rubbed her eyes on the edge of her apron. 'I'm that worried about Betty. It ain't right, someone being struck down by a kiddie's complaint.'

'No, my dear, it's not. All we can do is pray and I'm sure you've been doing plenty of that, as have we all.' Elizabeth squeezed Liza's arm as she walked past into the breakfast parlour.

Joanna followed, half-expecting the table to be bare but, despite anxiety and the fact that Liza was acting as housekeeper during Betty's absence, everything was as it should be.

'Sit down, Elizabeth, I'll fetch the coffee and so on from the kitchen. Liza has more than enough to do at present.'

Breakfast was a sombre affair and neither of them ate more than a slice of toast. The jug of freshly made coffee was finished – one never left a drop of that, as it was no longer available to purchase and was far too precious a commodity to waste.

They both jumped when they heard the back door open and close. Joe was back.

* * *

Di suggested they head for the recreation block, as it was far too early to turn in. 'I'm sure there's something we can cobble together to make a decent supper to go with our nightly cocoa.'

'Seems silly to be drinking cocoa in the summer but somehow not having it would be a sign that the Germans have got the better of us,' Millie said.

'I know exactly what you mean, old bean, as long as we've got something vaguely chocolatey then all's right with the world.'

When Millie told the others the plan, they were enthusiastic. Phyllis and Pamela came up with another idea, which was greeted with excited chattering. They were going to arrange a quiz of some sort.

'We'll organise the questions – you just have to get into teams of two. They won't all be based on general knowledge, geography and so on. Some of them will be challenges,' Pamela informed them with a smile.

'What sort of challenges?' Sally asked.

'Who can stand on one leg for the longest, hold their breath, balance a spoon on their nose and so on.'

'Golly, that sounds absolutely spiffing. Corp, Sally and I will arrange things in the recreation room whilst the catering corps prepare the food and drink,' Amy, the other new driver, said.

There was a groan at this reference to catering. The two unfortunate girls in charge of the kitchen were only there because nobody else had volunteered. These two had worked as orderlies in the NCOs' Mess and were the only girls with even a sniff of catering experience, so they'd been lumbered with the job.

'I'll supervise the supper and so on, Millie, whilst you find the necessary paper and pencils. It will be best if it's our corporal who steals the stationery,' Di said.

* * *

Everyone agreed that they'd had far more fun with their ridiculous quiz than they would have done if they'd remained at the party, being leered at and ogled by overeager airmen. Even the spam and piccalilli sandwiches had been devoured without complaint. Nobody moaned when Millie said it would be lights out at eleven, which gave them half an hour to dash over to the ablution block and then get to bed.

As always, Millie and Di double-checked that all the doors were locked, that no lights had been left on and everything was tidy before they headed for the Nissen hut.

'It's Sally and I who are on duty in five hours,' Di said whilst they were standing together in front of the sinks, cleaning their teeth.

'I've got so much clerical work to complete and hand in, I think I'll probably be up at the same time as you. Phyllis and Pamela are lucky in a way as they work more regular hours and never have to be on duty at night.'

'I'd much rather be driving, be outside most of the time, than stuck in an office typing all day as they are.'

At precisely eleven, Millie called out good night and then turned off the main lights.

It didn't take more than a couple of minutes to lay out the three biscuits – rectangular, straw-filled, brick-like objects that when side by side could loosely be called a mattress. The lumpy pillow and unpleasant rough sheets went on next and then the grey blanket. They only needed one at the moment, but hopefully there would be others issued in the winter as it was going to be freezing in the hut with only the one central, black metal stove supplying heat.

* * *

The alarm went off under Di's pillow so it didn't wake up anybody else. She'd left her uniform ready to put on and was dressed and heading across the concrete to the ablutions in five minutes. None of the girls showered or bathed before going on duty – it was just a lick and a promise at the sink, and something more thorough when they finished.

Sally was a few minutes ahead of her and had both their bicycles waiting. 'It's a lovely day. At least, I think it's going to be, but it's far too early to tell.'

'The birds don't care there's a war on and sing just as loudly as ever. If we pedal really fast, we might have time to grab something from the NAAFI whilst we wait for the chaps to come out.' Di was hungry. The spam sandwiches seemed a long time ago. 'It's eerily quiet at 4 a.m. Doesn't seem credible that bombs could be dropped here any day.' She frowned. 'It's so much easier for those of us working on the ground. I can only imagine what the flyers are going through.'

Di was thinking about Freddie. Obviously, she wanted him to survive what was coming, and for Ted and all the other boys too. She wasn't really sure if she would be any more heartbroken if anything happened to him than if Ted was killed. She shook her head. That just wasn't true. Ted was a friend but Freddie was far more than that already.

Sally touched her arm. 'Don't look so glum, Di, your young man's the most experienced pilot in his squadron. It's more than likely to be the new boys who'll be killed.'

She smiled sadly. 'Then we should be without fatalities here, as there are no new men. Everyone at Manston has been here since Dunkirk in June.'

'Exactly. Nothing for any of us to worry about. Come on, I'll race you to the MT. The winner gets to choose which lorry they drive today.'

'Right. You're on.'

Di won by a whisker and selected the slightly less ancient lorry. Sarge was waiting for them with their duties for the day. She was delivering Freddie's squadron and one of Hurries and retuning with the men who'd been on duty. Sally was taking and collecting the Australian Blenheim flyers. It would be good to spend a few minutes with Freddie if she got the chance.

* * *

Freddie was woken by his orderly at dawn.

'Good morning, sir, a lovely fine one it is too. Your tea's lovely and hot. Is there anything you need for today?'

'No, as usual you've left everything in place for me. Hopefully I'll be back tonight, unless we're put on permanent readiness again.'

'Righty-ho, sir.' His orderly, Brown, departed to deliver morning tea to his other officers.

Freddie could dress in the dark and still be confident that everything would be in the right place. Hardly seemed worth making the effort to look smart because once things kicked off, they'd be sleeping in their flight suits and all stink to high heaven.

During Operation Dynamo – what the fiasco at Dunkirk had been named – no one had shaved for days or been able to take a shower and certainly had not changed their clothes. He'd been so knackered, he'd stopped noticing how bad he smelled after a few days.

After he'd shaved, Freddie ran his hand over his jaw, checking he'd not missed anything. There would be a lot of sore heads, bloodshot eyes and moans from those bods he'd had to turf out of the party yesterday. Served them right for getting drunk when they knew they were on duty at dawn today.

His eyes were clear, he was ready for whatever was coming. He smiled ruefully. It didn't matter how much he washed his face, there were always faint black lines of embedded oil somewhere. It was easy to identify a flyer because of this, as ground crew, despite the fact that they worked with oil, always had time off to get a decent wash.

The mess was filling up, as much noise as normal, and as far as he could see, all the chaps were filling their plates with their usual enormous cooked breakfasts. That was a good sign.

'Morning, Skip, all bright-eyed and bushy tailed, I see,' someone said as he passed.

'Absolutely top hole, old boy, as I didn't get plastered last night.'

This was greeted by laughter and he was relieved there didn't seem to be any residual ill feeling for what he'd done.

Ted had saved him a place. 'Thanks, nobody seems to have a hangover, do they?'

'Neither is anyone binding about what we did. Once they were sober, the blokes would have realised we were right and be grateful that we stepped in when we did.'

'Nothing major must have occurred over the past two days, or the two squadrons on duty would have been scrambled.' Freddie took his place beside his friend.

'It's fine but windy. The Channel will be rough today, which means Hitler can't launch his invasion.' Ted wiped the last of the egg yolk from his plate with his bread and then washed it down with a slurp of tea.

'I still don't see an invasion is possible at the moment. Our navy's superior and with our support, I think together we'd have no difficulty stopping an invasion flotilla. Towing barges full of equipment and men is a slow task and would make them sitting ducks.'

'I agree. Which means, Freddie, that our job is going to be crucial. I have a nasty feeling that even the Jerries will work that out for themselves and the Luftwaffe will try and destroy us and our bases before the barges set out.'

'What a depressing thought, as Manston will be their first target. Any bombers heading for London and the docks will fly directly over us.'

'We don't have the advantage of numbers or experience, but there's one thing we do have that the Luftwaffe don't.'

'What's that?'

'We have ground control telling us where the bogies are, if we run out of fuel, we can land, and if we bale out, usually it's over our own country.'

'Not given that aspect much thought, Freddie. But you're right, thanks for pointing it out.'

'I say, Freddie, are you going to eat that breakfast?' The chap sitting opposite was already reaching out to take his plate.

'Bugger off, Chalky,' he said and held onto his meal in case his words weren't enough to deter the would-be thief.

Conversation ceased as he shovelled in the food before anyone else thought they could pinch it. Never a wise move to chat before you'd cleared your plate. The NAAFI was now fully functioning but was more for the use of non-combatants, as they had more time. There were now two bigger, better vans that circulated the base and kept the waiting airmen fed and watered.

The sun wasn't up but it was getting lighter by the minute. If the Luftwaffe were going to attack today, this would be the perfect time to do it. Those who'd been on duty all night would be hanging up their gear and waiting eagerly to be collected. There was always a slight hiatus when squadrons changed over, and he prayed that the Nazis weren't aware of this.

The lorries were parked, waiting for the men to emerge from breakfast. There was no sign of the drivers, but he thought they'd probably nipped into the NAFFI to grab something to eat. The catering at the WAAF billet was appalling.

From the noise coming from the rear of the vehicle, there were already men inside. The NCO flyers, and there were several of them, had to trek across from their mess as the lorries always waited outside the Officers' Mess.

He vaulted into the rear and was greeted by those inside. 'Good morning, boys, all feeling tickety-boo?'

A chorus of agreement came from the six occupants – three Hurry flyers, three Spits. The Aussie Blenheim chaps would travel separately as their kites were on the other side of the base.

'Excellent news. It seems quiet now, but it could be unpleasant later.'

Freddie slid onto the wooden bench, polished smooth by count-less backsides, and let the men continue to talk amongst them-selves. Being the highest ranked officer in this situation was a mixed blessing. Sometimes he felt he was intruding on his men.

A few minutes later, the lorry was full and Ted was squashed in next to him.

'Di's our driver today. She said she'll catch up with you later if we're not scrambled.'

'Something to look forward to.' Seeing Di always raised his spirits – she was his glimmer of hope in this dismal war.

It was impossible to continue the conversion, as in order to do so, they would have had to shout to be heard over the rumbling and roaring of the ancient lorry.

10

Joanna dropped her uneaten toast onto the plate and stood up slowly. She looked across at Elizabeth, who shook her head, as if anticipating that the news was going to be the worst possible.

With some reluctance, she headed for the kitchen. Instead of finding the twins in tears, they were smiling.

'Betty's a bit better, Aunt Joanna,' Joe said, and the knot in her stomach eased a little.

'That's the most wonderful news. How's Bert?'

'He's doing well and is already able to sit up and eat and drink a little. But then, he didn't have the measles nearly as bad as our Betty.'

'What did Dr Willoughby say, do you know?'

'He called in whilst I was there and I spoke to him afterwards. Betty's not out of the woods yet, but it's looking a lot better than it did yesterday.'

'I see. We just have to keep praying for Betty and hope that God's listening. How are you getting on with the pig, Joe?'

'No trouble at all; seems a shame the poor beast will be slaughtered in a couple months. He's a real character and likes to be scratched with a hammer between his ears.'

'This is farming country, Joe, and animals are raised to be eaten. As long as they have a good life whilst they're here, then that's the best we can do for them.'

'I've got a list of things Auntie Jean said I'm to ask permission to take when I go down this afternoon.' He offered the paper, but she shook her head.

'No, whatever they need, just take it. I mean it, anything at all, even alcohol from the cellar.'

'Fair enough. I need to pick up the muck in the field where Star's grazing and check that she's got water, collect any eggs, and I'm done here unless there's something else you want me to do.'

'I need both of you looking clean and tidy this afternoon when the solicitor comes. He'll want to speak to you, check that you're happy for me to adopt you. He's also going to speak to your grandmother, as she needs to give her permission.'

'Imagine that, Joe, in a few weeks we'll be Joe and Liza Harcourt.' Liza's happy smile slipped. 'I'm not going to say yes if your Sarah isn't happy. She might not want to have us as a brother and sister.'

'I've already written to her and nothing will proceed until I've had her reply. I'm sure she'll be delighted to welcome you to the family. She always wanted siblings and now she'll have them.'

'I think that will mean I'm more likely to be taken on as aircrew when I apply in a couple of years,' Joe said happily.

'Please don't talk about volunteering. You won't be fifteen until September so that's years away. Sarah's intending to come down for your birthday. As hers is the previous week, we thought to have a joint celebration.'

'Cor, a real party? Balloons, jelly, cake and that?' Liza said, scarcely able to speak for excitement.

'Yes to all of the above. It will have to be a fairly small do, but I'm hoping we'll have something even better to celebrate soon, as legalities should have been completed to make you part of the Harcourt family.'

Joe rushed off to complete his outside chores and Joanna left Liza singing in the kitchen while she prepared the vegetable soup for luncheon. The girl had a beautiful voice and had promised to join the church choir as soon as she was more confident with her reading.

When it was known in the village that she'd adopted the twins, people would say she was kind to give them a home, that they were lucky to be taken in by her, but it was the other way around. She was the fortunate one to have these wonderful youngsters about to become her children.

Elizabeth was pacing the drawing room, wringing her hands and looking apprehensive.

'It's good news, but Betty's still considered seriously ill. Bert's over the worst and he's definitely going to recover.'

'I'd be happier if it was Betty who was over the worst, not her disagreeable husband. However, it's not the dire news I was preparing myself for. Now we can enjoy the visit of Mr Broome and hopefully move forward with our plans to adopt the children.'

* * *

The solicitor arrived at exactly the time he'd stated in his telephone call and the twins both looked exactly as they should.

He hadn't brought his efficient secretary with him, which Joanna thought was rather odd but didn't like to ask the reason.

'Welcome, Mr Broome, we thought we would convene in the drawing room today. There is already tea and coffee as well as freshly baked ginger biscuits awaiting your attention.'

'Thank you, my lady, that all sounds quite delightful.'

He greeted Elizabeth and shook hands with Liza and Joe, which they found somewhat disconcerting but rose to the occasion.

'Might I enquire how Mrs Smith is progressing? I was sorry to hear that she and her husband have been so poorly with measles.'

'Bert is over the worst but Betty's still very unwell. Please, do sit down.'

Once they were settled, Liza poured tea and coffee and Joe handed the plate of biscuits around.

'Have you any more news about Lord Harcourt's interference in our affairs, young man?' Elizabeth demanded.

'The bank has been warned that they have a legal agreement with you both and, as far as I'm aware, there's nothing Lord Harcourt or the bank can do to change things.' Mr Broome hesitated and then continued. 'Of course, if by the end of the year the money from your stocks and shares is not forthcoming, then they are free to sell the debt to anybody. Is there any likelihood of there being a delay, my lady?'

'No, Coutts have assured me my funds will be coming in the next few weeks. I'm confident the matter can be settled long before the deadline.'

'That's a relief, my lady. Like you, I don't quite trust the new Lord Harcourt and fear that he might have an ulterior motive, that he covets the estates and house to go with the title.'

* * *

Di had had a few stolen minutes with Freddie and they'd exchanged a tender kiss before she'd had to rush off. After she had finished delivering and collecting the airmen, she returned the lorry to the MT and had to do a quick change in the rear of the vehicle from her overalls into her uniform. Her next duty was to drive to Hawkinge base and collect an officer of some sort and bring him back to Manston.

The officer she collected wasn't an active RAF member – he was too old. His dark hair was flecked with grey, and his neatly clipped moustache was silver. From the amount of gold braid, medal ribbons and so on, he was a very senior man indeed. He was also taciturn to the point of rudeness and didn't bother to return her crisp salute. He stood, gimlet-eyed, waiting for her to open the door and then didn't even bother to close it behind him but left her to do it. It was a great shame that all officers weren't like Freddie.

At the gate, she slowed right down and waited for the guard to check her papers. This wasn't a time to be lax with rules. The guard, wisely, didn't ask for the air commodore in the rear of the vehicle to show his. It had taken her the forty minutes of the drive to work out his rank from his insignia.

She didn't ask where he wanted to be dropped but drove directly to the admin building, jumped out, flung open the rear door and stood there saluting until he had no option but to clamber out. She then slammed the door behind him, shot back into her place and was away before he could ask her to do anything else. He might have demanded that she wait until he finished whatever business he had here, but she wanted a break, as her need for the loo was desperate.

Di checked her schedule for the day and saw that she wasn't needed for an hour unless there was a flap on. Ample time to get a meal at the NAAFI and still leave half an hour to cycle across to Freddie's squadron.

The NAAFI looked an unprepossessing place from the outside, as it was just an ordinary Nissen hut, but inside it had been given protection from the elements by an inner wall which was, of course, painted a dull regulation grey. This didn't prevent the place from being rather jolly and the appetising aroma of bacon and sausages wafted towards her.

The place was heaving with eager RAF personnel of both sexes and all ranks. There was also a sprinkling of civilians, as people from the village had got work here – usually in a domestic capacity. She spotted three of her girls eagerly tucking into a full breakfast. She was going to do the same, as the sandwich she'd managed to grab at dawn was now a distant memory.

Di nodded and smiled her way across the crowded space, moving easily between the tables until she reached the long counter, and the middle-aged lady behind it beamed.

'What'll I do you for, ducks?'

'If there's any of the bacon and sausages left then I'd love that. Also toast and tea to go with it.'

She took the tray across to the table where the girls had budged up to make room for her. 'I'm looking forward to this. I hope it tastes as good as it smells and looks,' she said as she sat down.

'It's scrumptious. We had the same as you, and you can see we haven't left a scrap,' said Mabel, one of the unfortunate girls landed with the job of catering for the twelve of them, with a happy smile.

'Golly, if our cooks prefer to eat here rather than their own food, then there's no hope for us,' Di said with a smile.

'Corp's got us training in the NCOs' Mess, doing actual cooking and not just peeling spuds like we were before.'

'That's good news for us all.' This was too much talk and not enough eating. Her plate was clean in minutes, the mug of tea drained, and she was ready to return the tray to the counter. In the NAAFI, the girls working there took care of the dirty crockery and cutlery but it was ingrained in them to clear the table before they left.

Bursting with energy after her breakfast, Di raced across the airfield, knowing she only had a quarter of an hour to spend with

Freddie before she'd have to be at the MT, change back into her overalls, and deliver whatever spare parts had arrived on the Annie – the Anson – just now.

The NAAFI van was just driving away when she arrived. Freddie must have seen her coming and was waiting to greet her. They walked a short distance away from the others so they could talk freely but were very careful to keep a respectful distance between them. No point in stirring people up.

'Good morning, I didn't expect to see you out of your overalls.'

'Hello, Freddie, I had to collect an air commodore from Folkestone. He had an overnight bag with him so either he's staying here or going somewhere else.'

He chuckled. 'I'd say that was obvious, sweetheart, but I know what you mean. Bigwigs are not good news.'

'I expect you'll be told all about it later. Did you get any flak from the men about ruining their evening?'

'Nothing at all. If anything, they're grateful they don't have a hangover.' He kept glancing towards the coast, squinting and tipping his head to one side as if he could hear and see something no one else could.

'What's wrong?'

'I know it looks peaceful, but—'

He didn't get to finish the sentence as the telephone rang, the airman came out and yelled, 'Scramble!' and then rang the bell to warn the ground crew to get the engines of the Spits and Hurries running.

Freddie was off, like all the others, running flat out to the hut to grab his chute before charging to his kite. He was wearing his flight suit and Mae West. Within three minutes, he was taxiing onto the bitumen runway.

A Spitfire was elegant when airborne but ungainly on the ground. It always amused Di, seeing the unfortunate flyer having to weave from side to side in order to be able to see. Two ground crew were obliged to sit on the tail as well when the engines were started. This didn't matter one jot as once they were up, according to those who flew in them, they were superb.

The noise was deafening. She held her breath as, one after the other, the beautiful planes soared into the air. She screwed up her eyes and peered out to sea, hoping she might see why both the Hurries and the Spits had been scrambled. The fighters flew so fast they were out of sight immediately, but she could hear the sound of dogfights taking place somewhere thousands of feet above.

The AAF, who flew the less-than-desirable Blenheims, had barely recovered from the horrendous loss of kites and personnel at Dunkirk. Was that why they hadn't been sent out to meet whatever danger was coming? Had those who had replaced the lost men also been Australians, or were there now other Commonwealth recruits amongst them? Then they too taxied onto the runway and, one after the other, followed the two squadrons of Hurricanes and the two of Spitfires.

The air was rent by the wail of the siren. For a moment, Di was disorientated, not sure which was the nearest shelter or ditch to hide in.

'Come with us, lass, there's a trench at the back. I can hear the buggers coming, so get a move on.' She followed the speaker and dived headfirst after him, and the others just ahead of them.

Not a moment too soon, as the distinctive drone of approaching bombers could be clearly heard. How had they got through? Hadn't the fighters been sent up to intercept them? She grabbed hold of both sides of her tin hat as if by holding it to her head she could actually stop it from being blown off.

* * *

Freddie listened to the instructions from the controller. There were a dozen bombers heading for the base and double that number of Me 109s protecting them. A Spit had only ninety seconds of ammunition. Once that was gone, you had to return to base to rearm and refuel. They climbed steadily and he saw their targets below.

'Tally-ho, chaps, let's get the bastards,' he yelled into the mic. The RAF expected a flight to remain in vic formation – flight leader at the front and the other kites positioned almost within touching distance of his wing tips. By giving the squadron permission to break formation, he was also breaking rules.

Freddie had got friendly with some Polish pilots who'd had experience of the Luftwaffe in the Spanish Civil War and they'd told him the British system was useless. The tail end Charlie – the unfortunate bod at the back of the formation – was quite often shot down and nobody would be any the wiser until they landed.

He dived. The G Force made him black out for a second, but he was used to this. He got the Heinkel III in his sights and opened fire. A satisfying cloud of black smoke indicated he'd hit his target. He'd enough ammo for one more attack. Sapper was screaming instructions through the headset in his helmet, but he ignored him. It was every man for himself in a dogfight.

The Me 109s – the German equivalent of their fighters – were engaging where they could. He emptied his guns into the cockpit of one of them. He was so close he saw the astonished look on the pilot's face before he died.

Freddie was now a sitting duck, as he'd got no ammunition. He had to return to base and rearm. He climbed steadily away from the fray, constantly looking right and left for danger. All clear, so he headed for home. The chatter on the wireless told him half the German bombers had got through.

It wasn't sensible to land his kite, as it risked being blown up. The reason the Luftwaffe were coming was to destroy the RAF. To do this would be essential if Hitler wanted to invade. He appeared to be alone and was flying above the cloud cover. He decided the best thing to do would be to remain airborne until the attack was over. He'd got enough fuel to stay up for an hour. He relayed the same instructions to his squadron. Better they avoided Manston for the moment.

Two of his men had gone for a Burton and he prayed they'd managed to bale out. For a moment, he lost concentration as his thoughts drifted to those on the base about to be bombed. He was worried about Di and Millie.

Suddenly, his kite rocked as he was hit. He saw a stream of tracer bullets in front of him. Bloody hell! A bastard German had crept up on him. Some instinct made him ram the stick forward. His Spit was nose-down; thousands of feet below him, he could see the ground.

His Sutton harness didn't let him down and he wasn't catapulted into the canopy. The straps bit into his shoulders. He was travelling vertically at a terrifying speed. For a second, panic almost overwhelmed him. His mouth was dry, sweat trickled between his shoulder blades.

The whole incident had lasted only seconds, but he was travelling ever faster towards certain death. If he didn't pull out of the dive, then he was a dead man – that's if the German fighter didn't get him first. Where the hell was the bastard? Had he followed him?

Somehow, Freddie pulled the nose of the Spit up and began to climb, twisting and turning, frantically looking for his attacker. He opened the throttle and added the emergency boost to assist the ascent. To his horror, he saw trails of white smoke coming from the engine. Then the beautiful Merlin engine packed up. The smoke had been the engine failing.

His breath hissed through his teeth. The fuel tanks in the wings of the kite were perilously close to the pilot. Every flyer's worst nightmare was being burnt alive.

As he got his breathing under control, he thanked God he was still alive – for how much longer remained to be seen. He now had to decide whether to bale out and ran through the procedure he'd learned. One – release Sutton harness. Two – disconnect helmet. Three – push back the canopy and roll the kite. Four – shove the stick forward and fall out headfirst.

Once out, you had to count before pulling the D-ring, but he was buggered if he could recall the exact number. If he pulled it too soon, then he would be hit by the kite, but if he pulled it too late, his chute might not open in time to stop him ending up like strawberry jam.

The Spit still flew reasonably well, although they were gliding in a rather ungainly way. He twisted his head from side to side and could see that apart from a few bullet holes, the cockpit was relatively unscathed.

He came to a decision. His kite might be salvageable if he landed it in a field; if he jumped out, it would continue its descent and could well end up crashing into houses and killing the occupants.

The fields rapidly approaching looked too small – far too small – but he was committed to a crash-landing, and it was too late to change his mind.

11

Joanna watched with interest as the solicitor interviewed the twins. He was respectful, treated them as adults and they responded to his approach. He asked the expected questions and they answered eagerly. She was proud of the way they'd developed since they'd been in her care.

It was hard to believe that she taken them in as little more than servants. Liza had been basically a maid, whilst Joe had been the equivalent of a boot boy. Look at them now – they were articulate, confident and soon they would be her son and daughter. Since Sarah had telephoned just an hour ago, saying she was delighted to be getting a ready-made brother and sister, there was nothing to stop the adoption going ahead.

'Now, is there anything you would like to ask me about the legalities?'

'We were wondering, sir, if our nan has signed something to say she's happy to let this go through,' Joe asked, and his sister nodded.

'I'm delighted to be able to tell you that a clerk from the office visited her yesterday and she has signed without demure.'

Joanna was delighted. 'So there's no reason this can't go ahead smoothly? How long do you think it will take?'

'As you know, I've already drawn up the necessary documents for you, my lady. However, there's also something for your future son and daughter to sign, which they can do now.'

'Capital, but you haven't answered my daughter-in-law's question, young man. When will the adoption be legal? We need to know because my future grandchildren are going to be baptised as soon as they are legally part of the family.'

'I apologise, how remiss of me. I'll file the papers at the court as soon as I have them and I don't anticipate any problems occurring. I'll arrange for Lady Harcourt to be their guardian in the interim so that she has the legal status of a parent.'

'Mr Broome, is this going to take weeks, months or possibly years? I'm still waiting for you to enlighten us.'

'As you can imagine, my lady, the courts are moving slowly, as so many of the people involved with their smooth running have already volunteered or been conscripted. Therefore, instead of taking a matter of days, it could be several weeks. I can assure you it won't be months.'

Elizabeth laughed. 'I believe that several weeks will, in fact, be months, but I'll let that go. Liza, Joe, everything will be in place in time for your birthday celebration.'

'Imagine, Joe, when Ma died and we went to live with our nan, we were ever so miserable. Now look at us – we've really gone up in the world. We won't be Tims any longer but Harcourt.' She turned to Joanna. 'We've talked about things, Aunt Joanna, and being part of the family won't make any difference to what we do here. If we were your real son and daughter, we'd still have to pull our weight, wouldn't we?'

This time, Elizabeth snorted instead of laughing. The solicitor was busy putting the papers away in his briefcase and was enjoying the exchange.

'You will be in every respect members of this family, child, and as such will no longer do domestic work. We've discussed this and we're going to arrange for you both to complete your education, either here with tutors or, if you prefer, at a boarding school somewhere.'

The twins looked horrified at the suggestion. 'Go away to school with all the posh kids? No thanks, my lady, we'll stay here where we belong. Tutors will suit us just fine,' Joe said firmly.

Joanna exchanged a glance with Elizabeth, as this was how they'd expected the conversation to go. They'd absolutely no intention of sending the children anywhere and knew they'd agree to the tutoring if the alternative was a boarding school.

'If that's everything, my ladies, I'll see myself out.' As the solicitor was speaking, they heard the distinctive wail of the air-raid siren coming from Manston and then, seconds later, the one in the village joined in.

'Quickly, we must go down to the shelter. Joe, are the outside men working today?'

'No, my lady, but Val and Joan are upstairs.'

The two ladies from the village, who were now in charge of keeping the house immaculate, were peering over the gallery banister, looking not at all bothered by the warning that German bombers were approaching.

'Don't dither about up there, you two, everybody must be safe. Even if it's a false alarm, it's about time we practised the procedure.' Joanna surprised herself by being so forceful and taking command. What a difference a war had made to her character. David wouldn't recognise her as the meek little wife he'd left a year ago.

The seven of them hurried through the house, into the kitchen and then through the back corridor to the door that led into the bowels of the house. She pulled the door open and reached round to switch on the light, thankful it came on.

'Liza, go ahead and open the door to the shelter and put on the light. Joe, call Lazzy. He needs to be with us.'

She turned to offer her support to Elizabeth, but Mr Broome had that in hand. The steps were stone, steep and narrow. The dog thought this a fine game and was bouncing around in excitement.

'Hurry up, Joe, I'll come last and close the door behind me.'

There was ample room for seven in the shelter, and candles and an oil lamp in case the power failed, plenty of blankets, cushions and books to read and board games to play.

'Oh dear, I've managed this very badly,' said Joanna. 'Someone should have made two flasks of tea. Also, I'm sure the French doors in the drawing room are still open, so anybody could come in and loot the house if we're down here.'

'Is that a door to the outside, my lady?' Mr Broome asked.

'It is – we think it was the way the Catholic priest used to come into the house when Oliver Cromwell was in charge. This is why my late husband chose this particular part of the cellars to convert. Joe, the bolt will be across, would you mind checking that the door opens?'

There was a long, padded bench down one side with ample room for five to sit comfortably. In the centre of the room was a table constructed from trestles. On the other side were shelves with a variety of tinned goods, mugs, assorted crockery, cutlery, a couple of saucepans and a motley selection of bowls. Thankfully there were four wooden chairs pushed under the table, so there was sufficient seating.

Joanna grimaced as she recalled David telling her the bowls were for anyone who wished to be sick, but they could be used for washing one's hands after using the primitive facilities. There were a dozen pottery jars with sealed lids containing water.

There was even a small, methylated spirit-powered cooker, which would do to heat soup or water to make tea.

At the far end, where the door to the underground passageway was situated, a cubicle had been built and an Elsan WC installed. She hoped she wouldn't have to use it, as to do so would be most embarrassing for herself and for those who would be obliged to listen to what went on in there.

'The door opens easy enough, Aunt Joanna,' Joe said cheerfully but then said something very rude indeed as the dog pushed past him and vanished into the darkness of the passageway.

'I'll go after him; he won't like it in the dark.' Before she could gather her wits, he too had vanished. They couldn't hear what was going on outside and both Joe and the dog could be running into danger. Her heart pounded and her hands were clammy.

* * *

Di closed her eyes as the bombs started to drop. The thump thump of the ack ack guns as they tried to shoot down the incoming German bombers and the rattle of machine-gun fire added to the terrifying experience.

Despite the fact that she was in a ditch, the shockwaves from the explosions knocked her sideways, her tin hat slipped over her forehead and for a moment, she couldn't catch her breath.

The raid continued for what seemed like an hour but was, in fact, only a fraction of that. The acrid smell of burning caught the back of her throat, then black smoke drifted overhead.

'Frigging incendiaries, we can't let things burn. I reckon the worst is over, even if the all-clear hasn't sounded,' the speaker, a senior NCO, yelled down the ditch to his subordinates.

They shouted back their agreement and as quickly as they'd arrived, the dozen or so men scrambled out, leaving Di alone. She wasn't a coward. She could drive a fire truck and help them put out the blaze.

She understood now why all the aircraft had taken off. If they'd been on the ground, they could have been destroyed. No time to worry about her friends, male or female, she had a duty to perform.

She was about to grab her bike when the scream of an approaching fighter made her freeze. Were they returning? Then she saw it was a Hurricane, one of theirs, and smoke was pouring from its engine. She held her breath as it crashed onto the grass beside the runway and skidded on its belly. There was the roar of a fire tender and an ambulance and a dozen men ran toward the burning plane. She watched in horror, believing the pilot must be dead.

To her astonishment, the rescuers pulled him out and he walked away from the wreckage. The bowsers had remained working, as not only their boys but planes from other bases landed to refuel and rearm.

Heart still pounding, she looked for her bicycle, which was unscathed, and she'd never pedalled so fast in her life. No time now to look around and see just how bad the damage was or if there'd been any casualties. All she knew was that one of the blazes was perilously close to the explosives store. There were two fire trucks, an ambulance and a couple of rescue vehicles housed just behind the MT.

'Sarge, what do you want me to drive to the fire?'

'Good girl, just the ticket. Take a fire tender to the dispersal huts. I'll not send a WAAF to the other one.' He pointed towards the flames near the explosive depot.

'Yes, Sarge, on my way.'

Fortunately, she'd had practice in the unwieldy vehicle and had no difficulty getting it into gear. The firefighters jumped aboard and Di put her foot down. She tore across the runway and brought the vehicle to a commendably smooth stop, as close to the fire as she dared.

Her job was to wait in the cab and be ready to move the truck when told. The heat from the inferno and the smoke made sitting where she was unpleasant – but not as bad for her as for the men putting it out.

The incendiary bombs had caused havoc in the dispersal area but with her timely arrival, the men had managed to save the most important hut – the one with the telephone. The latrine was a bit charred but hopefully still functioning. No hangars or aircraft had been damaged either.

It was all a bit chaotic for a while, but eventually the fires were out and Di drove the weary firefighters back to their base. It was her job to check the vehicle was still in working order and then to clean it down, but the men kindly offered to do this for her.

'No, you get on. You've done your bit,' the sergeant said firmly.

'I'll see if I can get the NAAFI van to add you to their round.'

She looked up as the distinctive roar of returning kites filled the air. She ran around to the runway to watch them come in. There should be twenty-four Hurricanes, the same number of Spitfires and twenty Blenheims. As the dreadful fighter-bombers, the Blenheims, hadn't actually been in action, she was certain they'd all have returned safely.

Having feelings for a pilot wasn't a comfortable thing, and she wondered if the boys flying the planes were as scared as she was worrying about one.

These unpopular aircraft had landed and were all present and correct on their designated spot on the apron. Half the fighter squadrons were already back, many of them looking badly damaged, but more were still coming back.

Di retrieved her bicycle and was about to ride across to the dispersal area but then decided against it. The flyers would be regrouping, waiting to debrief and she wouldn't be welcome.

Admin was the place to go, as somebody there was bound to know who'd returned and who hadn't. Not that she was entitled to this information, but she was sure somebody would tell her what she desperately wanted to know.

Her heart was thumping so loudly she could hear it, her hands were trembling and it was as if she'd swallowed a large stone. If any of the men she knew had died or been seriously injured, she would be sad but if either Freddie or Ted had failed to return, she would be devastated, and so would Millie.

She had to pass the NAAFI and changed her mind again. She needed a hot cup of tea and something to eat to calm her nerves before she found out who was missing. There were, she thought, at least four Spits and two Hurries unaccounted for.

As she propped her bike against the nearest wall, she heard her friend call out. 'Di, have you heard anything about our boys?'

They embraced and she shook her head. 'No, I'm pretty sure there are at least four missing Spits but whether they belong to Freddie or Ted I've no idea as I can't see from here. I'm going to get a cuppa and then ask admin if they can find out for me.'

'I do know that there have been no serious casualties on the base. I was driving one of the ambulances and we only had a broken arm, plus several cuts and bruises. The other one collected a few burns but nothing too bad,' Millie said.

'That's good news, at least. Actually, I don't think I want any tea after all. I couldn't swallow anything at the moment. If you come, too, I think we're more likely to get someone to speak to us, as you're a corporal and I'm only an LACW.'

'A leading aircraft woman is a junior NCO, as well you know. I was heading that way myself. It's going to be so difficult for both of us every time the men are scrambled.'

'Much harder for you, as you're married to one. I do care for Freddie quite a lot and obviously don't want anything to happen to him.'

'Not everybody falls in love as quickly as we did. We'd better hurry, as we're officially still on duty.'

Phyllis and Pamela were secretaries and they would be a good place to start. The admin block was noisy, people talking on telephones, in offices and corridors. They shouldn't be there getting in the way.

'Let's leave it, we could be put on a charge for dereliction of duty, Millie.'

'Unlikely, as I'm the most senior WAAF present. Nobody's taking any notice of us, so let's nip in and speak to the girls. We won't go anywhere else.'

Phyllis wasn't at her desk, but Pamela was. She'd been speaking on the telephone and looked up as they came in. She jumped to her feet and rushed over.

'Di, I'm so sorry. Your Freddie's missing. We're waiting for news. Ted's tickety-boo, Millie, but there have been least two fatalities, two more are missing, and two landed at Kingsnorth, near Ashford, and are on their way back now.'

She couldn't catch her breath. Her stomach lurched and for a second, Di thought she was going to be sick. Not Freddie – please God, not Freddie.

* * *

Freddie slid back the cockpit canopy and began his approach. The field he'd chosen had seemed long enough from a thousand feet but, as he glided ever earthwards, he began to have second thoughts. It looked dangerously short.

The wheels were up – a safer option in the circumstances. The kite shook as it hit the deck, but he was pleased with his landing. The Spit skidded along the grass. Everything was going splendidly, he was down to walking speed, when suddenly the kite was nose-down, the canopy slammed closed, and he was in the dark.

Was she on her back, had she turned turtle? He couldn't see a bloody thing. If he was upside down, then he was done for. God – what an ignominious ending – buried alive!

He grabbed the canopy and, expecting some resistance, put his full strength into shoving it back. It moved easily and the unnecessary force almost dislocated his shoulders. A wave of relief made him weak for a moment. They weren't upside down, but had slithered into what looked like a dry riverbed and were now nose-down in it. This hadn't been visible on his approach, and it was the overhanging plants and so on that had temporarily obscured his vision.

Despite the fact there was no smell of petrol – he was convinced he'd been out of fuel – he was desperate to get out. He grabbed the edges of the cockpit and heaved. He couldn't move. He was trapped. For the second time, panic made him incapable of coherent thought for a second.

He swore out loud at his stupidity. He hadn't released his harness – it was still tightly fastened around him. He pulled the pin and immediately was free. He was on his feet and about to jump when his head was thrown backwards. This time he'd forgotten to unhook his oxygen and radio. His flying helmet was still firmly attached to both.

Laughing hysterically, Freddie tumbled headfirst from the kite, landing safely on his shoulders and continuing the momentum into a forward roll. Not elegant but he didn't care. He was now minus a flying helmet and a Spitfire but at least he was alive – and in a wide ditch. He scrambled out and brushed the debris from his uniform.

He turned to find a group of villagers beaming at him. 'That was a close shave, son, I reckon you could do with a stiff drink in the pub.'

The speaker was a tall, thin chap with bushy eyebrows and a bald head. 'I need to ring the base. Is there a phone box in the village? In fact, I need to know exactly where I am. They'll send a lorry out to recover my poor old Spit.'

He moved closer to his upended plane now he was sure there wasn't going to be an explosion. The wings were more or less intact and resting neatly on the edge of the ditch. The engine and prop were buggered, but the wizards at MU, where the kites went to be repaired, might well be able to salvage what was still usable.

'There's no telephone box here, young man, but there's one in the next village, Willingham. Where are you from? Hawkinge or Manston?'

Freddie gave the helpful chap his name and he promised to have it relayed immediately to the base. Manston would send a driver to collect him and he hoped it might be Di. Seeing her lovely face would make him feel better, help him to push the ugly images from his mind. He just wanted to get back and find out how many of his men he'd lost.

12

Joanna shone her torch, full beam, down the steep steps leading to the passageway but could see nothing. However, she could hear Joe shouting the dog's name. His voice was getting fainter, so Lazzy was ignoring him.

'I'll go after them, my lady, shall I?'

'No, Mr Broome, I'm sure Joe will manage. He's a sensible young man and won't put himself in danger.'

Elizabeth was inspecting everything on the shelves, tutting and muttering, obviously not impressed. 'Whatever was David thinking when he stocked the shelves? What use is cocoa without milk, Marmite without toast and butter?'

Liza was also examining what was there. 'There's two tins of salmon, national dried milk, condensed milk and half a dozen jars with bottled plums and such. I didn't know there was any such thing as lemon barley powder, but it will go a treat in the water.'

'Well, if ever we're obliged to stay down here for any length of time, we won't go hungry. Mr Broome, could I ask you to see if the water is still fresh enough to drink?' Joanna asked the solicitor.

Whilst he fiddled with the stopper on the jar, she returned to her position at the top of the stairs. Then she smiled. 'How foolish – the dog can't get out as the end of the passageway has a door. They'll both be back in a few minutes.'

She was right and a somewhat chastened dog slunk in with his tail between his legs. Joe had obviously spoken very firmly to him.

'Could you hear anything?'

'Not a dicky bird, Aunt Joanna. If there were bombs dropping nearby then I'm certain I'd have heard something.'

'You do realise, Joanna, down here we won't be able to hear the all-clear?'

'I didn't until you kindly pointed it out to me, Elizabeth. Being under the house is all very well for safety, but there are definitely disadvantages.'

Joe grinned. 'I'll give it another quarter of an hour and then have a deco. Anyone want to play a game of whist?'

To Joanna's surprise, Elizabeth joined in and it was considerably longer than fifteen minutes before anyone thought of checking to see if it was safe to emerge.

Joe dashed off and was back almost immediately. 'All clear, and I reckon we could have gone up ages ago.'

What he didn't mention was the smell of smoke in the air. Manston must have been hit. Joanna hoped that nobody had been hurt when the bombs dropped. She pushed her thoughts away from the fate of the brave fighter pilots, as in every battle it seemed somebody was lost.

Nobody talked about what had taken place. Joe headed for the village, already late for his afternoon visit to the Smiths' cottage. She prayed he'd return with better news about Betty. Mr Broome departed also.

The ladies from the village had refused to go home at the usual time as they said they hadn't finished because of the raid.

'It won't take us a tick, my lady, and now the kiddies have gone to Norfolk there isn't a rush to get home,' Val said with a bright smile, but Joanna detected sadness in her eyes.

'Have they settled in with their evacuee family? It must be so hard for you to be on your own at home...'

The two exchanged a look that didn't bode well. 'It's like this, my lady,' Joan said. 'We need to do war work now we've got the time. We'll not leave you in the lurch but are just letting you know that we can't stay here if there's full-time factory work to be had in Ramsgate.'

'I understand. I don't suppose you know anybody who might like to take your places?'

'As a matter of fact, Doris, Enid and Aggie would like to take over. They've all got youngsters at home to feed and take care of who were too old to be evacuated but not old enough to be left on their own.'

Joanna was about to say that she didn't need three to help out but then stopped. Without Betty working as housekeeper, it would be terribly difficult to look after the land girls who were expected sometime in August.

'Thank you so much for finding someone to replace you both. If one of them doesn't mind doing heavy work – the laundry and so on – then as soon as the land girls do arrive, I'll be absolutely delighted to take them on. Tell them that at the next WVS meeting, we can have a quick chat afterwards.'

'We'll do that, my lady. Have you heard how Betty and Bert are doing? All the kiddies in the village are on the mend now. Sadly, Jimmy, the old boy who used to sit outside his cottage whittling wooden animals for the church bazaar, didn't make it. His funeral's Friday,' Val said sadly.

'Bert's making a good recovery but Betty's still very ill. One would think that a young woman of only twenty-five would be able to fight this off. I'll get Joe to take a condolence card to Mr Simmons' wife.'

'We'll come Thursday, not Friday, if that's all right. Because of the funeral, you know.'

'That will be fine. Good afternoon, ladies, and thank you for staying on and finishing your chores.'

Joanna retreated to the terrace, as from there the smell of the smoke spiralling up from the base was less noticeable and she couldn't see it either. Elizabeth followed her.

'Assuming that Betty gets over this, I doubt that she will be able to resume here as housekeeper for some time. Being so desperately ill will make her weak. I've heard of children going blind, deaf and in some cases mentally deficient.'

'Then let's pray that none of those things happen to her,' Joanna said. 'Are you suggesting that I take on all three ladies anyway?'

'I am indeed, my dear. You must be pragmatic about things. As far as I'm concerned, Liza and Joe are now my grandchildren. It's not acceptable for them to continue as domestic servants.'

'I agree that things must change, but Sarah did as much as Betty when she was here, both inside and outside the house, as well as fulfilling her duties as a fully qualified St John's ambulance member.'

'I don't want the children to feel that they are being exploited.'

'Exploited? Good heavens, how can you say such a thing? Since they started calling me Aunt Joanna, they no longer do anything I wouldn't have asked Sarah to do.'

'Very well, I grudgingly admit that you might have a point. But you do agree that their education, elocution and ability to mix with all echelons of society are paramount?'

'There's a war on, Elizabeth, and barriers between ourselves and others less fortunate have been lowered. Whilst we're on the subject – do you now want them to call you Grandmother?'

Joanna had said this with a smile, not expecting it to be taken seriously.

'I do indeed. I certainly don't wish to be called Nan or Granny but would be very happy to be addressed as Grandmother or Grandmama.'

'Then I shall become...' She wasn't sure what she wanted to be called. Sarah had always addressed her as Mummy. But despite saying she considered the twins to be her children, for some reason she wasn't ready to have them call her that.

Elizabeth sensed her dilemma; sometimes the old lady could be very empathetic. 'Why don't they call you Mother or Mama?'

'Do we have to decide now?'

The rattle of the tea trolley heralded the arrival of much-needed afternoon tea.

'I think we do, and we've got to stop Liza running about like a housemaid. It would be good for one of us to make the tea sometimes, don't you think?'

The suggestion was so ludicrous Joanna laughed, as did her mother-in-law.

She went to meet Liza. 'This is the last time that you wait on us like this. Your adoption might not be final, but as far as we're concerned, from today you and Joe are Harcourts.'

'Blimey – that's a turnup for the books...'

'That won't do, Liza. A Harcourt always speaks correctly and wouldn't dream of using either phrase. Please say it again,' Elizabeth said.

Liza took it in good part. 'Good heavens, I am most terribly surprised by that news.' She said this in an excellent imitation of Elizabeth's crystal-cut diction.

'Perfect, but trying to emulate me really isn't necessary. Be yourself, but with the rough edges smoothed away.'

Joanna helped put out the delicate porcelain cups and saucers, matching tea plates, sugar bowl and milk jug whilst Liza put the cake stand with the dainty sandwiches and scones in the centre of the table.

Normally the young girl would retreat and leave them to eat, but Joanna pulled out a chair and with some hesitation, Liza took it.

'I don't feel comfortable sitting with you.'

'You'll become accustomed to it. From now on, I wish you to address me as Grandmama and Aunt Joanna will now metamorphose into Mama.'

Liza had been straining the tea into the cups and slopped some on to the pretty floral tablecloth. 'I'm not sure I can do that. It doesn't seem right.'

'You and Joe will get used to the changes. Being legally adopted makes you as much my daughter as Sarah.'

Elizabeth nodded. 'I wish an adopted son could inherit the title, but unfortunately he can't.'

The conversation was interrupted by the noisy jangling of the telephone. Liza usually answered but Joanna shook her head. 'No, my dear, I'll get it. Sit down and enjoy your tea and talk to your grandmama.'

* * *

Di was stunned by the news that Freddie was missing, presumably shot down. Then she rallied. 'He's the best flyer at Manston. I refuse to believe that he's gone for a Burton. Thank you for telling us, Pamela.'

Millie guided her out with a gentle hand on her elbow and she was sure no one would realise how distressed she was. The thought that a young man so full of life, so intelligent and witty might be dead was unbearable.

'We both need that tea, Di, no arguments. It's an order.'

'I'm okay, just a bit shocked. I wish I knew the details but can hardly go in and ask. If anyone had seen him go down in flames, fail to bale out, then I'd have been told.'

'Missing is certainly better than confirmed dead. Remember that Ted has survived a couple of near misses.'

There were no empty tables in the NAAFI and anyway it was too noisy. 'If you don't mind, I'd prefer to sit on the grass behind the officers' accommodation block,' said Di. 'It's quiet there and we can pretend we're in the country and not on a base that's just been bombed.'

'Wait for me, don't go on ahead. We'll walk around together.'

Di put her bicycle under the tarpaulin that covered Freddie's motorbike. It would be safe there. She looked around and saw Millie's bike and did the same with hers. By the time she'd accomplished this task – everything seemed to be moving more slowly for some reason, including her – her friend was back.

Millie was carrying a tray with two mugs of tea as well as what looked like sausage rolls and iced fingers.

As expected, they had the area to themselves and she led the way to a patch of neatly mowed grass under the trees that edged the base. 'I can't see where the gate used to be, can you?'

Millie carefully put the tray on the ground before looking round at the fence. 'No, they must've used old chain-link fencing, as it's blended in perfectly. It was quite ridiculous having it put there in the first place. Sarah Harcourt's fiancé must have been mad to have done so.'

'He wanted to make it easier for Lady Harcourt and us; as he was being posted to Hornchurch, he wouldn't get into trouble.' Talking about trivial things was exactly what she needed to help her calm down.

Di flopped down on the grass and shuffled backwards until she was leaning against a tree trunk with complete disregard for any grass stains on her overalls. They were often covered in grease, so a bit of grass really didn't matter. Even from where they were sitting, she could hear machines and lorries, shouts and bangs, as men set about methodically rebuilding and repairing the huts at dispersal and the other damage done by the bombs.

'We really shouldn't be sitting here; they'll want all the drivers to help with moving materials about the base.'

'We've got time to eat and for you to recover from the shock.' Millie checked her watch. 'It's two o'clock – we'll get back on duty in twenty minutes. I hope no one's borrowed our bicycles.'

'I put them with Freddie's motorbike.'

She didn't think she'd be able to eat, but after drinking half the tea, she tucked in with as much enthusiasm as Millie. As always, they didn't chat until the food was finished. She wondered if gobbling down her meals like this would be something she'd do for the rest of her life.

'I was in the ditch behind the huts during the raid, where were you?' Di said.

'In the shelter. It was packed, hot and smelly. Would you believe that several airmen intended to smoke cigarettes? Fortunately, I was able to put a stop to it.'

'How long do you think it will be before we know about Freddie and the other men who are missing?'

'I'm not sure. Probably by the time we finish this evening. I'll take the tray back if you get our bikes out of hiding.'

* * *

Sarge was livid. 'Where the bloody hell have you two been? Sodding about, sitting on your arses drinking tea, have you? You're both going on a charge. You can forget further promotion by the time I've finished writing you up. I had to send two of my mechanics out with the lorries because of you two shirkers.'

There was nothing they could say that wouldn't exacerbate the situation, so they stood, penitent, rigidly to attention, eyes front, letting the stream of abuse wash over their heads. Eventually, the tirade was over. If all the lorries were already in use, then what were they going to be doing now?

Di exchanged a nervous glance with Millie, who shook her head slightly. They remained at attention for a further ten minutes and she was beginning to feel a bit faint. Sarge had left them standing there to answer the telephone.

'Stand easy. LACW 356, take the Austin to this address. Squadron Leader Hanover pranged his Spit and needs picking up pronto. Corporal, take the van and get over to the stores. They need stuff moving.'

They saluted, even though this was incorrect procedure as only officers were saluted. Di was frozen to the spot, hardly able to take in the news that Freddie was safe.

'He'll be pleased to see you. He's been waiting for some time.' He handed over the chit with the address. 'That's why you were both missing?' Millie nodded, but Di wasn't able to do anything sensible. 'You'd better get used to it. It can only get worse.'

She managed then to nod but was still incapable of speech. She was starting the engine of the Austin when she realised she should have changed into her uniform. When driving an officer, one should always be correctly dressed.

Freddie wouldn't mind and he certainly wouldn't report her. He must have been waiting a considerable time already and she certainly wasn't going to waste even a minute doing something unnecessary.

After checking the map, she saw that Willingham was the nearest village to where he was. Even without signposts, she was confident she could find it. She was about to drive away when someone banged on her window. She wound it down and a very dishevelled, exhausted-looking flight lieutenant was standing there.

'Hey, I need a lift pronto to Hawkinge. Sarge said you can take me on your way to pick up Freddie. I'm Ginger Jones.'

He didn't wait for her to argue but nipped around in front of the bonnet and jumped into the car. She could hardly argue with a senior officer and especially after what had just happened with Sarge.

'Freddie has been waiting ages already.'

'He won't mind, at least he's alive, which is more than I can say for two of my flight.'

'I'm sorry to hear that.' No wonder he looked tired. He was right to say that Freddie wouldn't mind waiting a bit longer. She wasn't sure if she should attempt a friendly conversation or leave him to his thoughts. She didn't know this young man well but had driven him back and forth several times. He was easily recognised because of his carrot-coloured hair.

'One of Freddie's flight has gone for a Burton too. But the other bloke that was missing has been picked up from the drink unharmed.'

'That's good news. So, we lost three men altogether?'

'That's right. Freddie's pranged in a field.' The young man slumped back against the door of the car, closed his eyes and fell asleep – at least she thought he was asleep, but he might just be avoiding having to talk.

Now she was really in trouble because she was improperly dressed with an officer in the car. She might well be demoted, but for the first time, she really didn't care about becoming an officer.

As long as Freddie was safe then she'd be happy to be returned to the lowliest rank of ACW2. She smiled. All this time, she'd been pretending he wasn't the most important person in her life but now she was forced to accept the truth. She was in love with Freddie.

13

Freddie refused the whisky he was offered in the pub but gratefully drank three cups of tea and wolfed down the same number of sandwiches made by the friendly landlady. Almost meeting his maker made a chap ravenous. He sat and talked with the villagers, caused much hilarity with his description of his efforts to get out of his kite, but after an hour or so, he thought he'd better make a move.

'Squadron Leader, someone will be coming to collect you and your aircraft as soon as they can arrange it,' the bod who'd first spoken to him said. 'The telephone was out of order at the telephone box, so he had to cycle to the doctor and use his. Hence the delay in bringing you this news.'

'Call me Freddie, why don't you? Thank you for arranging that. I feel much better after my prang and must get back to my kite. I don't want the local boys to start stripping it.'

'Good lord, that won't happen here. I'm chairman of the parish council and have two LDV standing guard.'

The local defence volunteers mainly consisted of boys too young to enlist and men ineligible for one reason or another. God knows what use they'd be if there was an invasion as, at the moment, all they had was an armband, no weapons to speak of, and some of them were too old to march, let alone fight.

'That's good of you, sir, but I need to be there myself. Thank you for your hospitality.' He didn't carry money so couldn't offer to pay for his food but thought if he did the landlady would probably be offended.

He sauntered the few hundred yards back to the field in which he'd ended up nosediving into a ditch. As expected, there was a group of scruffy youngsters staring longingly at his kite, but the presence of the two grizzled LDV was deterring them.

Freddie headed for the unkempt lads and addressed the leader, a shifty-eyed little bugger who was in need of a good bath and a haircut.

'Get lost, all of you. Looting is a hanging offence.'

They took one look at him and vanished, muttering curses under their breath. 'Shouldn't they be in school?'

'Those boys run wild and I'm sure any school's relieved they don't come. They don't live in our village but roam around the area looking for things to steal.'

It might be some time before a driver could be found to collect him – once admin knew he was alive and well, he wouldn't be a priority. He stood back, hands on hips, and stared at his poor old kite.

'The wings will have to come off for them to take her back to base.' He was speaking to himself more than the chaps guarding his beloved Spit, but the marginally younger of the two answered him.

'Dennis, the bloke in charge of everything – at least he thinks he is – has gone to organise a tractor to pull your plane out of the ditch.'

'Jolly good show. With any luck, when we get it out, it won't be too badly damaged. I need to retrieve my helmet and chute. I'll need them when I'm back on ops tomorrow.'

'You have spare Spitfires hanging about, do you? Thought they were in short supply,' the more grizzled of the two said sourly. 'Dennis has taken anything aluminium we've got, as well as all metal fences and gates.' He scowled. 'My missus gave him our saucepans and you can't get new ones for love nor money.'

'Dennis is only following government instructions and well you know it, Dave. Don't upset the young man, he's fighting to keep us safe from the Huns.'

'I did my bit on the Somme – it was supposed to be the war to end all wars – look at us now.'

Freddie left them to their conversation and went to make a closer inspection of his upended kite. He dropped into the riverbed and examined the nose from below. He was amazed the prop hadn't gone through it. It was remarkably undented considering everything.

Tentatively he pushed against the wing above him and nothing shifted. He scrambled out and decided he was going to recover his gear himself. The cockpit canopy was open, and it was almost within arm's reach. He checked the stability and decided he'd risk it.

The two old men were still arguing about the first war against Germany and he left them to it. Ten minutes later, he was back on the deck with his chute and his helmet in his hands. A job well done if he said so himself!

He shoved his helmet into his pocket and carried his chute across the field to the gate and then left it there. The sound of a tractor approaching meant a helpful farmer was on the way to extricate his Spit. He wouldn't let him do it unless he was quite certain it could be done without doing further damage. The fuselage was riddled with bullet holes but nothing his ground crew couldn't repair. He grinned wryly. Who was he kidding? This Spit was a write-off. She'd never fly again.

The man driving the tractor looked efficient enough and he'd certainly got plenty of ropes. 'I don't want to try this unless I'm certain we won't finish the poor old girl off.'

The man removed his cap and scratched his head. 'I reckon you're right, that there plane needs to be lifted out of the ditch, not dragged. Manhandling is what's required.'

Freddie pointed to the tail, which was resting in the field. 'What about putting a rope around that and then you pull it slowly? Would that work?'

'I reckon it might. I'm not climbing up no aircraft, young man, you'll have to do that.'

A rope was attached successfully around the tail and Freddie was sliding to the ground when Di called out to him. He almost ended on his nose.

'What are you doing? Haven't you had enough excitement for one day?'

'The farmer and I have come up with a plan to get my kite ready to be transported back to the base. I'm perfectly safe, so don't look perturbed.'

Luckily, he landed on both feet and didn't let go of the rope either. 'There, all tickety-boo. The farmer on the tractor is now going to pull my kite out of the ditch.'

Di didn't look particularly impressed by this information. 'Don't you think it would be better to leave it to the experts? Why don't you just get in the car and let me drive you back?'

'Oh, ye of little faith! Maths was always my strong point. I was going to study maths at Cambridge but saw how things were going in Europe so decided to join the RAF instead.'

'I don't see that being a mathematician is anything to do with being an idiot. Please, Freddie, don't do it. It looks perfectly happy there.'

'I've calculated the angles, length of rope required and the amount of force needed to pull it from the ditch.'

'Pulling it isn't the problem. Unless you're a magician, you're going to end up with your plane even more damaged and I'm sure it would be better to leave it where it is rather than do that.'

'I've sent for reinforcements and once she's moving, we'll walk forward, holding the wings steady as the tractor slowly drags her free.'

She looked at the rope, at him, at the tractor and then nodded. 'Okay, where do you want me?'

'As leader of the other group.'

'If we make things worse, we'll both be in trouble.'

He thought for a minute. 'If things go sideways then I'll take the blame. Your name won't come into it.'

'Good, because I'm in enough trouble already, but I'll tell you about that on the way back to Manston later.'

* * *

It had taken Di an extra hour to deliver her passenger and she was relieved she didn't have to return to collect him later. The last thing she expected was to find Freddie organising the rescue of his beloved Spitfire with the help of the locals and an ancient tractor.

Word had obviously spread and there was now a small crowd gathered, some to offer their assistance, no doubt, but most of them to enjoy the spectacle. She supposed that not much happened in this village, as it was sufficiently far away from the coast or a base to be at limited risk from bombing.

She held her breath as the tractor inched forward. The rope straightened, there was an ominous groaning and she tensed. If the rope broke, this would end in disaster and possibly Freddie's court-martial.

He must be well aware that if his extraction was successful, he'd be praised and called a clever chap, but if it failed, they would throw the book at him and say he was an idiot.

Her fists clenched. He was in the ditch, presumably attempting to guide the kite in the right direction. If the rope snapped, he would be crushed. Why was he so careless with his own safety? She blinked back unwanted tears. To lose him over something so stupid would be unbearable – to lose him at all would break her heart. What an extremely silly thing to have done – falling in love with a fighter pilot with a death wish was a recipe for disaster.

Watching was agony, but she couldn't look away. Slowly, the aircraft emerged from the ditch and seemed in reasonable shape, considering it had been shot at and had crash-landed. Once it was moving, she ran forward, along with half a dozen others. Now the extra ropes attached to the wings would come into use.

'Six of you with me on this side. Six of you on the other with the WAAF,' Freddie shouted, and they all did as they were told. 'Now, Di, grab the end of the dangling rope on your side and the rest of you there get in behind. I'll do the same on mine.'

She snatched up the rough hemp rope end, glad she'd had the foresight to pull her gloves on first. The fighter was protesting loudly at the indignity of having ropes attached to it and the sooner they accomplished this manoeuvre, the happier she'd be.

'Okay, everybody, start pulling steadily, but slowly, on my command.'

She leaned forward, the rope resting on her shoulder, both hands firmly around the frayed end. She daren't look back to see if the others were doing as he'd asked.

'Right – *now*.'

As they moved forward, the tractor continued to move at snail's pace towards the end of the field. His vehicle must weigh a fraction of the Spit and she had a nasty suspicion this could go horribly wrong.

* * *

Joanna almost went headlong over the dog as he rushed ahead of her. He had a tendency to bark at the telephone, as if telling it to stop ringing. She lifted the receiver. 'Goodwill House. Lady Harcourt speaking.'

'Lady Harcourt, it's Dr Willoughby. I've the gravest news. Mrs Smith is slipping away. If you wish to say your farewells, then I suggest you come down immediately.'

Joanna was unable to answer for a second then pulled herself together. 'Yes, Liza and I will come down at once. Is Joe there?'

'Yes, I've not told him. He's busy with the pig and chickens. There's no longer any risk of infection. Would you like me to collect you?'

The doctor lived in a manor house at least a mile on the other side of the village. 'No, it will be quicker on our bicycles,' Joanna replied as she ended the call.

The dog sensed her dismay and pushed his wet nose into her hand. 'Yes, Lazzy, it's the worst possible news.'

Liza was standing in the drawing room doorway and had obviously overheard the brief conversation.

'Shall I fetch your hat, Aunt Joanna?'

'No, thank you, I'll go as I am.'

Even Elizabeth was on her feet, her expression sad. 'I'm so sorry. Sometimes it's hard to believe there's a God taking care of us.'

Joanna was unable to answer. Her throat was clogged, her eyes gritty. Instead, she raised her hand to indicate she'd heard and then rushed out of the front door. Liza was close behind.

Twenty minutes after receiving the dreaded phone call, she was knocking on the front door of the Smiths' cottage. Jean opened it, her eyes red, her face blotched from crying.

'My lady, I can't believe this is happening,' Jean said as she stood aside to let them come in.

'Is she awake? Will she know we've come to say goodbye?'

'I'm not sure, my lady, but you never know, she might be able to hear you.'

'Is Bert with her? Will he mind us coming at such a difficult time?'

'He's shut himself in his room. He knows, but says he doesn't want to be with her.'

'I see. Would you be kind enough to fetch Joe? He'll want to say goodbye to Betty too. I assume that Mrs Jones is with her?'

'Of course she is, my lady. We've been taking it in turns to sit with her – it's all we can do now.' Jean's voice was gruff, and she swallowed noisily and mopped her eyes with an already sodden handkerchief.

Joanna reached out and squeezed her shoulder, then turned and drew Liza into her embrace. The girl was trembling, almost overcome with grief.

'Not now, darling, we must be strong for Betty. There'll be a time to cry afterwards.'

The sound of the back door slamming meant Joe was here. He appeared in his socks, his face white, trying not to cry. The two of them might be almost fifteen, confident and mature, but they were still children.

'Good boy, you remembered to take off your boots. Are you both ready?' They nodded and when she held out her hand to him, to her surprise, he clutched it just as firmly as Liza was clinging to the other one.

The cottage staircase was narrow, but somehow they negotiated it without being obliged to release their grip. The room in which Betty was lying was at the back of the small cottage. The door was standing open but the curtains were drawn, as if she'd died already.

Edith Jones was sitting by the bed, wringing her hands. Joanna drew the twins beside her. 'Joe, would you please pull back the curtains? It's a lovely sunny day and Betty would like to feel it on her face, I'm sure.'

He had to duck to go through the door – he'd grown at least two inches since he'd been living at Goodwill House. Both she and Liza walked through without the risk of being knocked out.

'Mrs Jones, why don't you take a break? Perhaps you could make a pot of tea for you and Jean whilst we sit with Betty.'

'Thank you, my lady.' The woman was on her feet and out of the room in seconds.

Her dearest friend, Betty, was scarcely recognisable. She appeared to have shrunk somehow in the past two weeks. It wasn't just that she'd lost weight, she was pale, like a shell of the vivacious woman Joanna had known for five years and loved like a sister.

The room was gloomy, and even the vase of pretty summer flowers on the windowsill didn't make it seem welcoming. It had the neglected look of a room that was rarely in use. The rag rug by the bed was faded. Apart from the wooden bedstead there was only a commode cupboard, three bentwood chairs and some hooks on the wall for clothes. Everything was tidy, but it was depressing. The curtains rattled back, letting in much-needed sunshine. Without being asked, Joe pushed up both windows and immediately the room was filled with fresh air and the sound of birdsong.

'You and Liza sit on the right-hand side – you can bring over one of the chairs from under the window. I'll sit on the left where Mrs Jones was sitting.'

Joanna was talking quietly, as if their voices might disturb Betty. Although she was certain her friend was no longer able to hear anything.

They sat on either side of the single bed. Bert had obviously remained in the principal bedroom. For some reason, this annoyed her. Betty should be in the big bed, not in the small room at the back of the house.

'Can she hear us?' Liza whispered.

'I don't know, but I think we should talk normally as if just visiting a poorly patient.'

Betty's breathing was shallow, her chest barely moving. How could a children's ailment be proving fatal to a healthy young woman?

She reached over and took Betty's hand. 'It's Joanna, dearest friend, come to see you. Liza and Joe are here as well.' Having been whispering, she then spoke too loudly, and her voice echoed around the sparsely furnished room.

Her friend's hand was cold, the skin felt papery beneath her fingers, like the hand of an old woman, not a vibrant twenty-five-year-old.

'Liza, Joe, hold her other hand. We want her to know that we're here, that we love her, that she's not alone.'

Strangely, it was Joe who reached out and his sister who hung back. He clasped Betty's hand in both of his. A shocking contrast between the two of them. His were brown, work roughened, healthy. Betty's were skeletal and white.

Then Liza leaned over and kissed Betty's forehead, sat back and began to sing 'Amazing Grace'. Her voice soared, the high notes perfect, the liquid sound filled the room as Betty took her final breath.

Joanna knew her friend was gone. They remained silent, still, holding the hands of someone who was no longer there. Then the curtains fluttered, and a blackbird began to sing sweetly outside the window.

'She's gone to heaven, children, that was her soul departing. She's with God now.'

14

_____

Freddie waved for the farmer to stop the tractor, as to continue pulling the Spit along on its belly would be counterproductive.

'Okay, chaps, you can let go of the rope now. Thank you for your able assistance.'

Di joined him under the wing of the wounded kite. 'Don't I get any thanks? Or did you think I was a man dressed in my overalls?'

His hand moved of its own volition and touched her cheek. Not very professional or sensible with so many people watching. 'I'd not mistake you for anything but a woman, even dressed in a flour sack.'

'Thank you, I think. Can we go now? I'm sure the LDV are quite capable of standing guard until the mechanics get here to dismantle it. You don't think it's going to fly again, do you?'

'Some of it will. Look, the wings are undamaged. There are bullet holes in the fuselage, but nothing that can't be patched. Even the prop's only slightly bent. Don't forget, if they're recycling old saucepans, then every scrap of this magnificent beast is worth saving.'

'Such a pity – but you did well to land without killing yourself. You can tell me all about it on the way back.'

He thanked the locals and was assured by Dennis – the man in charge – that no further harm would come to the kite and that it would be guarded day and night until the mechanics arrived to collect it.

There was something different about Di. Maybe he was imagining it, but twice she'd looked at him with what he hoped was genuine affection – hopefully, love – in her eyes. But he wasn't going to ask her and risk a negative response.

They'd been travelling for a few minutes in the car when she glanced across at him. 'Shall I go first? Do you want to know what happened at the base? I've some information about losses and so on.'

'Yes, from your expression it's not good news. Is Ted okay?'

'He is, but one of your men is dead. I afraid I don't know which one. Two of the Hurricane flyers are also deceased and two more are still missing.'

'Right, duly noted. What about casualties on the ground?'

'Nothing serious, a couple of broken arms, minor burns and the usual cuts and bruises. No aircraft were damaged, as they were all airborne when the bombs dropped. There's no serious damage to the runway but I have to tell you that only the latrine and the admin huts are undamaged at dispersal.'

'I'm sure they'll have everything replaced and in working order by tomorrow. Now, tell me why you're going to be put on a charge.'

She explained and he shook his head. 'Forget about it, Di, I'll throw my weight about a bit and sweet talk your sarge.'

'Having a senior officer as my boyfriend is a definite advantage. Would you like to tell me how you ended up in a field? Why didn't you bale out?'

She listened avidly and was suitably impressed by his saga. He made light of the real danger and emphasised his stupidity.

'At least you've got your chute and helmet, even if you haven't got anything to fly. If you've lost a man and two are missing, won't you be short of kites?'

'I'm hoping the Win Co will have that in hand. I intend to be operational tomorrow.'

'Surely you get a week's crash leave?'

'I wouldn't take it even if it was offered. I'm fully fit and they need all of us.' He closed his eyes for a moment, envisaging what was to come.

'Freddie, I was so scared when I thought you might have died. I really didn't want to get serious, but I think that things have changed between us.'

'Pull over, there's a place just ahead. We need to talk before we get back.'

She didn't argue and expertly parked the car off the road so they wouldn't obstruct traffic from either direction.

'Shall we get out and lean against the gate? The field's full of hops if the smell's anything to go by.'

Again, she followed his instructions and when they were on the passenger side of the car, hidden from any passing vehicles, she pointed to a conical roof a few hundred yards away. 'That's an oast house where they dry the hops. Kent's famous for hop growing. Did you know that families from the East End come down here and stay in huts whilst they pick hops? It's like a holiday for them. Do—'

Why the devil where they talking about hops? He'd far more important things to say. To stop her, Freddie kissed her. Her response was quite different from before. A highly enjoyable few minutes later, he raised his head and stared down at her.

'I love you, darling, but up until today, I didn't think you felt the same.'

Her smile gave him the answer he wanted. 'I didn't want to fall in love with you, but I have done so anyway. It's all very confusing. I'm not like Millie, I'm a careful sort of girl, not at all romantic, and yet here we are in an identical state to them.'

Freddie wanted to punch the air, to pick her up and twirl her around like a child but thought she might not appreciate that. 'Not quite the same. I'm not suggesting that we have a rushed marriage like they did. The last thing either of us want is to be in their situation. Now is just not the time to be having a baby.'

'Millie told me that after the first shock, she's actually pleased, despite the fact that she's going to have to give up her career. If Ted's shot down, then at least she'll have the baby to remember him by.'

'Time enough for children after the war.'

'I'm hoping there'll be a wedding before any children. I'm old-fashioned that way.'

'Do you want to get engaged? Make it official?'

'I rather think I do. I'd like to be named as someone who should be contacted if anything happens to you. I know absolutely nothing about your family. Do you have siblings? Parents?'

'I have an older, married sister, and younger brothers, both away at school. I've a nasty suspicion they might be joining me fighting Hitler before this lot's finished. My father works in the City and my mother, like Lady Harcourt, is a leading light in the village.'

'I have two older sisters, both of whom married appropriately – one to an incredibly rich industrialist who I think's a fascist and the other to a minor aristocrat – not quite as rich but thinks he's as important as the King.'

'Am I detecting some distance between you and your family? I take it you have no intention of marrying someone "suitable"?'

'Absolutely not! That's why Millie and I hit it off straight away, as we come from similar backgrounds. My people aren't as wealthy as they'd like everyone to believe, but Millie's family is extremely rich.

Both she and Ted have a private income from some departed relative, whereas I only have my meagre WAAF wages.'

'I don't have a private income but will inherit substantially on my father's demise,' Freddie said. 'God willing, that won't be for many years.'

'Now we have all the necessary information about each other, don't you think we should get on?' She smiled apologetically. 'It's not you that will be for the high jump, it's me. I've been gone ages and there are bound to be jobs waiting for me.'

'You're right, darling, but god knows when we'll be alone again.'

'It has to be possible to snatch a few moments as long as you're not flying. Are we sort of engaged now?'

He stepped in and pulled her close. 'There's no "sort of" about it. As far as I'm concerned, you're the girl I'm going to marry, you're the one I'm fighting for.'

* * *

Joanna guided the children from the bedside and gently escorted them downstairs. 'Why don't you wait in the garden? I need to speak to Bert.'

The blackbird they'd heard a few moments ago was still singing and somehow this was a comfort. Joe put his arm around his sister's shoulder and she leaned into him. Neither of them was crying – that would come later.

'I heard a car, Liza, let's go around to the front and see who it is.'

It was probably Dr Willoughby. The curtains should be drawn upstairs and she'd forgotten to do that. The undertakers and vicar must be notified, but that was something Bert ought to take care of. Jean and Edith met her in the kitchen.

'Are you going to tell Mr Smith, my lady?' Jean asked, obviously hoping it wouldn't be her task.

'I'm going to do that now. Jean, could you take the twins home? It would be better if they were away from here.'

'I'll just get my things. A lovely young woman like that, to die when she'd all her life ahead of her. It's just not right. Being killed by a bomb in a war is dreadful, but this is worse.'

'I know,' Joanna said, 'but I'm afraid that there are going to be a lot more sad occasions such as this, so we've got to accept what we can't change and move on as best we can.'

Even as she spoke, she knew she sounded hard, unfeeling, but if she gave in to her grief, she wouldn't be able to take care of her family. Joe and Liza needed her to be strong. She turned away and surreptitiously rubbed her eyes. As soon as she got home, she must contact Sarah. Her daughter would want to know and even though she hadn't come to her father's memorial service, Joanna was certain Sarah would want to come to Betty's funeral.

Dr Willoughby came in unannounced through the front door and joined her in the kitchen. 'A very sad day indeed, my lady. I need to write the death certificate and so on. I'll also speak to Mr Smith. I'll arrange for the undertakers to come and contact Mr Evans.'

'That's kind of you, doctor, I was going to walk down to the vicarage myself but would much prefer to go home. Bert refused to sit with Betty, which I find rather worrying.'

'He told me this morning that it's God's will that his wife should die, as she couldn't give him children. He said that he can now remarry and have the son he wants.' Dr Willoughby shook his head as if bewildered by this behaviour. 'There's no reason for him to be skulking in his bedroom, he's been perfectly well for the past few days. I realise now that he wasn't nearly as poorly as I'd thought. He can certainly take care of his own livestock and garden from now on.'

'What an absolutely dreadful thing for him to say – I'm shocked and saddened. I just hope he keeps his unpleasant opinions to himself, as Betty was loved by all who knew her.' She was as appalled by Bert's callousness as Dr Willoughby clearly was. 'I'm glad that Joe no longer has to come here. I rather think that we Harcourts will have nothing to do with him in future.'

'I agree. I'm trying – rather unsuccessfully – to convince myself that it was the illness speaking and not his true opinion. Time will tell, I expect.'

Joanna nodded and hurried out, determined to catch up with the other three. Jean would be walking so the twins would be walking with her. Therefore, if she cycled, she'd soon overtake them.

They were nowhere in sight. Unless they'd run, which was unlikely, they should be visible on the road and not already have turned into the drive. She increased her pace and almost skidded around the corner.

There they were, just approaching the house, and Jean was sitting on the crossbar of Joe's bike. No wonder they'd arrived so speedily. She wasn't sure she'd have agreed to travel in such a precarious fashion and was surprised that Jean had done so.

Lazzy bounded towards her, ignoring the others in his desire to be with his very favourite person. Despite the fact that the others probably did more for him and certainly walked him more frequently, the dog preferred her company. It could only be because she'd been the one to rescue him when he'd become trapped in the disused Victorian wing of the house a few months ago.

'Good boy, don't get in the way of my wheels or I'll fall off and you'll be hurt.' For a few moments, the joyous reception of her dog pushed aside her misery.

The others had heard her approach and were standing in a silent trio by the front door. 'We would have waited, my lady, but thought you'd be busy for a while,' Jean said.

'Dr Willoughby's taking care of everything. Joe, there's no longer any need for you to go to the cottage. Mr Smith has been well enough to do his own chores for some time.'

Jean had gone ahead and was already halfway up the stairs when the three of them entered the house.

'I thought as much, miserable old sod. I saw him watching from the bedroom and he looked perfectly fine to me.'

'Joe, kindly moderate your language. A Harcourt doesn't use such phrases.'

'Sorry, it's going to take a bit of getting used to, not being a Tims but a Harcourt.'

'I'm going to speak to your grandmother and tell her what's transpired. Then I suppose we'd better think about supper.'

Some impulse made her reach out and gather them into her arms. 'This isn't how I thought our new lives were going to begin. Betty would have been so happy for us.'

They hugged her back. 'I'll see to the supper. Joe has his outside things to do.'

Joanna was aware that they no longer called her Aunt Joanna but had yet to address her as Mama or even Mother. Maybe that wouldn't happen until the papers were finalised.

Elizabeth greeted her with a sad smile, and they embraced briefly. Joanna told her everything she knew about Betty's demise and her husband's appalling behaviour.

'I never liked the man and now my feelings are vindicated. He's living in a tied cottage that belongs to the estate, isn't he?'

'Yes, whilst he's foreman at Brook Farm, he's entitled to live there.'

'Then insist that your tenant farmer dismisses him. Then he'll have to leave the village, which is exactly what should happen.'

Joanna sighed. 'I can't think about that at the moment, Elizabeth. I need to telephone Sarah's digs and leave a message for her to ring me urgently. She'll be devastated – she didn't even know that Betty was unwell.'

'What an absolutely dismal day this has turned out to be and it started so well. There could well have been casualties at Manston during the raid, several of the brave young pilots might have perished. I do hope that our girls are safe and that Ted and Freddie weren't shot down,' Elizabeth said.

'As do I. We can hardly ring up and ask. I think I'll write a note to Millie, telling her about Betty. I expect they'll want to pay their respects too if they can get the time free.'

'I suppose it's a good thing that Betty didn't have a baby as now the poor little thing would be left in the clutches of that horrible man.'

'What are we going to do without her...?'

'Didn't the ladies from the village say that someone is ready to take her place if necessary?'

'Elizabeth, how could you think that? It isn't Betty's role as housekeeper I'm referring to, but the fact that she was my closest friend, that my children loved her much as I did. She made the last few years bearable and now I've got no one to talk to.'

'Tish tosh, my dear girl. You have me to talk to, and Liza and Joe. I'm certain there are suitable women in the neighbourhood you could spend time with if you so wished.'

Joanna looked at the old woman, realising that, despite their apparent closeness, they were still very much apart and had only their name in common.

15

Di dropped Freddie at the admin block, where he was greeted with slaps on the back, handshakes and even a few hugs. She watched this enthusiastic welcome for a few moments and then slammed the car into reverse and drove as fast as she dared to the MT, dreading what Sarge might say to her this time.

Her worries were unnecessary, as he wasn't there, and the friendly Corporal Miller was in charge. 'Sorry to have taken so long, Corp, but I'm here now.'

'Don't worry about it, as long as you're back. There's a pile of assorted items waiting to go across to dispersal. Take the van – it should be big enough.'

The flyers, those that had returned safely, were now sitting and lying a hundred yards from dispersal. This made sense, as the area was heaving with airmen putting fresh huts up. Her lips curved when she saw they hadn't removed the somewhat singed WC hut but put a second one next to it. The men would be pleased, as one between so many wasn't efficient or pleasant for them.

One wouldn't have known that a few hours ago, at least three of their friends had gone for a Burton – they were joshing and laughing as normal. The NAAFI van was parked on the edge of the runway and doing a brisk trade.

Di was back and forth across the base a dozen times, conveying items to the various building projects underway. Freddie was right to say that by tomorrow everything would be tickety-boo and the burned dispersal huts replaced with new ones.

The squadrons were scrambled a second time but there was no siren and the Blenheims remained where they were. She counted them out and all returned safely – thank god. She wasn't ferrying the pilots this evening so was able to finish her shift at eight.

Even though the huts were there, the interiors had yet to be finished and they needed tables, chairs and camp beds. This meant the men couldn't sleep at dispersal tonight, even though they were back on duty at four in the morning.

At least they would be able to sleep in a comfortable bed. If the Tannoy went off in the middle of the night, they would have to scramble from their billets. She and Sally were the designated drivers. The lorries were parked outside the WAAF accommodation at night in case of this eventuality. Di decided she'd sleep in her underwear tonight so she could be out and into the lorry in minutes.

Sergeant was now back on duty and appeared to have forgotten his previous disgruntlement. 'Things are hotting up. I doubt you'll get much sleep tonight. Sleep in your uniform, I should, just in case.'

'Righto, Sarge. It's good news that the two missing chaps were picked up from the sea unharmed.'

'It certainly is. Two new kites were delivered this afternoon by the ATA but that means they're still short of four. God knows when we'll get them.'

'Freddie thought they might be able to salvage most of his kite – but I think that was wishful thinking.'

After climbing into the cab of her designated lorry, she drove to the admin building. Phyllis and Pamela would appreciate a lift and she might be able to find out if Freddie was back on duty.

He must have been watching out of an office window and seen her approaching, as he bounded out of the door on her arrival. She dropped to the ground, delighted to see him.

'Are you operational, Freddie?'

''Fraid so, old bean, no peace for the wicked. If you've come to pick up your girls, they're both still busy typing up reports. You've got time for a cuppa in the NAAFI.'

'Then one of the new planes is yours. I was hoping you might be grounded for a day or two so we could spend a little time together. I've got a split duty tomorrow and have the afternoon free.'

Freddie slung his arm around her shoulders and she rather liked the weight of it. Even the fact that it raised a few eyebrows from those they walked past didn't bother her. She looked sideways and smiled up at him. 'I'm sure no other airman will dare to make a pest of himself now they know I'm spoken for by someone as important as you.'

He chuckled – she didn't know how he could be so relaxed after what he'd been through today. 'There are at least four officers of my rank and four more senior than I am.'

'Then perhaps I'm going out with the wrong person. Would you care to introduce me to somebody who's really important?'

Before she could protest, she was being thoroughly kissed; she was hot all over and flustered by the time he released her. Her cheeks were scarlet and she looked around nervously, expecting to see a dozen accusatory faces – but no one was looking in their direction. If they'd seen them kissing, then they'd ignored it.

'Freddie, you really mustn't do that so publicly. People will just think you're a fine fellow, but I'll be labelled as – well, I don't quite know – but something not very nice.'

'Darling, do you honestly think anybody cares what we do at the moment? They've got more important things to worry about – like an imminent invasion by the Nazis and the prospect of being bombed to buggery at any moment.'

'Well, if you put it like that, I suppose I can't argue. I think I deserve a bun as well as mug of tea, and you're paying.'

It was hot, smoky and noisy inside the NAAFI. But despite the place being full, she felt almost invisible, anonymous, in the crowd of grey-blue airmen.

'There's a table by the window. You grab it and I'll get what I can for us.'

The three airmen who'd just vacated the table nodded and smiled politely – no unpleasant leering today. Hastily, she pulled out one of the chairs and sat on it before anyone else could claim it for themselves.

Whilst she waited, she'd time to listen to the conversations of those sitting close by. She'd also time to notice she was the only WAAF in there. It would be so much easier when the full contingent of girls arrived, as the twelve of them would be less conspicuous.

Four ground crew were discussing the raid by German bombers. 'We got away lightly, all things considered,' one of them said gloomily.

'Our boys shot down three of the bombers and more than that of their fighters. Bloody Nora! Imagine what's going to happen to the rest of Blighty if we can't stop the Luftwaffe.' The speaker looked scarcely out of short trousers but was already a man, fighting for King and country.

* * *

Freddie managed to charm two sausage rolls, as well as the two sticky buns Di had asked for, from the server. There were no spare trays, so the girl behind the counter put everything on one plate and then turned the mugs so the handles were facing him.

'There you go, Squadron Leader, you'll manage those a treat now.' He had his coins ready, but she shook her head. 'Go along with you, you know the rule. Any of our boys who get shot down and come back safe don't pay.'

'Splendid – is that just for today or indefinitely?'

The girl, a pretty little thing with frizzy brown hair more or less under her cap, giggled. 'Blimey, just the first time you come in, we're not made of money.'

'Thanks, much appreciated.' He shouldered his way through the press of people, narrowly avoiding tipping the contents of the mugs over at least two of the chaps he passed.

'Here you are. You'll be pleased to know I didn't spill a drop. I also sweet-talked my way into not only buns but also sausage rolls. Aren't you impressed by my prowess?'

Her smile, as always, made him glad to be alive when it was directed at him. 'I'm amazed, Squadron Leader Hanover, and also ravenously hungry, so thank you.'

Di didn't object to sharing the plate and they ate in silence until every crumb was gone.

'I didn't have to pay for any of it. Did you know that returning heroes, such as I, get free food and drink on their first appearance after their derring-do?'

'Actually, I didn't, I'm not surprised they've established such a tradition. But I've a horrible feeling it might cost them a small fortune before this war's won.'

'I sincerely hope it does, as that would mean those shot down are returning to fly again.'

He would have liked to sit there and talk banalities for an hour, but Di was on her feet almost immediately after finishing the last mouthful of tea. 'I'm sorry, Freddie – Phyllis and Pamela will be wondering where I am. I must go. I'm on duty from dawn so might well see you then.'

He kept his arm firmly around her waist as they wove their way through the tables. She didn't object and he wanted to make it abundantly clear to all the chaps in there that Di was off-limits, that she belonged to him now.

She slipped from his grasp as soon as they were outside. 'Thank you for the refreshments, stay safe and no more silly heroics.' Then she was gone. How was it that even in her very unflattering overalls, she still looked stunning?

Freddie wasn't given to communing with the Almighty, but like every other bod, he sent up the odd prayer when things got difficult – it couldn't do any harm, even if it didn't do any good. As he strolled around to his room, he prayed that both of them would survive what was coming and would be able to marry and spend the remainder of their lives together raising a family.

God knows what he'd do with himself when the war was over – unlike some of the others, he didn't want to go into commercial flying. Maybe he'd take up that place at Cambridge and study architecture instead of maths as he'd planned to do. There'd be a lot of rebuilding needed if today's bombing raid was anything to go by.

As always, after bods had died, the remaining numbers of his squadron gathered in the mess and drank their health. They would speak fondly of their lost comrades for a while and then ranks closed and the poor chap was never mentioned again.

Only one of those lost would actually have a funeral his family could attend – it was being held in London somewhere. The other two poor bastards had gone down in the drink. The relatives of those men would have to make do with a memorial service.

The last thing he wanted was to stand in the bar, inhaling cigarette smoke, drinking warm beer and being slapped on the back for his remarkable escape and for two definite kills. But his men would want him to be there, so he had no choice.

* * *

As expected, when the lorry, driven not by Di but one of the new drivers – he'd not bothered to learn her name – trundled them across the strip, everything was as it should be. The dispersal huts were not only back but bigger and better than previously. Fortunately, as everybody had been airborne when the incendiary bombs consumed the wooden huts, nobody had lost essential flying gear.

'Lucky bugger,' Ted said as they examined his new kite. 'Almost worth being shot down to get one of these beauties. MK V, as I live and breathe. Faster, better engine and armaments. Worth pranging a MK I to get one of these.'

'Keep your eyes off it, old chum,' Freddie said. 'There have to be some perks for being in charge of you shower.'

His ground crew were equally thrilled to be looking after one of the newest versions of the Spit. The remains of his last one had been ignominiously piled onto the back of a lorry and driven somewhere to be either melted down or salvaged – the former, he feared.

There was no time to dwell on his burgeoning romance that day or the next. His squadron was scrambled half a dozen times, mainly to attack the Luftwaffe, who were bombing shipping in the Channel. It was relentless. They were either flying, or at fifteen- or thirty-minute readiness.

They snatched half an hour's shuteye when they could, grateful for the camp beds when they were lucky enough to nab one, or just collapsed in a deck chair or stretched out on the ground. Kites from other places in Sector 11 used Manston as a forward base as they had done during the debacle at Dunkirk.

A week after Freddie's crash, his squadron was still intact, two more MK Vs had been delivered, and the poor blighters flying the Blenheims had been the ones to suffer the losses. These Australians had answered the call for the Commonwealth to help Britain in her hour of need and had been given the worst possible kites with which to do it.

The offensive by the Germans continued and he eventually had a few moments, when he was at thirty-minute readiness, to speak to his beloved Di.

'I'm really sorry, Freddie, but Millie and I have got a three-hour pass to attend Betty's funeral so I can't stop.'

'I was sorry to hear about that. Such a tragic waste of life.'

They were standing just a few yards away from an interested crowd of spectators, but she ignored them and put her arms around his neck. He crushed her to him and kissed her. She tasted of engine oil – but she didn't seem to mind that he hadn't washed or changed his underwear for days.

'I expect Ted's told you that Millie's been forced to hand in her resignation, as she's now got the most horrendous morning sickness and can't do the job when she's constantly vomiting into a bag.'

'No, he hasn't mentioned it. Let me know how things go this afternoon.'

Di waved, clambered into the cab and was gone. As she drove away, the Tannoy sounded, the bell outside the admin hut was rung loudly, and those at immediate readiness were scrambling again.

* * *

Joanna, despite her misgivings, had tried to liaise with Bert, to offer financial and any other assistance he needed to plan the funeral, but he'd refused her help – or anybody else's, it would appear. The funeral was taking place and he wasn't holding a wake, there'd not be any gathering for mourners to reminisce and talk lovingly of a woman who'd lost her life so prematurely.

She was on the telephone speaking to Mrs Thomas, the chairperson of the Women's Institute, and for once, they were in total agreement. 'I think it a disgrace, my lady, that Mr Smith isn't having any sort of gathering after the service. Betty was an integral part of both the WI and the WVS. We must arrange something for her ourselves.'

'That's exactly what I was thinking, Mrs Thomas. We could have it here or we could use the village hall, as we did when we had the memorial service for those who died at Dunkirk.'

'I did make enquiries and unfortunately, the hall's temporarily out of use because of a leak in the kitchen,' Mrs Thomas said. 'I also asked the vicar if we could use the church hall, but Mr Smith has specifically said that this mustn't happen.'

'I don't understand that man's attitude. In which case, there's no alternative but to hold it at Goodwill House. The funeral's at two o'clock in the afternoon and there's a bus that comes through the village at three-fifteen. That will be perfect, as those who wish to attend can catch it. The twins and Jean are coming by bicycle, Lady Harcourt and myself are coming in the trap.'

'My word, my lady, I didn't know that you'd overcome your fear of equines.'

'I haven't, Sarah will be here and she'll drive us,' Joanna said 'It's a bit of a squash for three of us, but we'll manage.'

'We only have three days to organise it. Are you going to be able to provide sufficient refreshments?'

'I've got tea, coffee and sherry for those who want it. Liza and

Jean have been busy baking, so we'll have plenty of biscuits. On the day, we'll make sandwiches with whatever we've got and that will have to do.'

'I'm sure all the ladies will be happy to contribute to the buffet table,' Mrs Thomas said. 'At least if the event takes place away from the village, Mr Smith can't interfere or complain.'

Joanna replaced the receiver and stared thoughtfully at it for a few moments. There was something she had to discuss with Elizabeth immediately. Her mother-in-law was, as usual, sitting on the terrace with the dog at her feet, despite the sky being rent by aircraft landing and taking off at frequent intervals.

'How can you sit out here watching them fly out, knowing that some of them won't return?'

'I've become immune to the noise, my dear, and despite the reason for them being there, they are rather beautiful. Is something wrong – you look rather agitated?'

Joanna explained about Bert's recalcitrance and what she wanted to do. She also told her about the plans for the gathering. 'I'm going to speak to Mr Beattie, the tenant farmer where Bert's the foreman. I'm going to get him dismissed and then evicted. We don't want somebody like that living in Stodham, a constant reminder of his callousness towards Betty. Imagine, Elizabeth, how we'd feel if he married a girl from another village who didn't know the circumstances and he brought her to the cottage?'

'You have my full support, my dear, make your telephone calls. The ladies from the village, I'm sure, will be only too happy to help with the catering.'

After speaking to Mr Beattie, she was satisfied that he agreed with her and Bert Smith would be sacked. Her next call was to the solicitor. Mr Broome was only too happy to set in motion the eviction.

'You do realise that when he loses his position, he'll immediately be called up?'

'I do, but perhaps being in the army might knock some sense into him.'

'In which case, I'll inform the authorities at the same time I issue the eviction notice,' Mr Broome said. 'Presumably, he'll be given his marching orders today?'

'Yes, the farmer's going to see him immediately. Dr Willoughby was happy to confirm that Bert has been malingering and could have been back at work a week ago. That's more than enough reason for him to be dismissed.'

'Before you go, my lady, I've had somewhat concerning news from the bank.'

Her hand clenched on the receiver. 'What is it?'

'Although there's a legal document stating that your mother-in-law has until the end of the year to pay off the debt, they have now decided they want the full amount by September.'

'How can they do that? You said we have the law on our side. Do I need to ask who's behind this? I assume it's Peter Harcourt.'

'I'm afraid it is, my lady. He's got a team of London barristers working for him and they insist that they've found a loophole in the agreement. Obviously, we can fight this, but they've got money and resources on their side.'

'What can we do to prevent him getting the estate?'

'Is there any chance that the funds will be available by then?'

'I don't know, but if they aren't?' Johanna asked.

'Then the bank can sell to Lord Harcourt. And once he has his hands on the debt, it's anybody's guess if we'll ever prise the estates from him.'

'This is an absolute disaster...'

'I apologise unreservedly, my lady, for my part in this. I should never have contacted him. If he wasn't aware that he'd inherited the title, then things wouldn't be as they are now.'

First her beloved friend had been taken from them, and now they could lose Goodwill House. No – this wouldn't happen. She would do whatever it took to save the house and keep her family safe.

16

Di had been shocked by Freddie's appearance. He looked exhausted, thinner than he'd been just a few days ago, and both his hands and face were etched with oil – at least, that's what she thought the black lines embedded in his skin were.

A week had passed since his crash, and he'd been flying every day since. Each time the Tannoy screamed over the base, the bell outside the dispersal hut rang, her heart was in her mouth. The Australian flyers had lost four of their men and six of their planes – she'd heard talk that these horrible kites were going to be taken out of frontline duty. Not before time, as they were not fit for purpose.

Millie had left already, moved to the little cottage half a mile from the base, and Di missed her best friend dreadfully. The Wing Commander had summoned her to his office and promoted her to the rank of corporal. She now occupied the cubicle that Millie had used, Pamela was an LACW, and this was some small compensation for not having Millie with her.

Sarge had given her permission to use the Austin and she was picking Millie up at her cottage on the way past. Di had paid special attention to her appearance, as she didn't want to let Betty down.

She didn't need to go in, as Millie was waiting at the gate – she was shocked that her friend wasn't in uniform.

'I don't think I've seen you in mufti, Millie, you look quite different.'

'I would have liked to have worn my uniform one last time to honour Betty, but the quartermaster insisted that I handed everything in. I had to go to the village dressmaker to get this frock – someone had ordered it and then changed their mind – it's not ideal but all I could get.'

'You look very pretty in blue. It goes perfectly with your auburn hair. Don't forget that Jean, at Goodwill House, is a seamstress. I'm sure she'd make you something if you can get the material. You can ask her later when we go to the wake.'

'I should be wearing black, or uniform, like everybody else. People are going to think me very disrespectful, turning up in such a bright colour.'

'You've got a black armband, that will have to do. You look very pale; will I need to pull over in a hurry for you to be sick?'

'The lady next door said if I just have an arrowroot biscuit with a weak cup of tea for breakfast then I'll not be so ill,' Millie said. 'I started yesterday and it seems to be working so far.'

The car was causing an obstruction on the main route to the base, so the sooner they got moving, the better.

As they approached the village, Millie sniffed and dabbed her eyes. 'Every time the boys are scrambled, I burst into tears. It really isn't good for the baby, but there's nothing I can do about it.'

Di studied her friend more closely. 'I thought pregnant women were supposed to put on weight, but you've definitely lost it. I suppose it's the nausea. Even if I was thinking of spending the night with Freddie, seeing the state that you're in has convinced me not to do it.'

Millie's shook her head. 'At the moment, I really wish this hadn't happened. I hate being on my own in the cottage, cut off from everything I've come to love and with nothing to do but dwell on my predicament and the fact that Ted might die at any moment.'

Di felt useless, unable to help her friend or offer any constructive suggestions to make things easier for her. Being so isolated wasn't a good thing for any young wife and especially a pregnant one with horrible morning sickness.

'Freddie said that the experienced flyers know what they're doing and are less likely to be killed,' she said. 'It's the new boys with only a few weeks' training and no combat experience at all who are so vulnerable.'

'What a very depressing conversation, and it's entirely my fault.' Millie sat up straighter and pinned on a not very convincing smile.

'Golly, we're going to a funeral of a good friend who died suddenly and in tragic circumstances. Of course we're both going to be feeling miserable.'

Di parked in front of the village hall, along with three other vehicles. A church bell was tolling, one sonorous peal at a time. There was a steady stream of villagers heading for the church, which was hardly surprising, as Betty had been loved by all who knew her.

'Look, that's the trap from Goodwill House, and I recognise those three bicycles propped against the tree close by. We've not seen anyone from there for ages. I wish it was in better circumstances.' Di put her arm through Millie's, hoping in so doing that the congregation would recognise her as the previous Corporal Cunningham and understand why she wasn't in black.

'I wonder why Mr Smith isn't waiting out here with members of the family for the coffin to arrive. In fact, shouldn't Mr Evans be here too?' Di said in a whisper as they were about to enter.

'Look, the vicar and the coffin are already there. No wonder everyone's so quiet.'

The church was full, but the pews reserved for family mourners only had one person – a youngish man who must be Mr Smith.

The service was brief to the point of being disrespectful and from the expressions of others in the congregation, they agreed. There was no eulogy, nobody got up and spoke about Betty and how much she'd been loved and what she'd done for the village, only Mr Evans was able to say anything about the lovely young woman in the coffin at the front of the church.

Two hymns were sung, prayers were said and then the undertakers appeared from the vestry. The congregation stood and the vicar led the sad procession of just the coffin, bare of flowers of any sort, and Mr Smith filed from the church.

The two Lady Harcourts and Sarah Harcourt, plus the twins and Jean, followed and then everyone else dropped in behind them. They walked solemnly to the prepared grave. Betty was lowered into the dark hole as Mr Evans said the appropriate words.

Di watched Betty's husband, waiting to see him show some emotion, toss a flower into the grave or a handful of dirt – but he did none of these. He nodded to the vicar, ignored those who might have wished to offer their condolences, and walked off as if this was just another day.

Her cheeks were wet, and she stepped forward to take a turn at the graveside and wish her friend a safe journey. Then two ladies appeared with baskets of carefully arranged posies. One by one, the real mourners took pretty bunches and tossed them onto the coffin.

By the time everybody had done so, the coffin was invisible beneath the sweet-smelling summer flowers. People were openly crying, expressing their grief but also their anger at how the funeral had been conducted.

Millie was no longer with her, and Di saw her hurrying around the side of the church, no doubt to have some privacy whilst she was sick. Joanna beckoned her and she hurried over.

'Poor Mr Evans had no choice but to conduct the service as Mr Smith demanded. I could see that you're as angry as everybody else.'

'Yes, his behaviour's unforgivable.' Di blew her nose loudly. 'Millie's not in uniform because she's resigned from the WAAF. She's expecting a baby, and you can't remain in service when you're pregnant.'

'I did wonder,' Joanna said. 'I hope you can come back to Goodwill House. Sarah doesn't have to be back at the hospital until tomorrow and I'd like you to meet her.'

'The service was so brief, we've still got two hours before we have to return to the base. We've got two spare seats in the back of the Austin if you and Lady Harcourt would prefer to travel with us?'

'Thank you, I certainly will, as I really don't enjoy anything to do with horses. Sarah gets her enthusiasm from her father.'

* * *

Joanna told her daughter that she'd be travelling back in the car. 'Are you going in the trap, Elizabeth, or will you travel in comfort with me and the girls?'

'It was a trifle cramped with three of us on the seat on the way here, my dear, but as you'll not be with us on the return journey, it will be most enjoyable. It takes me back to when cars were a rarity and everybody travelled by carriage.'

'Go ahead, Mummy. I'll have a chance to chat to my grandmother on the way.'

'All right, Sarah darling, I'll see you all at home. The ladies from the village left on the cycles a while ago, so hopefully they'll have the tea urn on by the time everyone arrives.'

Joanna dodged through the press of people waiting at the bus stop and crossed the road to find Millie and Di. The howl of the

Tannoy at the base was followed almost immediately, it seemed to her, by one fighter after another roaring into the sky. She waited, holding her breath, for the siren to go off, warning them that bombers were on their way.

'Lady Harcourt, over here. If we get off immediately, we'll beat the bus. If that arrives before we get onto the road, then we'll be held up for ages behind it,' Di called.

The vehicle was in motion almost before she was settled on the rear seat. 'The bus driver and conductor are going to have a shock when faced with half the village wanting to get on for just two stops,' she said with a smile.

They drove past a dozen or more people who'd decided to walk and not wait for the omnibus. 'I'll help with the refreshments, my lady—'

'Joanna, please, Di, we're friends, are we not?'

'I hope so. But returning to my previous comment – it looks as if the entire village will be coming to Goodwill House and you're going to need help.'

'Thank you. With you, plus Sarah, Liza and Joe, as well as the two ladies from the village, we should manage. When my daughter had her engagement party, there were more than a hundred guests...' Her voice faltered as she recalled that Betty had been there and now they'd never see her again.

Millie had wound the window down and was looking out anxiously. Joanna wasn't sure if the poor girl was trying not to be unwell or checking to see if her husband was on his way back to Manston.

'Millie, I think there might be half a dozen ensembles in Sarah's wardrobe that would fit you until you can get something else made up. I'm assuming that you had to hand in all your uniform and don't have anything with which to replace it.'

'You're right, my... Joanna. I think I was lucky that the quartermaster allowed me to keep the underwear I had on. Goodness knows what they do with it, as I hardly think second-hand knickers would be very popular.' The girl managed a small smile. 'And thank you for the offer. Ted's found me some parachute silk and I'm busy sewing underwear and nightwear from that.'

'I'm sure nobody would dare to complain about whatever they're given. Once they've been laundered, they'll be perfectly acceptable to their next wearer.'

What an extraordinary conversation to be having on such a miserable day – but talking about knickers, Di supposed, was better than the alternative.

'I have to ask, Joanna, why were there no flowers, no eulogies and such a short and impersonal service?' Di asked as she wound down the window and waved her arm up and down to indicate she was turning left into the drive.

'Bert Smith's glad that Betty has died. He blames her for not providing him with a son and told Dr Willoughby it was God's will it happened so he could remarry.'

The girls exchanged a horrified glance. Millie recovered her voice first.

'How absolutely appalling – from what Betty told me, he wasn't a particularly nice man, but this beggars belief. Thank goodness the ladies of the village provided those lovely posies.'

'There will be flowers on the grave as soon as it's filled in. Smith will be leaving the village in the next day or two and then we can take care of Betty as she should be. I'm sure she has a sister and that her parents are still very much alive. I have a nasty feeling they weren't even informed of her death.'

'Then I hope someone does that. I can't imagine the pain they'll feel when they hear that their beloved daughter has died, been buried, and they didn't even know.'

Di was out of the car as soon as it was stationary and would have opened the door for Joanna, but she shook her head. 'No, I'm neither old nor in any way your superior. Look out, here comes the dog and he's bound to jump up.'

Lazzy skidded to a halt in front of Di, who'd been terrified of dogs when she'd first arrived at the house. When she'd been attacked by a man determined to rape her, the dog had saved her. From that point on, she'd overcome her fear of dogs – at least this one. She leaned down and held out her hand. Lazzy danced forward and the two of them were happily reunited.

* * *

Joanna needn't have worried about there being enough food, as most of the women brought something to add to the buffet table. The smell of the food upset Millie's delicate digestion, so she was unable to help but did spend some time with Jean ordering some new clothes. They would have to be made to allow for her expanding waistline, but she was sure this was well within Jean's capabilities.

Everybody gathered in the ballroom and the vicar asked for silence. He then prayed for Betty, Liza sang 'Amazing Grace' again and half a dozen people walked to the front and spoke lovingly of the departed.

Di and Millie slipped away halfway through because Di had to be on duty and Millie wanted a lift back to the cottage.

'This is going very well, Mummy,' Sarah said, 'but Betty should have been here to enjoy it with us. Thank goodness you offered to hold something in her memory. We all needed cheering up after that dismal service.'

Sarah, like all of them, had changed over the past few months. Being a medical student, living in digs on her own, whilst worrying about the safety of her fiancé, Angus, had turned her into a mature and accomplished young woman. Joanna was very proud of her daughter.

'A funeral is meant to be sad, Sarah, but regardless of the service, nobody will ever forget Betty. I can see her, hear her, even though she's not here any more.' They were both overcome, so she hastily changed the subject. 'It must be difficult for you, wondering what's happening to Angus.'

'To be honest, I don't have time to worry about anything apart from studying and working on the wards. We've agreed we've just got to get on with our own lives for the moment and when this nightmare's over, we'll get married, regardless of how far into my training I am.'

'If neither your grandmother nor I can be present, you have my blessing, of course, but if you can give us even a day's notice, we'll be up to London to at least act as your witnesses.'

Sarah hugged her hard. 'No, Mummy, I don't want you or Grandmama anywhere near the capital, as it's going to be far too dangerous once the bombs start falling.'

Perhaps now wasn't the time to remind Sarah that being so close to a RAF base and the coast was equally dangerous.

* * *

Freddie lost his two new flyers the first time they were involved in a party. One, Milo Giles, baled out safely and was picked up but had broken both his legs so wouldn't be returning for months to active duty. The second poor sod, George Caton, hadn't been so lucky. Having been back to full strength, they were now down two flyers and two kites. He was supposed to have sixteen kites and a dozen spare men but hadn't had that luxury for months.

Today, there was a balloon unit being set up at the far end of the strip. Not barrage, thank god, but hydrogen-filled balloons about five yards long which would be released to drift to Germany and drop propaganda leaflets. Bloody stupid idea, total waste of time and money in his opinion.

He scowled down the strip at the silver balloons bobbing about in the wind. If they let them go when they were being scrambled, it would be a disaster for everyone. Why the hell did the War Office think dropping bits of paper would do anything but create litter? If Germany dropped pamphlets on England, then he was damn sure they'd be used as bog paper.

Ted was now his second-in-command as he'd been promoted to flight lieutenant. There were others in the squadron with more experience, older, but nobody objected. He was popular in the mess, the best flyer and chaps listened to him when he spoke. Having his best friend ready to step in if anything happened to him was a small consolation for Freddie – the squadron would be in good hands. There was supposed to be a rule that one only flew thirty ops before getting stood down for a period of R&R. He wasn't exactly sure how many he'd flown, but it must be well past that by now.

The forty-eight hours Manston had had recently would be the last free time any of them were going to get for a while. He was missing spending time with the woman he loved, but binding about it wouldn't help.

'Skip,' Chalky White yelled from the admin hut at dispersal. 'You're wanted on the blower.'

It sounded urgent, so Freddie approached at the double, shot into the hut and snatched up the receiver. 'Squadron Leader Hanover speaking.'

'Good show. Bad news, old boy, get over to admin immediately.' The line went dead and he stared at the silent receiver. What bad news? Why didn't whoever it was tell him immediately? Were they sending a car or was he expected to run?

Ted was talking to his ground crew and he beckoned him over. 'Something's up, don't know what. Got to go to admin pronto. Is your horrible bike anywhere about?'

'Over there, be my guest. I'll take care of things – don't look so worried.'

Ted's bicycle was infamous – it was falling apart but at least today the tyres were pumped up, even if the brakes were non-existent. He was a few inches shorter than Ted, but his legs must be the same length, as he'd no difficulty reaching the pedals or the ground.

He dumped the bike outside the door when he arrived at the admin building, confident nobody would pinch it. There was no point in checking his appearance, as he looked appalling, as did all his men. He strode in and there was an NCO waiting for him. 'Come with me, sir, there's some bigwigs waiting to speak to you.'

The door to the Wing Commander's office was open and he was almost blinded by the amount of gold braid on the uniforms of the three very high-ranking officers in there. They didn't look particularly agitated – they were lounging about, drinking coffee and munching buns. His heart slowed to a more sensible rate. The bad news couldn't be that bad.

He stopped in the doorway, came to attention and saluted crisply. 'Squadron Leader Hanover.'

'Come in, don't footle about in the doorway waving your arm around,' one of them said with a smile.

The Win Co nodded towards the empty chair that completed the circle. There were no other men of his rank present – if he'd been called in for a chinwag, why hadn't they?

'I expect you're wondering why you're here and what the bad news is. Your squadron's being posted to Hornchurch. The gen is that the Luftwaffe are preparing to attack London and the fuss in the Channel is just a diversion.'

Freddie nodded but said nothing and allowed the anonymous air commodore to continue.

'We need you to be in the air in an hour. Instructions have already been sent to the orderlies to pack. The NCOs will need to get a move on, as they've got to do it for themselves.'

'Right, sir, understood.' There had been little point in sitting down, as he was now on his feet and out of the room without the formality of his entrance.

He went into the adjutant's office and was connected to the dispersal hut. He got Ted on the other end of the line and gave him the bad news.

'You haven't got time to see Millie, old boy, I'm afraid. I'm arranging for transport to collect the NCO pilots as they've got to sort their own gear. I'll be back in a few minutes.'

'Bloody bad luck – just as I've got Millie settled,' Ted said. 'I'll get things organised this end. If you see Di, ask her to explain to my wife, will you?'

Freddie deliberately pushed all thoughts of Di from his mind. He had a job to do. He had to concentrate on his duty. The lives of his men and of possibly hundreds of civilians depended on him being fully focused and not worrying about the woman he loved.

17

Di barely had time to get out of the car and change into her work overalls before Sarge told her she was to collect some of Freddie's squadron and return them to their accommodation.

'What's going on, Sarge?'

'No idea, Corporal, just get the damn lorry over there.'

He was obviously in one of his tetchy moods, so she just nodded, ran round to the lorry and clambered into the cab. The NCOs, sergeant pilots, scrambled into the back. Ted raced up to the window.

'We're being posted to Hornchurch. Please take care of Millie for me. Tell her I love her and I'll be in touch when I can.'

'Of course, I'll go down when I'm off duty. I've only just got back from the funeral.' She was talking to an empty space, as Ted had vanished.

She delivered the men, reversed so she was facing in the correct direction, and waited for them to reappear with their hastily filled kitbags. It didn't seem fair that they had the same responsibility as an officer but none of the perks.

The last chap threw his bag into the rear of the lorry and

followed it headfirst as she was already pulling away. There was obviously a flap on in London and Freddie's squadron was needed there urgently.

She parked in front of the dispersal huts, making sure she was off the strip. This was an emergency, and it wasn't professional of her to be thinking about getting out to find Freddie before he left.

The problem was solved as he appeared at her window, just as Ted had earlier. He opened the door and she tumbled out into his arms. They were hidden from view by the bulk of the lorry and the open door.

Their kiss was passionate, desperate even, and neither of them wanted to end it. 'I'm going to miss you terribly, Freddie, please take care and write to me if you have a moment.'

His voice was gruff. 'You write to me as often as you can, darling. I doubt I'll have the time to reply, but know that every word I read will mean so much to me. If anything happens, then you'll be informed, as I have you down as my fiancée.'

'I love you.'

He kissed her again, hard, but too soon, he released her and rushed off to do his duty. She wiped her eyes on her gauntlets and climbed into the cab. The Spits were ready to depart, and the deep throaty roar – the power – of the Merlin engines rocked the lorry.

It would be even more cramped in the tiny cockpit with their bulky kitbags stuffed in behind the seat. God knows what would happen if one of them had to bale out. She remained stationary until the last fighter was airborne and then engaged first gear, drove across the runway and headed back to the motor pool.

Manston seemed strangely empty with only one squadron of Spitfires – they still had the somewhat depleted squadrons of Blenheims and also the Hurricanes. The siren howled but she ignored it and continued to the MT. If bombs dropped, then she'd be needed to drive a fire tender or an ambulance. Millie's departure had left them shorthanded.

When she'd contacted Victory House, she'd been told to prepare for the arrival of a dozen more girls who this time would be accompanied by a sergeant, and she assumed at least one of the girls would be a driver.

The remaining aircraft screamed into the sky and almost immediately she heard in the distance the sound of gunfire.

'Not going into the shelter, Corporal?' Sarge asked as he emerged from his office.

'No, I can't hear any bombers. I think it might be a false alarm – again.'

'Let's hope so. I wonder which squadron will come to replace the one that's left. It might well be Hurries – they're the workhorses, not as pretty or as fast as a Spit, but from what I've heard, they've had more kills.'

She noticed the mechanics were still working and had also ignored the warning. There was no raid and, one by one, the fighters returned. They didn't rearm and refuel, so whatever the emergency had been, it was over. Thankfully they'd returned with no losses.

Freddie's squadron was still depleted. She supposed the gaps would be replaced by more inexperienced, vulnerable young men. It must be horrid for Freddie and Ted to welcome new flyers, knowing they might well die the next time they were scrambled.

The all-clear had eventually sounded – the person in charge must have been asleep, as the squadrons had been on the ground for some time when it went.

'Sarge, if there's nothing else for me to do this evening, could I possibly leave now? I want to tell Millie what's happened.'

'You go. It's been a difficult day for both of you. When do the new girls arrive?'

'Tomorrow, I think, but I'll get an official notification when they're on the train, as I'll have to arrange for somebody to collect them.'

She waved to the guard as she pedalled through the gate and on arriving, brought her bike inside the hedge that bordered Millie's cottage.

Millie took some time answering the door. 'I didn't expect to see you again today, Di, but I'm so glad you've come. I keep thinking about Betty.'

'Afraid I've got more bad news. The squadron's on its way to Hornchurch. Ted asked me to tell you that he loved you and will write to you as soon as he has a moment.'

Millie took the news better than she'd expected. 'I'd guessed as much, as they left before the siren and none of them came back. We both knew they wouldn't stay at Manston for much longer, but as I've got friends here, I'm happy enough.'

'Good show. I was thinking that even if you can't be a WAAF, maybe you can still do your bit by joining the WVS and the WI.'

'Joanna asked me if I'd like to help out at Goodwill House when the land girls come next month, and I'm going to do it if I stop being sick all the time.'

Di couldn't stay long, as she had things to organise for the arrival of the new contingent. As she cycled across the base, she thought about who might be coming. Would there be a qualified cook? The food they were eating was awful – the girls were doing their best, but they only knew how to cook a couple of things successfully. Even they sneaked off to the NAAFI when they had a moment, in order to eat something palatable.

She was glad Millie was going to help out at Goodwill House. Being a housekeeper wasn't ideal, but it would mean her friend wouldn't be on her own and worrying about Ted all the time. Di, obviously, was thinking about Freddie but she was fortunate as she had her work to keep her mind busy and therefore had less time to dwell on what might happen.

* * *

Joanna slowly adjusted to the new reality – that of not having Betty as part of the household any more. Sarah's flying visit reminded her that she had so much more to lose than a good friend.

The twins had bonded with their older sister, and it had raised her spirits hearing the three of them eagerly planning their joint birthday celebrations in September. Now the house was quiet, but things had changed and not just because of Betty's death.

They all ate together – sometimes in the kitchen, sometimes in the breakfast parlour or on the terrace – but sharing the past tragic two weeks had created a more solid bond. Jean was now part of this group and the more Joanna got to know her, the better she liked her.

Even the constant noise of planes landing and taking off at Manston no longer bothered her. She was resigned to what was coming and had made plans accordingly. The shelter in the cellars was now freshly stocked and in the unlikely event that they were trapped down there for any length of time, they certainly wouldn't go hungry or thirsty.

A few days after the funeral, Liza was in what used to be David's sanctum, but was now their study, with the charming old gentleman Joanna had employed to be the twins' tutor. Joe was busy outside. Elizabeth was taking a nap on the chaise longue in the drawing room, and she and Jean were planning the menu for the next few days.

'Joe said he'll kill a cockerel, Joanna, as there are half a dozen of them now and two hens are broody and both sitting on a clutch of eggs. The yard will be overrun with cockerels by the end of the year.'

'It's amazing that a young man who grew up in the East End has adapted so well to country life. The cockerel should be sufficient for the five of us for three days at least.' She counted on her fingers as she spoke. 'Roast on day one, cold with salad and new potatoes the next day, and a hearty soup with dumplings on the third.'

'The kitchen garden's doing well, and we've got more than enough soft fruit and vegetables,' Jean said. 'It's a shame there's not sugar available to make jam.'

'We can bottle the plums, greengages and cherries without using sugar, so at least we'll have those in the winter.'

Jean laughed. 'Do you know how to do that? I certainly don't. I'm sure that either Val or Joan would be glad to do it for us.'

'I'm sure they would, but we must both learn how to do it ourselves – I'll also get Liza to join us when we do it. I'll ask one of them to teach all three of us soon. I wish I'd had a more practical upbringing, and I'm determined that my children will know how to do everything in the kitchen and outside.'

Joe had come in from the yard and overheard her last remark. 'Everything? I think that's rather ambitious. Do you want me to learn how to bottle fruit and Liza to kill a chicken?'

'I don't see why not,' Joanna said. 'The world's changing and I'm going to keep up with it. If women can fly fighter planes, drive lorries, ambulances and even fire engines then I'm quite sure anything's possible.'

'I came in to tell you that I said George, the old chap from the village who comes in to do the kitchen garden, can take half a dozen eggs as well as his usual vegetables. I hope that's all right.'

'You're in charge of the outside, Joe, I trust you to make sensible decisions. As far as I'm concerned, you're quite old enough to have that responsibility. Goodwill House might well be yours in the future, as Sarah told me she's only too happy to hand it over to you.'

His answer was drowned out by the dog barking ferociously and a man yelling curses. Joe was outside first, but she and Jean were close behind.

Bert Smith was being pinned against the wall by the dog. 'Get this blasted animal off of me. I'm warning you; I'll come back with my shotgun and finish him off, you see if I don't.'

Joanna had been dreading a confrontation like this. He'd had his eviction notice yesterday and would have to vacate the property within a week.

'Mr Smith, I suggest that you go home before my dog savages you.'

'Go home you say? You stuck up bitch, it's all very well for you in your grand house, but because of you I'm homeless and unemployed. You'll not get away with this. I never liked you nor wanted my wife to be your servant.'

Joe had hold of Lazzy's collar but was having difficulty holding him. The dog was frantic. He didn't need to understand the words to know that Bert Smith was a threat to his mistress.

'Nobody wants you in the village after the way you behaved. The authorities are aware that you no longer have a reserved occupation so you can expect them to send you your papers. When they come, you'll no longer be either unemployed or homeless and actually be doing something useful with your life.'

This was hardly placatory, but Joanna wasn't afraid of this bully and had no intention of being cowed by his threats.

He shouted more abuse, made more menacing remarks, ranted on about getting his revenge but then stomped off, followed closely by the dog, snapping at his heels.

Her knees were weak, her hands clammy and she was grateful for Jean's arm around her waist to escort her inside.

'You sit down, Joanna, what you need is a stiff drink and a strong cup of coffee.'

'Just coffee, thank you, it's far too early to drink even after what just happened.'

Whilst she recovered, she ran through what he'd yelled. 'Do you think he'll really come back with a shotgun and kill my dog?'

'I think you should report it to the Constabulary,' Jean said. 'He threatened Lazzy and you with physical harm.'

'Haven't I done enough to the man? I really don't want him to be incarcerated because of me. His appalling behaviour might well be motivated by grief.'

Lazzy bounded in and immediately shoved his huge shaggy head in her lap. 'Good boy, clever boy, you did so well. Joe, make sure he doesn't wander off on his own for the next day or two, just in case.'

'There's shotguns and things locked away in the study. I should be able to use one of them.'

'Good heavens, I don't want you to shoot anybody. That said, Sarah used to shoot for the pot, and it might be sensible for you to be able to do the same. I'm sure there's someone in the village who'd be happy to teach you.'

Jean offered to make the report to the police, although Joanna believed it to be unnecessary and merely a formality. As they were about to sit down for supper, Lazzy jumped up and looked towards the front of the house. Minutes later, they heard a car pulling up.

'Oh dear, what now? Nobody with any sense calls at dinnertime,' Elizabeth said crossly.

* * *

Freddie had told his squadron to make their own way to Hornchurch. No flying in formation, just common sense and navigational skills required. He circled the strip and the green light came on for him to land. Half an hour later, all the chaps were down but so far hadn't been guided to their designated place on the base.

At Hornchurch, the Spits were housed in blast pens scattered around the base. This should mean that in the event of a German attack, the kites would be protected. It took longer to taxi everyone to their place than it had to fly there from Kent.

The two sergeant pilots were accommodated elsewhere – bloody silly having this segregation, in Freddie's opinion. He would be accommodated in Astra House and the other facilities were in an equally smart brick-built building. A van arrived to ferry them all to their billets; he left his kit for his new orderly to take care of and went in search of the Officers' Mess. It was here that any chap not at readiness would be sharing the gen with his fellow flyers.

Ted had said he would join him but wanted to write to Millie first. Freddie thought it was his duty to garner all the information he could about the base and the men on it, the man in charge and anything else relevant, before he dealt with personal matters.

The bar was almost empty, no one propping it up as would be the case at night, but there was a table by the window with three bods, drinking coffee. They looked up as he entered and one of them called out.

'Join us, you must be the new lot. We need all the help we can get.' The speaker was a redheaded flight lieutenant and indicated the empty chair.

'If there's a spare cup, coffee would be perfect. I'm not going to be popular if I say that I'm not a heavy drinker and neither do I smoke cigarettes. I do, however, enjoy a pipe occasionally.' He strode over to join them. 'I'm Freddie Hanover, just arrived from Manston.'

The redheaded chap jumped to his feet and to his surprise, slapped him on the back. 'Bloody hell! I was, briefly, CO there.'

Freddie laughed and pumped the man's hand. 'I know who you are. You're Angus Trent, engaged to Sarah Harcourt of Goodwill House.'

By the time he'd explained his close connection to the Harcourts and brought Angus up to date with his future mother-in-law and grandmother-in-law, they were the best of friends.

'I can't believe there's two of you just arrived and both engaged to girls who also lived at Goodwill House,' Angus said, not for the first time. The other two chaps had left them to swap anecdotes and wandered off to join a few other officers more eager to drink and enjoy themselves.

Ted arrived and was equally surprised and delighted to meet Angus. 'It's busier and noisier here than at Manston, but the accommodation's better.'

Angus had ordered a second pot of coffee, as well as a plate of freshly made sandwiches with recognisable fillings. There was a slight hiatus when this arrived and they, as all RAF bods did, ate whilst they had the chance.

'There's something you need to know. When we're on readiness, we get moved to Rochford – it's living under tents and very basic. You and your chaps are to be rostered on for Rochford from 4 a.m. tomorrow.'

'At least it's decent weather – I can imagine it's none too pleasant in the rain,' Freddie said as he poured himself another cup of coffee.

'Bloody horrible at all times,' Angus said. 'Just the NAAFI van for food, incredibly basic and unpleasant ablutions...'

'There's no need to elaborate, we get your gist. I suppose it's a grass strip as well, which can't be ideal when it's wet.'

They were binding about everything, including being separated from the women they loved, when the other chaps strolled off.

'Time for dinner. We're supposed to be in our best blues, and on our best behaviour, but since Dunkirk things have relaxed and we go as we are.'

'At least we won't be scrambled tonight.'

'Don't be too sure, Freddie, if there's a flap on, we'll all be scrambled.'

18

Di had put Pamela in charge of making sure the necessary bedding was neatly stacked on the empty beds in the hut. Her promotion was working well, and Di was confident everything would be in place when the new WAAFs arrived today. She'd been on duty for three hours already and was in her overalls, not her uniform.

'It's going to be strange having our billet fully occupied, Corp,' Pamela said.

'It will make things so much easier having a sergeant as well as the two of us in charge. When it's all tickety-boo in here, please check the billet for the sergeant.'

'I already have that on my list. Thank goodness the ablution block's fully functional. Only having three working WCs, two baths and two showers for so many would make things more difficult.'

Di laughed. 'I don't know where you lot were trained, but Millie and I were somewhere with only the same amount as we've got now for more than a hundred of us. Now *that* really was unpleasant.'

Phyllis had taken her friend's promotion remarkably well and the two older women, who'd been really difficult when they'd first arrived and were living at Goodwill House, were no longer surly but totally reliable and good team players. Di intended to recommend Phyllis the next time a promotion was available.

All the girls would become aircraft women first class after completing six months without being put on a charge of any sort. She wished that she knew exactly who was coming to join them at Manston. Did Victory House send the trades that Manston needed, or were the girls just randomly selected?

'I'm relying on you to ensure everything's as it should be. Sally's going to collect them at midday, as I've got to drive an air commodore to a meeting in Ashford. I might well be there all day as I've got to wait to bring him back.'

'Don't worry, nobody will let you down. I hope—'

There was no time for her to finish her remark, as the air-raid siren wailed at the same time as the squadrons were scrambled. Did she have time to cycle to the MT before bombs were dropped?'

'Get into the shelter, make sure anyone on duty joins you.' Di didn't wait to see if her order was carried out but hopped on her bike and rode flat out down the edge of the strip, knowing she could be put on a charge if caught. She had put on her tin hat – so she wasn't breaking every rule.

She was within a hundred yards of her objective when the unmistakable sound of a low-flying aircraft approaching made her veer off the bitumen and fling herself face down on the grass that ran alongside.

Not a moment too soon. The terrifying rat-a-tat-tat of machine-gun fire advancing made her flinch. She daren't look up. If she kept her face to the dirt, the German pilot might not realise she was a human target. A face was easy to distinguish from the air – she prayed her grey-blue overalls would be camouflage enough.

How long had he been firing? Freddie had told her his kite only had ninety seconds of ammunition. Surely the sound of bullets hitting the runway had been going on longer than that? She almost wet herself at the scream of fighters arriving directly overhead. The noise was deafening and the ground reverberated. They were so low that if she rolled over, she'd be able to wave to the pilots.

Then, as suddenly as it started, it was over. The German fled, hotly pursued by two Spitfires. The end was inevitable, and she watched in fascination as the enemy aircraft burst into flames and spiralled into the sea.

The boys on the base who'd shot it down performed a victory roll as they flew over the base. This was strictly forbidden, but it still happened, and she didn't blame them for celebrating. They'd certainly saved her life.

The siren sounded the all-clear and she staggered to her feet and picked up her discarded bicycle. The runway was pitted with bullet holes, as was the ground, no more than three yards from where she'd been spreadeagled.

She wasn't sure if anybody had seen what had happened, apart from the two flyers, and she had no intention of telling them. With any luck, as she'd been face down, the pilots wouldn't have been able to identify her. If she'd done as she was supposed to and gone into the shelter, then she wouldn't have put her life in danger.

Sarge greeted her as he always did. 'You're to take the Hillman. You should be in your uniform – not your overalls.'

'I know, but I thought I might be needed to drive a rescue vehicle so didn't change. My intention is to drive back to my billet and then collect my passenger. I don't expect he'll want to leave until the squadrons have been debriefed.'

They were now returning and landing one after the other before taxiing to their places on the apron.

'Fair enough. I got one of the erks to give the car a bit of a spit and polish. Don't want any criticism from a bigwig.'

'I'm glad I know the way to Ashford. Even with a map, it's a bit tricky with no signposts.'

Sarge chuckled. 'Won't do a bleeding bit of good stopping the Huns – they'll land on this coast and then march straight to London.'

'I heard removing signposts and station names is to stop spies who parachute in.'

'Very likely – some bloke in the pub the other night said half a dozen nuns had dropped in near Hastings the other day. They were men in disguise and were captured by the LDV.'

Di laughed. 'That sounds highly unlikely, but it makes a good story.'

It was good to talk about something else and not have time to review her near demise. It was entirely her own fault, as she should have gone into the nearest shelter or ditch like everyone else.

* * *

The senior officer she was collecting was very relaxed, insisted on sitting next to her and immediately pulled out a packet of Kensitas and lit one with his lighter. At least his cigarette wasn't one of the evil-smelling Woodbines which the airmen smoked as they were cheaper.

He sensed her disapproval and laughed. 'Sorry, my dear, you'll just have to put up with it. I'll open a window if you like.'

'Yes, if you don't mind, sir, that would be splendid.'

He wound the window down and immediately his hat flew off his head because she'd wound down her window at the same time as him. His cap vanished into the road. She applied the brakes so violently he almost went through the windscreen, which didn't improve the situation.

Before he could yell at her, Di was out of the car and running back to collect the wretched object. She thanked her lucky stars it was unharmed by its unexpected journey. On her return, she dropped it into his lap, slammed the door, engaged the gears and drove off, all without saying a word.

They travelled in chilly silence for several miles and then he finally spoke to her. 'Not your fault, Corporal, and you handled the situation well. Are you familiar with the route?'

'I am, sir, my fiancé crash-landed in a village close to Ashford last week.'

'From your demeanour, I gather he was unhurt.'

She risked a glance in his direction and smiled. 'It's a pity I can't say the same for his beloved Spit.'

'Pilots are more important than planes. I'm afraid it's going to be a long day. I've got a meeting at Kingsnorth, then another with some brown jobs in Hastings, back to Hawkinge and then home. Hope you brought your knitting.'

'I don't knit or sew, sir. If I have your permission, then I'll offer my services in the MT at whatever base we're at for however long you think you might be.'

'Good show. Make sure you fill the tank at each stop and don't go more than a few miles from where I'm involved with a meeting.'

'Very good, sir, I'll check back to see if you're ready to depart every half an hour.'

He was quiet for a bit and then shifted suddenly, making her jump. 'I say that Hanover fellow must be your fiancé. He's got a bit of a reputation – one of the best pilots we've got.'

She couldn't prevent her happy smile at hearing Freddie's name mentioned so glowingly. 'Yes, Freddie's my fiancé. My best friend is married to Flight Lieutenant Thorrington.'

'Good god! I've heard about him too. Well, well, well – Thorrington's already an ace. Let's hope the two survive this war. We need men like him to fight the Luftwaffe.'

The guard at the gate of Kingsnorth base gave their ID papers a cursory glance and then waved them through. Even on a base she'd never visited before, finding the admin block was relatively easy, as it was always the biggest building and invariably brick-built and not a wooden building or a Nissen hut.

After dropping her passenger, Di found her way to the motor pool and was disappointed not to be needed. 'Enjoy your free time, Corporal Forsyth, I don't reckon you get much of it if things are the same in Manston as they are here,' a friendly sergeant told her.

'I'll be in the NAAFI if anything changes. I brought a book with me but really didn't expect to have time to read it.' It was good to have a few quiet minutes to herself and to be thankful she hadn't been shot that morning though her own stupidity.

* * *

Joanna was about to stand up and investigate who the unexpected callers might be, but Liza was already at the door. 'I'll go. And I'll tell them to come back when we've had our supper.'

'No, don't do that. Just ask them to wait under the portico and then come and tell us who it is.'

'Joanna, I'm shocked at the lack of manners nowadays,' Elizabeth said sharply.

Since Betty's funeral, there'd been a distinct chill between them, and Joanna feared this was her fault. Losing a dear friend had brought her closer to Jean, who understood Betty hadn't just been an employee but someone very dear to her. Her mother-in-law just couldn't grasp the fact that one's housekeeper could also be a friend.

'I think I'll go anyway and see for myself who it is. As the sooner I deal with it, the sooner I'll be back to eat this delicious roast chicken. Please continue with your meal whilst it's still hot. There's no need for all of us to have cold food.'

Jean nodded but instead of picking up her cutlery – which Elizabeth did immediately – she picked up the two plates. 'I'll put a bit of greaseproof paper over each of them and pop them in the slow oven. They'll be piping hot when you and Liza return.'

As she approached the front hall, she heard a man's voice and not one she recognised. Liza was inviting whoever it was in, so it must be someone important. The first man was grey-haired, wearing a trilby, a smart trench coat and she suspected that he must be a plainclothes policeman. Who else would arrive in a big black car and disturb one's evening unannounced?

'Good evening, I am Lady Harcourt. How can I be of assistance?'

The senior man stepped in, followed by a younger version of himself, but this policeman limped badly and needed a stick to hold himself upright.

'I'm sorry to disturb you so late, my lady, but when the report about the threats to your life arrived on my desk, I came at once. I'm Chief Inspector Williams and this is my sergeant.'

He didn't bother to introduce his companion by name, which she thought was impolite and it set her hackles up. 'There was absolutely no necessity for you to do so, Chief Inspector. Mr Smith made threats, but he was upset at the time. His wife died tragically very recently. I'm absolutely certain he won't act on his words.'

She looked pointedly at the open door and his eyes narrowed. 'He certainly won't, as he's been arrested. I'll not have any riffraff threatening to kill a Harcourt on my watch.' He waited to see if she was going to comment and when she didn't, he continued. 'Lord Harcourt might not be here to take care of you, but I can assure you...'

'I thank you for your consideration, Inspector, but I'm quite capable of taking care of myself and my family. Also, my husband might be deceased, but there's a new Lord Harcourt. Therefore, although your diligence and interest are appreciated, neither are required. Good evening, and thank you for coming. A telephone call would have been sufficient.'

She caught the eye of the sergeant, who was trying not to laugh. Williams reminded her of the objectionable Mr Culley – David's solicitor – who'd she'd disliked on sight and no longer employed.

'I suggest that you release Mr Smith immediately, as I have absolutely no intention of pressing charges or of making a witness statement of any sort and neither have any of my family or staff.'

Liza had been standing by the door and now pulled it fully open. The nameless sergeant grinned at her and then, with remarkable speed for someone who was lame, vanished through the door, leaving his superior no option but to follow.

'Goodness, you soon sent them packing,' Liza said. 'I don't like Bert Smith but he doesn't deserve to be put in prison.'

'Quite right, Liza. If I'd known making the report would result in such a heavy-handed action, then I wouldn't have allowed Jean to do it. Too late to worry about that now and I'm absolutely ravenous. Shall we return to the others and enjoy our supper?'

* * *

That night, as she was settling down to sleep, Joanna thought about what had transpired that day. Had she been premature in dismissing the policeman and not taking Bert's threats seriously? Then she recalled that she'd mentioned Peter Harcourt and regretted that remark, too.

The patronising chief inspector had obviously known David quite well to believe he had the right to step in and act as her protector. The only place they might have mingled was at the Freemasons Lodge – not anywhere she'd chosen to visit, even when invited to a Ladies' Night.

Would Williams take it upon himself to seek out the new Lord

Harcourt? Had she made another enemy who might threaten the wellbeing of her family?

Another problem was that Joe and Liza were no longer addressing her as Aunt Joanna but equally they still weren't calling her Mama or Mother. In fact, they were carefully avoiding using either. Tomorrow, she must take them to one side and ask them why they were so reluctant to do so. More pressing, perhaps, was to restore a good relationship with Elizabeth.

Her mother-in-law was a cantankerous old lady in her late seventies, born a Victorian and brought up in a very wealthy family. It was inevitable that the two of them would have differing views. Hers, she hoped, were more in keeping with modern times, but she couldn't expect Elizabeth to adjust so readily to how things were in 1940.

19

Di eventually returned to Manston at dusk and thought it had been a waste of a day. Driving a senior officer about the country was all very well, but she'd much rather have been delivering parts, ferrying pilots or even driving the bowsers that refuelled the planes.

No bombs had been dropped or kites lost, for which she was thankful. The only positive thing about the day was that she'd managed to buy some Basildon Bond writing paper and now had a chatty, loving letter to send to Freddie. She didn't need to know his exact address, just his name, rank and number and the base where he was would be sufficient to find him.

She'd promised Ted she'd look in on Millie, but she daren't do so, as she needed to get back and introduce herself to the woman who would now be in charge of the two dozen girls and women billeted there.

This evening, she carefully pushed her bicycle into the designated place along with three others, rather than dumping it against the wall of the hut as she usually did. The blackouts were down but it was still light enough to be able to see without the use of her torch.

She hesitated for a moment, not sure whether she should nip into the hut and check everything was as it should be or go immediately to the main block where, from the noise, everybody was.

The first thing she saw on entering their sleeping accommodation were the extra greatcoats, waterproof ground sheets and tin hats hanging from the pegs. The second was the fact that the office was now obviously in use – the sergeant had already put out her personal possessions on the desk.

So far, so good. She was about to leave when she heard someone crying. It was coming from the dormitory and she pushed open the door and saw a huddled shape crouching on the floor between two of the beds at the far end of the space.

'I'm Corporal Forsyth. What's wrong? How can I help you?'

The girl looked up, her face blotched and her expression wretched. She gulped, shook her head and continued to cry. Di dropped down beside her.

'Come on, old thing, this won't do. I need to know what's wrong but first I need to know your name.'

'Daisy Jones. I mean ACW2 931, Corp.'

'Well, that's a start. What's your trade?' It seemed safer to ask something easy to answer rather than delve into the reason for the girl's distress.

'I'm general duties, but Sarge says I'm to work in the stores. I don't know nothing about what's in there. I thought I was going to be doing cleaning and such.'

'Is that why you're crying?'

Finally, the girl stopped snivelling and sat up. 'Of course it ain't, I ain't that dopey. I didn't get a chance to say goodbye to me fellow and now he's gorn off to Africa and I'll never see him again.'

'You can write to him. I can assure you he's a lot safer in Africa than my fiancé is flying a Spitfire. Buck up and dry your eyes. A lot of us have got sweethearts dotted all over the place and we just have to lump it and get on with things.'

Her bracing words seemed to do the trick. Daisy stood up and only then did Di see the girl was tiny – scarcely over five foot – but despite her diminutive size, her uniform fitted her perfectly.

'Golly, most girls your size would be swamped in that. How come yours fits so well?'

'Cor, Corp, ta ever so for noticing. I was a seamstress in a sweat-shop in Poplar so altered it meself.' The girl grinned and lifted the skirt to reveal her silky summer knickers, known as twilights. 'These came down almost to me ankles. Blimey, we didn't half laugh. I made two pairs from each one and gave the spares to me sister.'

'I didn't hear you say that, Daisy, as I could put you on a charge for misuse of equipment and theft.'

The girl's horrified expression made her laugh. 'Don't worry, I'm not going to, but I suggest you don't tell anyone else your secret.'

She directed Daisy to the ablutions to wash her face and tidy her hair before they both slipped through the blackout on the main door and into the building which housed not only the mess, but also the recreation room and officers' accommodation.

At first, she couldn't pick out the sergeant or the corporal but then saw Pamela sitting at a table with two strangers. Neither of them had on their uniform jackets so their stripes couldn't be seen, but it made sense that Pamela, if she wasn't sitting with her best friend, Phyllis, would gravitate towards the other NCOs.

Daisy rushed off to join her friends and Di headed for the hatch to see if they'd got anything left – not that it would be pleasant to eat, but needs must. To her delight, there were two new girls working in the kitchen and something smelt delicious.

'There you are, Corp, we've got a tasty stew in the warmer for you and fruit pie and custard for afters.'

She held out her tray and the girl placed two steaming plates of absolutely wonderful food on it. She couldn't help beaming. 'Thank you, I can assure you that you two are going to be the most popular girls here. I take it you're both fully trained cooks?'

'I've worked in the family café since I was a nipper and Gladys worked in a posh hotel. You'll get decent meals from now on. And we'll train up the two girls who've been doing their best.'

Di carried her treasures across to the table she'd spotted on the far side of the mess. 'I'm Corporal Forsyth, sorry I wasn't here to meet you, but I've been dashing all over the country with a bigwig all day.'

She had given all the newcomers a quick scan as she'd walked across the canteen and they seemed a decent bunch. She was glad to have someone take over the paperwork, a task she didn't enjoy and wasn't particularly good at.

She didn't ask if she could join them, she was entitled to sit wherever she wanted. Pamela smiled. 'I've shown Sarge and Corp around and told them everything they need to know.'

'Good show.' Di put her tray down. 'I'm absolutely starving, so introductions will have to wait. Excuse me whilst I enjoy the first decent meal we've had since we arrived on the base – that's if you don't count the food we buy from the NAAFI.'

Joanna, on reflection, decided to leave things as they were with her mother-in-law. It was quite likely that Elizabeth might say something, do something, that just widened the rift. There was enough anxiety and worry in the world at the moment without making things worse in her own household.

She didn't even broach the matter of her new son and daughter calling her Mama or Mother – they too would come to a decision on their own without her intervention. Fortunately, she heard no more from the patronising police inspector and neither did she have any further unpleasant encounters with Bert Smith.

A week after the funeral, the village hall was back in action, and there was to be both a WVS and WI meeting held that afternoon. Joe was left to keep an eye on Elizabeth and she was walking to the village with Jean and Liza.

'We've only got two bicycles in working order now,' Jean said sadly. 'Do you think we might be able to buy some puncture patches in Ramsgate? The ironmonger in the village has sold out and said he won't be getting any more.'

'Joe's sure he will find what we need in one of the barns. Things have been tossed in there for years and there might well be an old bicycle he can dismantle and then use the rear wheel to replace the one that's got a flat tyre.'

'I don't mind the walk, it's a lovely day and it's only half an hour. We can always catch a bus back if we time it right,' Liza said as she paused to peer into a hedge. 'Look at that, a nest and it's full of little birds.'

'Don't disturb them, my dear, or the mother might not return to feed them.'

'I've been in the country for months and I still don't know much about it. Joe's a real country boy now and knows the names of everything.'

'Then get him to teach you,' Joanna said. 'We might not have theatres, shops or cinemas as they do in a big city but we have so much more.'

Liza laughed. 'I wouldn't want to be living in the East End – the bombs are going to drop there any day. Do you think the ones aimed at Manston could fall on us? We're no more than half a mile as the crow flies from the edge of the base.'

'It's possible, but there's no point in dwelling on what we can't change. Let's concentrate on things we can influence...'

'What, like rolling bandages and knitting balaclavas and gloves for the sailors?'

Joanna shook her head. 'I know it seems a pointless exercise, Liza, but sometimes doing something mundane helps us to stop worrying about things we can't do anything about. Neither of today's meetings will be at all boring, and I'm so glad you've decided to become a junior member of both.'

'Well, I'm a Harcourt now, and it's expected of us, isn't it? Joe and I won't ever let you down.'

'I know you won't, any more than Sarah will.' She flinched as the air-raid siren began to howl. 'We're halfway between home and the village. I think we should just get off the road and hide behind the hedge in the field.'

'Fat lot of good that will do if they drop a bomb on us,' Jean said but didn't argue.

They found a piece of ground free of nettles and thorns and settled down to wait. One after the other, aircraft from the base roared into the sky.

She was quite sure the fighters at both Hornchurch, where Sarah's fiancé, Angus, was based, and where Millie and Di's young men were, would be even busier than here.

The dogfights seemed much closer today – the noise of machine guns, the scream of the engines, was getting closer, she was sure of it. Liza shifted nearer and the girl was shivering. Joanna put her arm around her but for some reason wasn't frightened herself. When had she become so brave? Jean leaned forward and peered out from their leafy sanctuary.

'There's a dive bomber heading this way. Thank god we had the sense to hide. I wouldn't put it past the bastards to machine-gun innocent women if they could.'

Instinctively all three of them huddled further into the flimsy protection of the hedge. The noise got louder and then the force of an explosion sent them backwards into the ditch. They landed in a tangle of arms and legs. Seconds later, there was a second explosion and then the smell of burning.

'Quickly, we can't stay here. If this hedge catches fire, we'll be roasted alive. I'm pretty sure one of the planes has crashed in this field.'

'It's a good thing it hasn't rained recently, Joanna, as crawling along here would be even more unpleasant,' Jean said from behind her.

'We can wriggle out by the gate.'

'What if there's a German with a gun waiting to shoot us?' Liza asked.

'Whoever was in that crash will be dead. No one could have survived what we heard.'

The ominous crackling of wood catching fire gave her the necessary impetus to increase her pace and lead the three of them out of the ditch and into the lane. The hedge was now alight. It was as dry as tinder and would burn fiercely.

Jean was the last to emerge from their temporary shelter and, being taller than either Liza or Joanna, was able to look back. 'Holy cow, our boys shot down the bomber.'

'Jolly good show.' Joanna wasn't sure celebrating any man's death was civilised but she was glad none of them had been injured, apart from their dignity and clothing.

'Let's hurry to the village. We can get cleaned up and so on when we get there. That was quite an adventure, wasn't it, Liza? Joe will be jealous that he didn't share it with us.'

'He's welcome to it. I almost wet myself, I was so scared. I don't think I'd be any good joining the services. I hope there's something a bit safer I can do when I'm old enough to volunteer.'

'Let's trust this war is over before that happens. I sincerely hope I don't look as disreputable as the two of you.'

Jean's new felt cloche, which she'd admired, had a large hole in it. Joanna's stockings were also laddered and there was a large amount of the ditch and hedge attached to her clothing.

Liza, who hadn't graduated to wearing a hat as she still wore her hair in pigtails, had ripped the front panel of her frock and appeared to have lost a pretty, beaded buckle from one of her shoes.

They both turned to look at her and she knew they'd laugh. 'Your hat's on back to front and you look more like a scarecrow than the most important lady of the village,' Liza said, giggling, and the pinched look in her face began to fade.

'Let's not do anything about it. I think the ladies will be amused to see us in our disarray.'

If David could see her, hear her remarks, he would be turning in his grave. Not for the first time, she felt a wave of relief that she was no longer living a half-life with a man she'd never really loved.

* * *

Di regaled the new arrivals with her recent near-death experience and, as she'd hoped, it broke the ice wonderfully.

'That's exactly what I'd have done,' Sergeant Joyce Dickinson said. 'Duty first, regulations second is my motto, and obviously yours too. I think we're going to get along famously, Corporal Forsyth. I was impressed by the efficiency of your record-keeping and all of your small group of girls are highly satisfactory.'

Di nodded as if she'd expected praise. 'I can see that my request to have trained cooks has been answered. Do we also have at least one extra driver?'

'We do, AWC1 Maureen Brown is an experienced driver and has been working as a dispatch rider at a base in Norfolk. She requested a transfer to Kent so she can visit her parents occasionally – they live just outside Folkestone.'

'A motorbike rider – jolly good. Sometimes it's quicker to send someone on two wheels rather than take a car and it uses far less petrol.'

'There are two more clerical staff, and the rest are general duties so will be sent wherever they're needed.'

'I met Daisy Jones and she told me she was going to be working in the stores.'

'Ah, yes, I meant to send Corporal Rhodes to find her. She's a volatile young lady and heard from her young man that he'd been posted as we caught the train.'

'My fiancé is a squadron leader and has just been moved to Hornchurch. I told her to concentrate on being a good WAAF, write him lots of letters, and just get on with it like we all have to.'

Sergeant Dickinson smiled sympathetically. 'My husband's somewhere in Africa – he was a reservist in the army and recalled in September. I've not seen him since then. I immediately enrolled myself in the WAAF and have been fortunate to be promoted.'

Di explained about Millie and got permission to leave the base for a couple of hours. It was almost dark, but her night vision was excellent, and she was able to see well enough to cycle down to the cottage. Obviously, not a glimmer of light came from either of the windows that faced the road.

She knocked on the door but also called out. 'Millie, it's me. Sorry to call so late but I've only just got off duty.'

The door opened, sending a shaft of bright light spilling out into the night. 'Quickly, I've not got the blackout on this door and I don't want the warden screaming at me.'

Once inside, Di embraced her friend and then stood back to look at her. 'Gosh, you look a lot better than you did yesterday. I expected to find you crying in a corner.'

'I did cry a bit but am resigned to having Ted somewhere else,' Millie said. 'He could be on the other side of the world so I'm fortunate that he's just outside London. It might be possible to go and see him occasionally – not now – but sometime in the future when I'm feeling better and things aren't quite so dangerous.'

Di didn't like to disillusion her friend. If she thought things were dangerous now, then she was going to be absolutely horrified when the balloon went up.

'I had a near miss this morning when the sirens went. I'll tell you about it, but can I put the kettle on? I didn't have time for a cup of tea.'

After spending a pleasant couple of hours in the cottage, she was satisfied that although Millie was suffering from morning sickness, she was otherwise in good spirits. She'd been shocked to hear about Bert Smith's threats and the attitude of the local CID.

'Oh, I didn't tell you that Joe came to see me. Joanna has invited me to live at Goodwill House if I'm prepared to take on the role of housekeeper. I'm going to do it, as I really don't like being on my own.'

'No wonder you're tickety-boo. What about the sickness?'

'Joanna understands I might have to dash off occasionally and is quite happy with that. I don't have to start until the land girls come and that will be at the end of the month. The woman who organises the accommodation for the girls is calling next week.'

'What about this place? Will you keep it on or hand back the key?'

'I'll wait and see how I settle in at Goodwill House; if it works out, then, of course, I'll not need the cottage.'

'So, good news all round,' Di said. 'I couldn't be happier with the new sergeant. I'm not sure when I'll be able to pop down again, but I'll come when I can.'

'Don't worry about me, you've got more important things to do, like not getting machine-gunned by a German.'

They hugged, and this time Millie turned off the hall light so there wouldn't be any breach of the blackout regulations when the front door was opened. It was now very dark indeed and there were no lights on Di's cycle.

The lane was relatively straight, and she knew where she was going, so she decided to risk cycling virtually blind. If Freddie and the boys could use their instruments to fly at night, then she could use her sense of direction and common sense to do the same. She smiled to herself.

She prayed she wouldn't be flying either over the handlebars or into a ditch. More by luck than skill, she arrived at the entrance to the base. The barrier was down and as she'd never returned so late before, she wasn't sure of the correct procedure; she really didn't want to be shot as an intruder.

After propping her bike against the guard hut, she walked around and rapped sharply on the door. There was a crash of falling furniture, a barrage of very rude words and then the door opened.

'What the bleedin' hell do you think you're playing at? Almost broke me neck from shock,' a very cross guard snarled at her.

'Don't speak to me so disrespectfully. I'll put you on a charge.'

He shone the feeble beam of his torch from her face to her stripes. She almost laughed when she heard an audible gulp.

'I beg your pardon, Corporal, no offence meant. I never expected no one to bang on the door at this time of night.'

'None taken. Please log me in. I signed out just over two hours ago. Corporal Forsyth.'

She was still smiling when she let herself into the silent accommodation hut. It was too late to write to Freddie, but she certainly had plenty to tell him when she did so tomorrow.

20

Freddie was told by the intelligence officer – the spy – that his squadron wouldn't be moving to Rochford base the next day but would remain at Hornchurch until it was back to strength. As the men hadn't been told about the proposed move, only he and Ted were aware. He sent word to the NCO pilots to be on duty at seven the next morning. He was able to speak to the others in the Officers' Mess.

'Let's hope it takes a few days to find us the extra men and kites, Ted, and that we've got time to give them a bit of flying experience before they're involved in a party.'

'I was talking to Stan, his batman told him the two empty rooms on his corridor would be occupied by four new blokes tomorrow,' Ted said. 'Like him, they'll be pilot officers – the lowliest of the low – but unlike him will have bloody zero combat experience.'

'I've not been told about these men or about any new kites. No doubt the CO will inform me tomorrow. Did you get your letter posted to Millie?'

Ted beamed. 'I did. As we don't have to be up at dawn tomorrow, you've got time to write to Di. Rochford sounds pretty grim and the thought of being out there for several weeks doesn't appeal.'

'We left so quickly this morning it just didn't occur to me that Angus Trent was stationed here. Bit of good luck knowing someone, as he was able to give us the necessary gen.'

When he got a moment, Freddie wrote a long letter to Di. He was glad that this time he had something pleasant to tell her, as he was unlikely to be doing anything particularly dangerous for the next few days. His cheerful new orderly promised to post the letter tomorrow.

* * *

Freddie received the good news that there were two spanking brand-new Spits waiting to be collected from a factory near Southampton and that two of his men would be ferried directly there in a taxi Annie by an ATA pilot. The Air Transport Auxiliary were doing a great job and had released experienced flyers for active duty by delivering and collecting kites, people and goods and taking them to where they were needed.

The men were milling about in the blast pen that held their precious fighters and he raised his hand for silence. He explained that they wouldn't be on combat duty until the squadron was back to full strength. 'Right, Stan and Dave, I want you to collect the first of our new kites. Do you think that you can find your way back from Southampton without getting lost?'

'Too bloody right, Skip, it'll be a doddle. Does that mean Dave and I get to keep the kites, or will the new bods get them?'

'They'll be yours. No point in giving them to the inexperienced sprogs. Might be a bit of a waste.'

There was no need to say any more, as everybody was well aware that the life expectancy for one of these chaps could be frighteningly short. Sometimes they were only part of the squadron for a day before going for a Burton. If these flyers survived their first party, weren't shot down or didn't prang their kite, they had a good chance of living for at least a few more weeks. He couldn't afford to lose brand-new aircraft on their first flight either.

The two men left in decent weather, but the Met chappie said it was closing in and heavy rain and strong winds were forecast for Hornchurch, which was a concern. Once all his squadron had familiarised themselves with their ground crew, put their Mae Wests, chutes and so on in the correct place in the locker room, they were free to drift off to the bar, recreation room or their billets, but they weren't allowed off base.

Ted, as his second-in-command, and the other flight commander remained with him in the blast pen despite the torrential rain, anxiously awaiting the arrival of the two kites. Although they wouldn't be scrambled, as far as he knew, he'd been told it was quite possible they might be sent up on reconnaissance missions or in pairs to intercept any lone Bf 109s that had somehow evaded the active squadrons and the barrage balloons.

'I'm going to ring Sapper again, Ted, he must know where they are. He'll be speaking to them on the RT and both of them are proficient at instrument flying.'

'That's no bloody good in this weather, Freddie. I think even you or I might find it difficult to find the field with visibility so poor.'

The other men drifted back, as anxious as he and Ted were that Dave and Stan were still missing. The RT system in the planes was iffy at the best of times and in this sort of weather, the two chaps might well be unable to communicate with the controller. They certainly wouldn't be able to see the strip or the landing lights.

Then the familiar drone of an approaching Spit could be heard, despite the racket of the rain. Freddie moved to the edge of the strip, mentally crossing his fingers and hoping that both landed safely.

'God, there's only one. Where the hell's the other bloke?' Ted said as he screwed up his eyes and looked into the gloom.

'If he'd crashed then I think we'd have heard. Let's hope he landed somewhere else and will turn up when the weather improves,' Freddie said, sounding more confident than he felt.

The Spitfire was flying blind and had done well to find Hornchurch at all. Instead of landing, the silly sod beat up the base, a practice strictly forbidden. Doing victory rolls at one hundred feet was dangerous and stupid.

'He's not changed the pitch of his prop,' Freddie said. 'He's over-revving the engine and the whole bloody thing will be covered with oil.'

'The racket he's making will have been heard by everybody. Neither of them is a complete novice, so I don't understand why something so basic could have been forgotten.'

Freddie was livid and intended to let whichever one of the two it was know exactly how he felt. When the kite taxied into the blast pit, he was waiting. Dave pushed back the lid and hopped out onto the wing.

He took one look at the icy-faced officers waiting to greet him and his happy smile faded. Freddie told him in no uncertain terms exactly what he thought of him. The embarrassed young man apologised profusely and slunk off.

The telephone jangled noisily and one of the erks answered it and then poked his head around the door. 'The other bloke landed at Kenley by mistake, sir. He's tickety-boo and will be back tomorrow.'

Freddie smiled at this piece of good news. His squadron was complete, and they could get back to full operational duties.

* * *

Joanna walked into the hall as if she was looking as smart and well turned out as usual. She no longer wore her WVS uniform unless doing something official. None of the other ladies had bothered to buy the very unattractive frocks – they had better things to spend their coupons on.

'Good gracious, my lady, whatever happened to the three of you?' Mrs Thomas, the chair of the WI, exclaimed loudly.

'We were literally pulled through a hedge backwards. Or rather, if I'm going to be absolutely accurate, we crawled through it forwards.' After explaining exactly what had happened, they were plied with hot tea and custard creams – a real treat to have those biscuits. Everybody had taken shelter in the cellar of the Brewery Tavern, which had been converted into somewhere safe for the villagers who didn't have their own Anderson or Morrison shelters.

'That blighter almost hit the church tower, he was flying so blooming low,' Joan said.

'Well, our boys got him and he's dead in the field, so, ladies, if you'll excuse us, we'll try to repair the damage to our appearance before the meetings begin.'

She was surprised that she was so calm, as it wasn't everyday one was shot at by a German aircraft.

This was the first time they'd got together since Betty had been ill and only a week since the funeral. They did their best to be cheerful, but the mood was subdued. As Liza had predicted, everybody was either rolling bandages, knitting or crocheting something – no idle hands allowed.

Mrs Thomas kept her meeting short and then handed the assembled women over to Joanna. Her main focus was on being ready to support anybody who might be bombed out.

'Mrs Evans is coordinating the collection of essential items at the vicarage. If anybody is unlucky enough to lose their home and its contents, there should be sufficient for them to take to wherever the authorities find them accommodation.'

'Do you think we'll be bombed, my lady?' The speaker was one of the older residents, a widow whose three sons had moved away to find employment many years ago. Until the outbreak of war, there'd been little to do in the country apart from working on the land.

'Not deliberately, but we're perilously close to the base as well as only five miles from Ramsgate. It's perfectly possible that in a raid the bombs might well go astray. Make sure you have everything packed to take to whatever shelter you're going to use. It's really important to have your ration books, identity cards, insurance documents and so on in the bag you take with you.'

'What about if there's bombs dropped on Ramsgate? Do we go there to offer our assistance or leave it to the Red Cross and their local WI and WVS groups?'

'An excellent question, Mrs Thomas, and I've given it much thought myself. As long as the telephone lines are still working, then I'm sure someone from the council in Ramsgate, or a member of one of their groups, will contact one of us if they need us to step in.'

'I reckon you'll be asked to take in homeless families, my lady, what with you having such a large empty house and all,' someone else said sharply.

'I'll be having a dozen land girls billeted with me from the end of the month. Unless I opened the Victorian wing, I'd not have any room. I will, of course, do what I can if the circumstances demand it, as must we all.'

The meeting disbanded promptly at four o'clock. Each time they held a meeting, there were fewer younger women present. All those who were able to work now had full-time employment at one of the manufactories in Ramsgate.

As Joanna was ruefully examining her ruined hat and gloves, Mrs Thomas joined her. 'I'm not sure that we'll be able to do anything of any use in an emergency with our membership so depleted. I should think the average age of those that are still active members of either group is around sixty. We'd be more a hindrance than a help, don't you think?'

'I agree. Our ARP warden is in his seventies, our police constable might not be past retirement age, but he can scarcely get about the place safely. He won't be able to deter looters if we had any.'

'The LDV,' Mrs Thomas said, 'is made up entirely of old men and boys. Those who still work on the farms around here have failed to volunteer. At least they would be younger and fitter.'

'There are no men under thirty working on my farms as far as I know. They've either been conscripted or volunteered, which is why the land girls are so desperately needed. The remainder of my park is going to be ploughed up, and all farms have been told to bring every spare acre into production as soon as possible.'

Liza, who'd been helping with the washing-up, came over to join them. 'I know it was fine when we came but there's black clouds rolling in from the sea. If we hurry, we'll catch the next bus, which should be here any minute. If we don't, then we're going to get drenched.'

'Then I won't keep you, my lady,' Mrs Thomas said. 'As you know, my son-in-law and daughter have a market garden a few miles from here and they too have been asked to grow more tomatoes and so on. I wonder if any of your land girls might be able to work there.'

'Mrs Dougherty, the area organiser, is coming to finalise the arrangements next week. I'll mention it to her, but I don't think she has anything to do with the allocation of the girls, just their billeting.'

'I understand, and it's quite possible the authorities are already aware of their need for extra hands.'

Afterwards, Joanna, Jean and Liza had to run for the bus, but the driver saw them coming and waited for them to arrive. Their dishevelled appearance did not go unnoticed, and they received several sympathetic looks as they found their seats. They'd not been travelling for more than a few minutes when the skies opened. The rain obscured the windows outside and soon they were steamed up on the inside, making visibility impossible.

'We're going to have to run when we get off,' Liza said cheerfully.

'I hardly think it matters how wet we get, my dear, our appearance is already unsatisfactory after our encounter with the dive bomber.'

'At least the rain has put out the fire in the hedge. I hope that too many nests weren't destroyed by it.'

'The birds will rebuild somewhere else and have another clutch. There are far more important things to be sad about than a few unfortunate fledglings,' she told Liza firmly.

Was the war making her new daughter become more sentimental or was Joanna becoming harder?

* * *

Di was enjoying the new regime. Having somebody senior to herself made things much easier for her, as she didn't have to be constantly thinking about her responsibilities. There was now a sergeant, two corporals and a LACW to manage the wellbeing and behaviour of only twenty women.

The next two days sped past, and she didn't have a free

moment to visit Millie. She had received another long, funny letter from Freddie, who obviously had far too much time on his hands. They were still waiting for one more pilot to join his squadron and two more Spitfires – once they had those, they'd be posted for several weeks to Rochford, which didn't sound any fun at all. He certainly wouldn't have access to any of the luxuries he had now.

The weather had been appalling for the middle of July, with torrential rain and rough seas. The sergeant at the MT said at least it stopped Hitler from invading, as the barges would sink if they were towed into the Channel at the moment.

'That's the only good thing about pouring rain, Sarge,' Di said cheerfully as she collected her chit for the day. The duties listed could obviously change according to circumstances, but today she wasn't ferrying airmen but taking the van to Hawkinge in Folkestone to collect some parts that were needed and couldn't be delivered by the ATA any quicker.

'Call in at Ramsgate Station on the way back, Corp, there's a few parcels coming by rail that need collecting.'

Pointing out to him that Ramsgate was in the opposite direction didn't seem a sensible option, as he was in one of his tetchy moods again. If the parts were wanted urgently, then it made more sense for her to deliver them to the hangar where the ground crew were waiting and then go on to Ramsgate.

The journey to Folkestone and back was a round-trip of about forty miles, and for once the paperwork and the items themselves were ready to be picked up and she didn't have to hang around. The wipers were barely making a dent in the water trickling down the windscreen, and consequently driving was slower and more hazardous than usual.

On arriving at the hangar at Manston, she reversed into it. She didn't need to get out, as the men had the rear doors open and were snatching out the items eagerly. She was thanked and praised for bringing them so promptly, even though it was her job to do so.

She decided to return to the MT and inform Sarge that she was now on her way to Ramsgate. It was just possible something more urgent had come up in her absence.

Instead of being cross that she'd brought the parts before going to the station, he rushed over to speak to her. Her heart sank. His expression was grave. Had Freddie had an accident?

'Thank god you did it this way, Corp. We had a call from someone called Violet a couple of hours ago – she's a neighbour of Millie's. She ran to the base in the rain to get the message to me.'

'Oh no – from your face, it's bad news.'

'Millie's been taken to hospital. It seems that she's lost the baby.'

'How absolutely dreadful – can I go and see her after I've collected the parcels?'

'You don't have to ask, love, Millie's one of us. You give her our love.'

Although initially Millie hadn't wanted this baby, she must be devasted to have lost it. Di was pretty sure she would be in pieces.

She was in and out of the station in record time and then parked in a side street near the hospital. She bounded up the steps and went to the reception area.

'Mrs Camilla Thorrington was brought here a little while ago. I think she might have had a miscarriage.'

The woman behind the desk checked the records and nodded. 'You're fortunate, it's visiting time. She's in Ward 5, Women's Medical.'

The hospital was spotless, the nurses were immaculate in stiffly starched aprons and frilly caps, but the smell of boiled cabbage and disinfectant lingered everywhere. Di followed the signs and arrived at Ward 5.

There was a staff nurse sitting at the desk by the door and there were eight hospital beds arranged on either side of the long room. She saw Millie halfway down, looking pale and sad. She was concerned that there was a glass bottle of blood hanging next to her bed. She must have haemorrhaged to need a transfusion.

'I've come to see Mrs Thorrington,' she announced to the staff nurse.

The young woman smiled sympathetically. 'Go ahead, I think she saw you come in.'

Di hurried across and, ignoring the chair put neatly beside the bed, sat on the bed instead. She leaned forward and hugged her friend. 'I'm so very sorry. What frightful luck. Does Ted know? Do you want me to try and get in touch with him?'

'The consultant said it's quite common in the first few weeks and doesn't mean that future pregnancies will end the same way. It should have been straightforward, but I was unlucky and lost quite a lot of blood.' Millie sniffed and wiped her eyes, recovered then nodded towards the bottle by the bed.

'I can see. Thank goodness Violet was able to fetch help. What about Ted, you didn't answer that?'

'Someone at Manston has already contacted him and because they're not on active duty for another couple of days, he's got leave and is coming to see me. He's getting a flip from Hornchurch to Manston with an ATA flight, and they'll return him as well.'

'That's jolly good news. I suppose I'd better sit on the chair before the staff nurse comes over to tell me off. I'm so glad you're not feeling too devasted.'

'I'm sad, of course I am, but to tell the truth, a part of me is a little relieved,' Millie said. 'The war's getting closer every day and maybe now is not the time to be bringing a baby into the world.'

This made absolute sense to Di, and she thought she'd feel the same way. 'Will you re-enlist?'

'Definitely, but I want to train for something more challenging than driving. Ted's told me about the plotters and the girls who work in the home chain and I intend to apply to join one of those groups.'

If Millie was leaving Manston, Freddie had gone already, then she thought she would do the same. 'That makes sense. We have both loved being drivers but doing something more skilled now seems a good idea. Maybe we can train together and get sent to the same posting. When will you be discharged from hospital, do you know?'

'A week if I recover my strength and so on. Will you speak to the new sergeant for me and see how I go about applying to be in special duties? Are you really going to do the same?'

Di nodded. 'I was already considering asking for a transfer. Being a driver without you isn't the same. I need something more interesting to do.'

Suddenly Millie's face lit up. Di didn't need to ask why. She jumped up and saw Ted striding toward the bed. He nodded briefly at her as he passed. She hurried out, leaving them together.

21

Freddie was glad he could give Ted permission to visit Millie in hospital. If this had been Di, he would have been desperate to be with her and offer her comfort. Losing a baby wasn't easy, even if it hadn't been planned. In between the heavy rain, he got the men to fill sandbags and stack them up along the sides of the blast pad – you could never have too much protection in his opinion.

He was called to the telephone, and it was the controller, saying he wanted two kites up immediately as they'd had word that there were bombers incoming, but the radar was on the blink because of the weather and the blips on the screens were inconclusive.

'It's bloody horrible up there, Sapper, I can't believe any Huns will be coming at the moment.'

'I agree, Freddie, but someone's got to go up and have a deco.'

'Right, it had better be me. I'd send Ted but he's just got compassionate leave for twenty-four hours.'

'Then let's hope your lot aren't scrambled in your temporary absence, old boy.'

Thoughtfully, Freddie replaced the receiver. Was it wise for him to take this reconnaissance flight and leave his men leaderless? He shrugged – he was the best flyer and the most likely to succeed, and he really didn't want to lose anyone else when they were almost up to full strength.

He needed a wingman and thought he'd get Stan to accompany him, as the young chap needed to redeem himself in the eyes of the squadron.

Ten minutes later, they were taxiing out onto the runway and waiting for the green light to take off. He could barely see it through the rain. The RT crackled and hissed and then the controller's voice was just about audible and comprehensible.

'The possible sighting's over the East Coast. I'll give you the vectors.'

Freddie was given a series of directions that he followed precisely. He was flying mainly on his instruments as the weather had continued to deteriorate and although scarcely five o'clock, it was already almost dark enough to be night.

He'd seen zero Luftwaffe and thought the whole thing was a total waste of time on everybody's part. The Observer Corps dotted along the coast were excellent, as were the girls and men manning the radar stations, but sometimes they got it wrong and this, he was sure, was one of those times. Thank god the rain had stopped, although the fog wasn't much better.

Stan had remained with him as he should have, and acquitted himself well. Suddenly his kite was illuminated by searchlights. Stan screamed over the RT.

'Look out, Blue Leader, there's a balloon straight ahead of us.'

He looked up and just in time heaved on the control column and barely avoided becoming ensnared in the balloons, which were there to deter low-flying German fighter-bombers.

The controller had inadvertently sent them into the middle of the Harwich balloons and only after he'd finished swearing did he realise he'd left his RT on transmit and every word had been heard by the controller and the WAAF plotters in the control room.

He'd be eating a lot of humble pie and doing a fair amount of grovelling when he got back for that rookie mistake. No doubt Stan was sniggering to himself because this time he wasn't the one at fault, it was the CO.

As they approached Hornchurch, heavy fog had settled over the base and visibility was almost nil. They didn't have sufficient fuel to go in search of somewhere else, so it was land here or crash somewhere else.

'You go down first, Stan, I'll follow.'

In the few minutes it took his wingman to land, the thick fog had turned into a green pea soup. The flares put out to light the runway were completely invisible from his approach height of 800 feet and he was going to have to land using just his instruments.

There should have been a low light, known as the Chance Light, at the far end of the flare path but for some reason this too was invisible. His under cart was down. It was now or never.

Here goes – he was landing blind on a strip he'd only used once. On the plus side, he knew roughly where it was and there'd be no other kites in his way in weather like this.

Freddie hit the deck hard. At least he was down, but now he had to stop without hitting anything. He braked hard and his gallant Spit slowed, didn't veer off at a crazy angle and by some miracle, he managed to pull up before he careered into the fence at the end of the strip.

He thought it wise to leave his kite where it was as at the moment, even his ground crew would have difficulty finding him and it. He pressed the release button on his harness, unclipped his helmet from the oxygen and RT, pushed back the hood and heaved himself out.

The only way he was going to find his way back was if someone directed him. He yelled into the filthy, yellow choking fog and immediately got a response.

'Follow my voice, Skip, we're heading for the mess. We've joined hands like kiddies to make sure no one gets lost.'

Some wag responded – he didn't recognise the voice. 'We'll all be bleeding well lost with you at the front, Stan.'

This was enough to guide him in roughly the right direction and within a few minutes, he joined the human chain and, with much joshing and tomfoolery, he eventually staggered into the mess to spend a riotous evening drinking rather more than he usually did.

The next morning, the pea soup had cleared, the rain also, and it was a perfect summer's day. Freddie made the required telephone calls to the control room that had heard him using such appalling language last night and his apology was accepted, but ungraciously.

He hung up thinking the man whose idea it was had been at fault and almost caused himself and Stan to go for a Burton, but it was considered far worse that he'd used bad language. The whole system was insane, but he couldn't do anything about it.

The RAF was mostly run by a lot of buffoons with no combat experience, who'd fought in the last war when things were different. Initially, they'd been expected to fly with collar and tie – but that had now been abandoned.

That afternoon, the remaining bod he was waiting for turned up and instead of being an inexperienced sprog, he was someone battle-hardened who'd been out of action for a few weeks after a nasty prang.

Freddie now had thirteen fully functioning kites and fifteen flyers. This would at least give him some flexibility and he could rotate his men so everybody got a couple of hours' respite. Things had been bad enough during Dunkirk and would be even worse when the Luftwaffe stopped attacking the convoys in the Channel and turned their attention to the RAF.

Ted returned, sad but pragmatic about the loss. 'Millie's re-enlisting and wants to become a plotter. Di's going to ask to do the same so they can stay together. I'd much rather she was working somewhere safe than living on her own in that little cottage.'

'I thought she was going to be housekeeper at Goodwill House?'

'She was – but I'm not sure it would have worked out, as she's not a domestic minded sort of girl.'

'I don't think Di is either – our ladies are better suited to life as WAAF and will make excellent plotters.' He was surprised Di hadn't written to him about her plans but they'd agreed until the war ended they had to do whatever was needed to help the war effort. Not that either of them had much choice, as they were both at the disposal of the armed services for the duration.

* * *

Joanna received a telephone call from Dr Willoughby, telling her the sad news about Millie. 'Is she very upset?'

'Indeed, my lady. But I would say that on balance, she was relieved once she'd got over the shock. They'll be keeping her in for a few days but from what I've heard, she's already been visited by Corporal Forsyth and her husband.'

'I'm sure that will have cheered her up no end. If you see her, please give her my best wishes for a speedy recovery.'

One thing she did know was that Millie was unlikely to take up the position of housekeeper now – in fact, if she was a gambling sort of lady, then she'd put her best hat on Millie re-enlisting immediately.

When she informed the family of this news, Jean made a suggestion that was greeted with enthusiasm by everyone. 'I really don't think this house needs a full-time seamstress, Joanna, but we certainly need a housekeeper, as once the land girls are here it's going to be difficult getting enough of the rationed food to feed them.'

'Tommy, the gamekeeper at the farm where Bert Smith used to work, reckons I'm going to be a good shot. I'll be able to keep Good-will House supplied with rabbits and pheasants,' Joe said.

'Rabbits you can shoot at any time, young man, but remember game birds can only be shot in season, which isn't now.' Elizabeth was always ready with helpful advice.

'He's explained that to me – and there're roe deer in the woods and I intend to have a crack at one of those in the autumn.'

Liza punched her brother on the arm. 'You're not shooting any deer. Rabbits and birds are bad enough.'

'Don't be so soft, sister. You eat lamb, pork and beef, deer meat's venison. I can't see any difference.'

'Please don't argue when we're eating,' Joanna said, giving them both a stern look.

Joe chuckled and for a moment, he no longer seemed like a boy but the man he would become in a year or two. 'Fair enough, we'll have a blazing row afterwards.'

Elizabeth pursed her lips, but the others laughed as he'd intended. Joanna still hadn't had the opportunity to question the twins about their reluctance to call her Mama or Mother and she did so dislike being anonymous in their conversations.

'Joe, Liza, if you don't want to call me Mama or Mother, then please return to calling me Aunt Joanna.'

The two exchanged a glance. Liza blushed and looked at her plate. Joe cleared his throat.

'It's like this, neither of those mean anything to us. What we want to do is call you Ma because that's what you are now.'

She blinked furiously, not wanting to spoil the moment by

crying. 'Of course, how silly of me. Yes, I'm very happy indeed to be addressed as Ma.' She looked across the table. 'Elizabeth, I take it that you will be happy to be called Grandma?'

The old lady was gazing out into the garden and appeared not to have heard. 'Elizabeth?'

'What? Please don't raise your voice, Joanna, it's most impolite.'

'I beg your pardon. Liza and Joe are going to call us Ma and Grandma as they were uncomfortable with our alternatives.'

'I'm not surprised. As long as you start addressing me as something, I'll be satisfied.' She smiled with genuine affection at the two of them and they responded in kind.

'Grandma, I thought I'd take the trap out this evening as Star needs the exercise and it's been too wet today,' Joe said. 'Would you like to accompany me?'

'I should love to.'

Now Joe had got things started, his sister was eager to join in. By the end of dinner, Joanna thought she'd been addressed as Ma, and Elizabeth as Grandma, a dozen times – in fact, so often that it was already beginning to become a little tiresome.

* * *

The next few days, she was busy with Jean, telling her everything she knew about running the house. This wasn't a great deal, as Betty for the past five years, and a Mrs Gregson before that, had taken care of everything.

'Don't worry, Joanna, I'm a practical sort of body and will soon learn what I don't already know. I'm also a good cook, as well as being a seamstress. With the three new ladies from the village coming daily to do the cleaning, and the two old biddies who do the laundry and ironing, I'm sure we'll be able to manage perfectly well.'

'It's a nuisance that Val and Joan have left to work full-time in Ramsgate, but their replacements are good sorts and will be ideal,' said Joanna.

'Doris, Enid and Aggie don't want full-time jobs, so working here for a few hours every day suits them fine.'

'Mrs Dougherty, the lady in charge of finding suitable billets for our new lodgers in this area, is coming tomorrow. It's good we have everything in place now.'

'Joe said that the girls can use the mare and the cart for transport – is that right?'

'I've checked with all my farms and they have barns and paddocks where Star can be stabled or turned out during the day. If they don't have bicycles, it's going to be a long walk to even get to where they'll be working.'

'I wouldn't fancy being on the land in the winter, but the other seasons would be grand,' Jean said. 'Do they lay them off when there's nothing to do?'

'I've no idea. I'm going to find out everything tomorrow, hopefully. Won't it be jolly having the house full of girls again?' Perhaps then the emptiness caused by Betty's loss would be less noticeable.

Elizabeth returned from her jaunt in the trap in better spirits and seemed much livelier than she had been over dinner. Being forgetful and dozing on and off all day were, Joanna was sure, just a part of getting older and nothing to worry about.

The next time she bumped into the doctor, she would just mention it to him so he could reassure her. They would be going to church in a couple of days and he was bound to be there. If she invited him back for lunch, she'd find an opportunity to take him aside and raise her mild concerns.

* * *

Di spoke to her sergeant that evening when everybody was in the recreation room, either playing cards, knitting, engrossed in a book or just chatting about their day. After she explained about Millie re-enlisting, she broached the subject of her own future.

'What do you think, Sarge? They wanted me to put my name down for special duties and were quite miffed when I didn't. Would I be accepted to be trained in one of the more specialised areas?'

'I'd think they'd bite your hand off. Only girls with the sort of education you and your friend have are suitable for those positions,' Sarge said. 'Would you like me to speak to somebody on your behalf?'

'That would be spiffing. Thank you. I heard Daphne saying that she can drive and used to ride her brother's motorbike and would much prefer to be driving than working as a cleaner. I'm sure it wouldn't take long for her to convert and that would mean the MT wouldn't be short when I leave.'

'I should think you could teach her – after all, you're very experienced and a senior NCO.'

'I'll ask my sarge tomorrow, but it took us three months to qualify so I doubt Daphne will be allowed to do it in a couple of days.'

'True, but neither of you could drive and that makes a big difference.'

'You're right, Sarge. I'll go and speak to Daphne now as if she's really keen, then maybe we'll be allowed to get a bit of practice in behind the hangars when we have time free.'

Three days after this conversation, Di heard that her application to transfer for training for special duties had been accepted and that she'd receive her travel documents in the next couple of days.

As soon as she was discharged from hospital, Millie had caught a train to Hornchurch and was staying in a B&B. Hopefully, to spend a few precious hours with her husband.

That night, the telephone jangled in the sergeant's office outside the dormitory. Di was closest so hurried out and picked up the receiver.

'Corporal Forsyth speaking, how can I help?'

'Just a minute, Corp, I've got a call for you.'

'Di, I thought I'd speak to you rather than write,' Freddie said. 'How are you? Have you heard anything yet?'

'How wonderful to hear your voice, Freddie. Yes, I heard this morning and will be leaving for wherever I'm going to be trained tomorrow or the next day. More to the point, what about you? Why haven't you moved to Rochford?'

'That's why I'm calling, darling. We're transferring at dawn tomorrow and I'll be incommunicado for three weeks. We're supposed to get a day off but without transport I won't be able to go anywhere. The chaps spend their free time asleep or at the local hostelry. No doubt I'll do the same.'

'You won't be able to write to me or telephone me, as wherever I'm posted will be top secret. I'll have to contact you.'

'You never know, you might be here. That's what Ted and Millie are hoping. There's a queue of chaps waiting to use the telephone, so I'd better go. Being a squadron leader won't save me from their wrath if I don't hang up. Take care of yourself, darling, and I love you.'

'You do the same, Freddie, and I love you too.'

He'd broken all the rules getting connected to this particular line but, in the circumstances, she doubted anyone would follow it up. It was worth the small risk just to hear his voice. It might be weeks or more until she could see him, but at least he was still in England and not posted overseas like so many other servicemen.

* * *

Daphne had passed the required standard for a WAAF driver after two days of intense instruction from Di and Sarge.

'That girl's a natural. Going to be handy having two who can ride a motorbike. Much quicker to send one of those with a message or a small package.'

'I've enjoyed being here, Sarge, and I want to thank you for making me so welcome,' Di said. 'I'm going to miss Manston but am very excited about doing something different.' She had been going to say *more important* but had decided that wouldn't be tactful.

'You'll be missed and so will your friend. Good luck with whatever you're going to be doing.'

With a tinge of sadness, Di cycled across the base for the last time. She was going to miss the girls she'd got to know over the past few months but was more than ready to move on. There was nothing to hold her here now that Millie had gone as well as Freddie.

She'd been able to borrow the Austin for a couple of hours and drive to Goodwill House and say her farewells there. The twins were unrecognisable from the badly spoken, ill-educated East Enders that they'd been when they'd arrived. In a few months, Joe and Liza Tims had ceased to exist and would be known by everyone in the neighbourhood as Joe and Liza Harcourt. It seemed as though life was changing for everyone.

22

Freddie was even less impressed with the forward base than he'd expected. Mind you, the fact that the tents were sagging with water, the ground was squelchy and there was not a single dry chair or camp bed to sit on, added to the overall lowering of spirits as they taxied off the grass strip into position.

'Bloody hopeless place, Skip,' one of the sergeant pilots grumbled.

'There's a war on, in case you haven't noticed, so stop binding and get your kit stowed.' Freddie was in a foul mood and hadn't time for anybody's complaints. He'd had a blinding headache for the past two days and aspirins just didn't touch it. It had started when he was on his last op, and he thought it might have been something to do with his heavy landing in the fog.

He certainly wasn't going to speak to the medic, as he'd no intention of being grounded. Therefore, he'd grin and bear it, but it was making him bad-tempered.

'I reckon there's a full flight parked in this dismal place, Freddie,' Ted said with his usual cheerful grin. 'I've only gone up with a full flight of thirty-six once before. Will you be leading it or is there someone more senior here?'

'Haven't the foggiest, but I'm going to find out. You'd think, wouldn't you, that as this base is here permanently, they'd at least have built some huts by now?'

'Cheer up, it'll look better when the sun comes up,' Ted called after him.

'Well, it couldn't look any worse.'

On checking, he discovered he was indeed the most senior officer at Rochford so therefore would, if directed to, be leading the Spitfires. If only his bloody headache would ease off a bit, he could actually enjoy the prospect of a sortie in charge of a full flight.

They weren't scrambled until later on in the day and only his flight of four was ordered to go up in pursuit of an unidentified aircraft flying near Dover. Freddie, leading his men at 6,000 feet, immediately saw what looked like a seaplane with civilian markings but then, just above it, were several Messerschmitt Me 109 fighters. This meant the seaplane was definitely a bogey.

'Tally-ho,' he yelled, that being the universal phrase to indicate they were to attack the enemy. As he led the dive, the Germans saw them coming and split into two. Only then did he realise his squadron was outnumbered six to one. The sky was full of Me 109s.

Freddie set his sight on one of the bogeys and with his first burst of machine-gun fire he saw the bullets go into the fuselage of his opponent. He had no time to finish the Hun, as two Me 109s were behind him.

The most effective way to shake them off was to climb in a tight spiral and, on doing this, he was pleased to see his pursuers stall and abandon their chase. He'd got one Me 109 and was determined to get another before he ran out of ammunition and fuel.

Three thousand yards ahead, another German fighter was

heading for him. He remained on the same course, as did his opponent. He steadied his kite and opened fire at the last minute.

The German returned fire and then Freddie's prop hit the Hun's fuselage as he screamed past. His hood was pushed in. The engine shook fiercely and then cut out. Smoke, the most dreaded sight of all, began to pour from the ruined engine.

Freddie held the plane steady with the stick between his knees, and with both hands tried to push the hood back. It wouldn't budge. He was trapped inside the cockpit and the acrid smoke was making breathing difficult. He couldn't bale out. He would have to crash-land – again. Would he be lucky a second time, or was this going to be the fatal crash every flyer dreaded but expected?

Thank god he'd been heading for Blighty when the collision occurred. He'd glided in a crippled Spit before and prayed he could do it again before he got roasted alive.

Visibility was minimal – he held the kite in a reasonable gliding position until things began to flash past. A post rushed by a wing tip and then his kite slammed into the ground.

The Spit bounced into the air before hitting a second time and sliding at speed through a series of fence posts bordering a field of some sort. His harness was cutting into him and he hit the release pin. He needed to get out, and get out fast.

Freddie had only seconds left before the flames in the engine engulfed the entire plane. Frantically he hammered his fists into the hood and finally it splintered. He pulled himself out of the smoke-filled cockpit and staggered away from the crash until he was a safe distance. He'd no intention of being blown up if it exploded, after having survived the most hideous of prangs.

Once he'd regained his breath, he checked his injuries. His knees were bruised, his hands bleeding heavily from smashing the hood open, his lip was cut and his eyebrows were somewhat singed, but apart from that he was more or less all right.

The posts he'd seen were anti-invasion barriers put in to deter German gliders. He was bloody lucky not to have gone for a Burton. A number of locals had now gathered to watch the burning kite and admire the lucky pilot who'd managed to escape.

Then the air was rent by the sound of machine-gun ammunition exploding. 'Stand clear of the aircraft. Move back, all of you. There's still a lot of high-octane fuel in the tanks.'

He didn't need to tell them twice, as they scattered immediately. A young woman approached him.

'I've telephoned Manston and told them about your crash-landing, and an ambulance and fire engine are on their way.'

'Right, thanks. Where exactly am I?'

'This is Gunston Farm, near Ash, just about five miles from the base. Would you like to come back for a cup of tea whilst you wait?'

Surprisingly, he was able to walk on his injured knees but was becoming concerned about the amount of blood he was losing from his hands. The farmer's wife wrapped both hands tightly in tea towels, added bandages, and told him to put them on his chest, above his heart.

'I'm a member of St John's so I do know a thing or two about first aid. Did you hit your head?'

'I don't think so, but I've the most appalling headache. I don't suppose you've got any aspirin?'

Plied with hot tea with plenty of sugar, four aspirin and a sofa to stretch out on, Freddie drifted off and didn't fully awake until the ambulance men banged on the door. Somehow, he managed to regain his feet without using his hands to help him up.

Then his knees gave way, and he didn't remember anything else until he woke up in hospital. Both his hands were bandaged, a flagon of the red stuff hung by his bed on a metal stand and was dripping into his arm. His knees hurt, but not as badly as they had.

If it wasn't for the bloody pain over his eyes, he'd be ready to return to ops as soon as his hands recovered.

A wave of relief washed over him. He would see his darling girl again and that had been doubtful at one point.

* * *

Joanna was on the terrace with Elizabeth, waiting for the arrival of the area organiser for the Land Army. Mrs Dougherty would find nothing wrong with the accommodation, the staff or anything else at Goodwill House.

'I find it quite extraordinary, my dear, that I've become immune to the noise of the aircraft landing and taking off continually,' Elizabeth said. 'The constant howl of the air-raid sirens in the village and on the base have also become commonplace.'

'I think a lot of the aircraft we hear are just coming in to refuel and rearm and then continuing with whatever they're doing in the Channel. Actually, I was going to talk to you about your refusal to come down to the shelter yesterday. I know so far there've been no bombs dropped anywhere near us, but we still need to go down to the cellar as a precaution.'

'I really don't care if a bomb drops on me, Joanna. It's different for you and the children, but I'm an old lady and quite ready to meet my maker if necessary.'

'There are women in the village in their nineties who still live on their own, do their shopping and take an interest in the village as they've always done. I don't know exactly how old you are but, as far as I'm concerned, seventy-something means you've still got another twenty years to live!'

'I promise that I'll come down when the real bombing starts. Now, I think I can hear a car approaching. It must be your Land Army person.'

Joanna took a deep breath, inhaling the wonderful scent from the roses that were flowering in profusion in the beds below the terrace. Even though the park had been ploughed up and planted with potatoes, they still had the garden to enjoy. This had been her project, and David had indulged her passion for growing flowers for the house.

The perennial borders had a few tulips showing amongst the shrubs and permanent plants. When the Bentley had been in use, the chauffeur had driven armfuls of flowers to the church on a regular basis. But there were more important things to do nowadays than worry about floral displays inside the church or anywhere else.

She waited until the small Hillman had driven around to the front of the house where it was no longer visible from the terrace and then went to greet the woman who would decide whether she wished to place two or three teams of land girls in the house.

'Good morning, Mrs Dougherty, welcome to Goodwill House. Would you like to look around outside before coming in?' She offered her hand, and it was shaken firmly.

'Good morning, my lady, I'd love to spend time admiring everything, but I've two other places to visit today and both of them are a considerable distance from Stodham.'

'Then come in, and my daughter will show you the four rooms in which the girls will be sleeping. They also have their own sitting room upstairs, a bathroom and two WCs. Each room also has a wash basin for teeth cleaning and so on.'

Liza appeared and Joanna was proud of the way the girl introduced herself and offered her hand to be shaken. She left her to show the visitor around and went to collect the tea that Jean was making.

'You don't need to look worried, Joanna, this is a palace compared to where some of the girls will be billeted. I don't think you'll be making a profit from the arrangement, but you'll be doing your bit for the war and that's what counts.'

'As long as we don't make a loss, and I'm depending on you for that, Jean. Otherwise, I'll offer to take in families who lose their homes when the raids start. Land girls will be housed somewhere suitable by those who run the organisation. Destitute families will be relying entirely on those better placed than themselves.'

'Maybe we can do both, there's plenty of spare rooms in the empty wing,' Jean said.

'Since I had the access to the Victorian section boarded up, it no longer seems part of the house. It's cold, draughty and unpleasant, but I suppose to those with absolutely nowhere to go, even this would seem acceptable.'

She'd thought that Mrs Dougherty would stop to discuss what would be expected of her after the inspection, but this wasn't the case. The brisk, middle-aged woman just handed over a manila envelope full of leaflets and information.

'Everything you need to know, my lady, is in here. This place is perfect in every respect, as it's central to the places the girls will be working. Your son said that your horse and pony cart will be available for them, but I doubt that any of them are familiar with horses.'

'I thought all country girls were, even if they don't ride themselves. Many farms still have working horses and at least four small-holdings in the neighbourhood use a horse and cart for transport.'

Mrs Dougherty laughed. 'Oh dear, I'm afraid you've been misinformed if you think the girls who'll be coming will be country girls. I'm not exactly sure who they'll be, but I certainly know that the majority are from the cities. They will have received a two-week basic training somewhere – but that's all.'

'I see. If they've joined your organisation, Mrs Dougherty, then

I'm sure they'll soon learn whatever they need to do their job satisfactorily. My son will teach them how to harness and drive Starlight.'

'He was telling me that the Ministry of Agriculture has asked for you to bring more of your grass into production. I've no doubt that Mr Beattie, of Brook Farm, will be designated to do that, as he already looks after the potatoes planted at the front.'

'I assume that will be the case. Therefore, it makes sense for some of the girls living here to take care of the land under production at Goodwill House. Mrs Thomas, a friend in the village, asked me to enquire if market gardens would be eligible for your help?'

'Indeed they are. I believe there are already two in this neighbourhood where your girls will be working.'

The woman left, saying that the twelve expected had just arrived for their basic training and would come directly to Goodwill House in two weeks. This meant that her home would be full by the end of July, and Joanna couldn't wait.

* * *

Di had her travel warrant in her haversack along with her personal documents and other important items, her kitbag was over her shoulder, she'd handed back her two sets of overalls and was dressed smartly in her usual uniform.

She was heading for the bus stop just outside the gates and had about fifteen minutes to spare before it was due. As she was striding past the admin block, Pamela rushed out and beckoned to her frantically.

Di changed direction and hurried across. 'What's up? Surely they've not changed their minds about me leaving today?'

'No, I've just seen some paperwork from yesterday. Your Freddie crash-landed his Spit a few miles from here. He's in Ramsgate Hospital. I don't think he's too badly hurt.'

It was as if the world stood still for a moment whilst Di absorb this dreadful news. 'Thank you for telling me. I could have got on the train and might not have known about his accident for weeks. Now I can visit before I leave and then blame my tardy arrival on the transport situation.'

She heard the grinding of gears and the rattle of a bus approaching, so she said thank you a second time and then ran for the bus. There were three airmen waiting to get on and they made sure it didn't depart until she arrived.

One of them offered to put her bag in the luggage space but she shook her head. 'No, thank you for asking, but I'm able to do it myself.'

Luckily there were seats and gratefully she took one and shuffled across to the window. It was market day in Ramsgate and there would be dozens of women waiting to clamber on when they stopped in the village.

The bus rattled to a halt at the stop nearest to the hospital, and Di grabbed her bag and jumped off. She doubted it was visiting time, but she wasn't going to leave until she'd seen Freddie and discovered if he was badly hurt or not.

The receptionist offered to look after her kitbag whilst she went in search of Freddie. When she arrived at the ward – in a different part of the hospital to the one she'd visited so recently when Millie had been a patient here – there was a gaggle of white-coated doctors doing the rounds.

She knew better than to attempt to gain admittance when this was happening. She leaned against the wall outside, her heart thumping, her hands clammy, praying that Pamela's assessment of Freddie's injuries had been correct.

The consultant and his entourage were coming out. She stood to attention – to be seen slouching by someone so important just wasn't on. To her surprise, the group stopped in front of her.

'Would you, by any chance, be coming to visit Squadron Leader Hanover? He mentioned he had a fiancée in the WAAF.'

'Yes, sir, I'm Corporal Forsyth. Is he all right?'

'The injuries he sustained from his accident yesterday are trivial, he lost a lot of blood but that will soon sort itself out with the transfusion he's getting. He's determined to discharge himself and I want you to persuade him to remain put. I'm not happy about his headaches and need to investigate.'

'I'll do my best, sir, but I can't promise I'll be able to change his mind. I didn't know he was getting headaches, but I'll certainly ask him about them and report back.'

'Good girl, do your best.'

'Am I allowed to visit even though it's not the official time?'

'Go in, go in at once. Time is of the essence.' The consultant gestured to one of the junior doctors. 'Tell Sister that Corporal Forsyth can visit as long and as often as she wishes.'

Di smiled her thanks and walked into the ward with some trepidation, not wanting to be harangued by an irate sister for disturbing her ward.

'Corporal Forsyth, Squadron Leader Hanover will be delighted to see you. He's been telling us all about his accomplished fiancée.' The sister in charge of the ward greeted her, not at all bothered by an unexpected visitor.

'Thank you for allowing me in. I have to report in London today so couldn't wait until visiting hour.'

Freddie was halfway down the long room, sitting up in bed. Apart from the transfusion in his arm and the bandages on his hands, at first glance, he looked fine. Then she noticed his eyes were swollen and puffy, and he seemed to be having trouble focusing.

'Darling, I hoped you'd be able to see me as I'm in this hospital. You look very smart. Are you on the move?'

'I am. I'll find a chair and then you can tell me what happened.'

23

Freddie hadn't expected his lovely girl to actually visit him, but he'd hoped. Now, here she was, and he watched her move gracefully from the ward to collect the chair she needed. He felt bloody awful, but seeing Di made everything seem better. She reappeared carrying a chair and put it down beside his bed.

'Why don't you draw the curtains around the bed, darling, they'll still be able to hear us but at least we'll have the illusion of privacy.' He spoke quietly in the vain hope that his inquisitive neighbour wouldn't be able to hear and then pass it on to the person next to him.

'Good idea. I expect the other patients will be cross that you've got a visitor and they haven't.' Her reply was equally quiet – maybe if they sat close together and whispered, they wouldn't be over-heard. 'Your consultant said you intend to discharge yourself. I'm assuming that's wrong. You don't look well enough to be out of hospital and certainly not well enough to fly.'

'He looked so horrified when I said it that I've reconsidered,' Freddie said. 'If he can do something about the pain above my eyes whilst I'm here, then it'll be worth hanging about for a day or two.'

'Your eyes are very puffy. The doctor said he wants to do an X-ray of your head to see what's going on. Have you had this pain for long?'

'I don't want to talk about my ailments, sweetheart, don't you want to hear how I ended up in this mess?'

His intention had been to make it seem amusing, but from her expression she was finding the story far from funny.

'Please, Freddie, I don't want to hear any more. It's a miracle you survived, and I know that as soon as you're given the all-clear you'll be back in that wretched plane and next time you might not be so lucky.'

A student nurse appeared with a tray. 'Sister said you might both like a nice cup of tea and some biscuits.'

'Thank you, that's exactly what we could do with.' Freddie winked at Di. 'It's like a luxury hotel in here, so why would I want to leave earlier than I have to?'

They'd forgotten about the eavesdropper in the next bed.

'Here, nursie, what about my cuppa? I'm parched,' he called out from the other side of the curtain.

'You'll have to wait until teatime, Mr Welham, like everybody else. Squadron Leader Hanover is a hero and almost died yesterday fighting to protect people like you.'

There was no further interruption from this Mr Welham during the all too brief visit.

'I've got to go, Freddie, or I'll be put on a charge,'

'At least I can sleep easily for the next few nights as I know you'll not be back on ops. I don't know where I'm going to be sent for my training, but it could be anywhere in England. I'll find out when I report to Victory House.'

'I love you, darling, and having you in my life makes this bloody war almost bearable.'

She leaned across and kissed him. 'I love you too. Please

promise me that you won't hurry back to your squadron until you're given a clean bill of health.'

'I promise. If the quacks can sort my headaches out, then I'll be a better flyer, so it makes sense to remain put for the moment. I get a week's crash leave anyway, and I'll definitely take that.'

She kissed him again and rushed off. He was as overcome as she. Neither of them knew if they'd ever meet again.

* * *

Freddie's X-ray was noisy but not painful. The empty glass bottle had dripped the last of the blood into his arm and was removed from beside his bed and the nurse who took his vitals said his blood pressure was back to normal.

'When will I get the results of the X-ray, do you know?'

'The ENT specialist is on his way to see you. I expect he'll be able to tell you.'

Sure enough, a white-coated MO appeared. 'Look here, young man, these pictures are absolutely frightful. How long have you been suffering from headaches?'

'A few weeks, but it's not always as bad as this. It seems to be aggravated by climbing steeply and diving, which are part of the job of a fighter pilot.'

'I'd say that you've been suffering for a lot longer than that. You've got acute sinusitis and I'm going to sort this out for you. It's too late tonight, but I'll be here first thing in the morning. It won't be pleasant, my boy, but it'll be worth it.'

Being moved to a theatre should have warned him about what was coming. The ENT chap had a tray of terrifying instruments and an assistant.

'I'm going to put cocaine inside your nostrils and then drill a hole through into the antrums to drain the fluid.'

Freddie had no idea what an antrum was and didn't really want to know. The assistant dabbed cotton wool soaked with cocaine inside his nose and it made his whole face tingle. He was warned again that what was going to happen wouldn't be pleasant and that it would be better if he closed his eyes and tried to relax.

There was an excruciating, stabbing pain and then some sort of fluid was pouring from his nose, as if a tap had been turned on. The room began to roll as if he was back in his kite. He lost his sense of balance and orientation. From a distance, he heard the old chap say with some alarm in his voice, 'Good god, it must have been a cyst.'

If someone hadn't been holding his head, he thought it might have become detached from his body.

'All right, Squadron Leader, it's finished. Keep still for a moment. I'll get you back on the ward and you will be feeling just the ticket in a little while.'

He must have passed out, as the next thing he knew, he was back in his old place in the ward, dripping with sweat and with the bedclothes pulled up to his chin.

'Here, sir, you need to take these pills. Do you want me to help you?'

Somehow, he managed to open his eyes to see a different nurse standing there. Obediently he opened his mouth and swallowed the pills. He didn't come round for a further fourteen hours and the only good thing about waking up was that there was no longer a terrific pain across his forehead and around his eyes, but the rest of him was limp and he felt as if he'd been run over by a steamroller.

* * *

Di did, in fact, know her posting was to RAF Leighton Buzzard in Bedfordshire. It would probably have been all right to have told Freddie, but she thought she'd better stick to the rules. She'd been relieved that he wasn't going to be flying for a while, which meant she could settle into her training before having to start worrying about him being killed.

Eventually, she arrived at Leighton Buzzard Station and looked around for signs of any RAF transport. There were a couple of other WAAF and four airmen also waiting but she had no time to talk to them as the lorry arrived.

She tossed her kitbag into the back and jumped in and took her place beside the two other girls. They were about her age but looked nervous and their uniform was still pristine, unlike hers. The driver yelled that they'd have to wait for another train and then they'd be off.

Half an hour later, a further two airmen scrambled in and the driver pushed up the tailgate, fastened it, and dropped the canvas that obscured the back. Then conversation was impossible because of the noise, but she was content to sit in silence.

When she reported to the guard room, as expected, the first thing she noticed about the camp was that it was heavily camouflaged. Everywhere was festooned with a heavy green fabric, making it look from above like the countryside. Di knew this must be a very secret destination indeed, but the other two girls were puzzled.

They were to be accommodated in what used to be a workhouse, but it wasn't as bad as expected. After settling in, the three of them went to get a meal and were then to report back to the main building.

'I'm Di, Corporal Forsyth, and I'm retraining. I've been working as a driver since January.'

The taller of the two, with light-brown permed hair and crooked teeth replied. 'I'm Jenny North and this is Emily Watson. Have you any idea what we'll actually be doing? I know we're all Clerks Special Duty, but apart from that, I haven't the foggiest.'

'Well, I'm sure we're about to find out.'

In the main building, they were sent to the new intake briefing room, which held around thirty people, mostly WAAF but a few airmen too. The first thing they had to do was sign the Official Secrets Act.

It was explained to them that they were to be part of the RDF chain – this meant range and direction finding. She would either be an RDF Operator, a Filter Room Plotter or an Operations Room Plotter. And Di learnt that she was to be a Filter Room Plotter.

The group remained as one for the first two days and the lectures covered how the system worked. She learnt about radio waves, goniometers and a lot of other technical things. No wonder one had to have a good education to become part of this group.

They watched films showing an Operations Room that was dominated by a large table. The girls surrounding it wore headsets and were moving counters and markers about the table with a long pole. This room seemed calm and well-organised.

Then she watched a film of the Filter Room, and it was the complete opposite. Her throat constricted, it was if a large stone had lodged in her stomach, what she was seeing was almost manic activity.

The girls were packed about the table pushing, shoving and removing counters, there were officers barging through them putting down arrows or changing the information on the metal raid plaques. There was a balcony with officers also with telephones shouting down instructions, identifying aircraft, then checking the incoming information. It was hectic but exciting and despite her nerves, she was confident she'd made the right choice to retrain.

Finally, they were split into their specialised training groups. Di prayed she'd be able to master the technique and not let herself and the WAAF down. She had an advantage over the other nine girls, as she was experienced in the ways of the WAAF and already a senior NCO.

The place where she was to be trained was an exact replica of II Group Filter Room, which was at Fighter Command headquarters at Stanmore. Over the next two weeks, things got easier, and by the end of her intensive training, she was both fast and accurate and, although not wishing to blow her own trumpet, thought she was by far the most proficient in the group.

Di was to be sent to Stanmore – a real honour as normally, she learned, only experienced plotters were posted there. She couldn't believe her luck, as being based at Stanmore meant she might well be able to see Freddie occasionally.

The first thing she did when she got to London was to find a telephone box. She asked the operator to connect her to Hornchurch and after a few clicks and whirs, a cheerful young woman answered the telephone. Immediately, Di pressed button A and heard the coins drop into the box.

'I'm most dreadfully sorry to bother you, I'm Corporal Forsyth. My fiancé, Squadron Leader Hanover, is based with you. Could I leave a message for him? I think he might well be at Rochford.'

'Just a minute, Corp, I'll check.' There was a clatter as the receiver was put down on the desk and Di verified that she had sufficient pennies to put in the slot if she had to hang on for some time.

'I'm sorry, Corp, he's not on the list. He isn't based here.'

'What about his squadron?' She gave the relevant information and the girl went away again, this time she returned more quickly.

'Yes, that's at Rochford. I'm really sorry, but he's no longer with them.'

* * *

Joanna had received the legal papers confirming that Joe and Liza were now Harcourts and was busy arranging a small celebration. The twins had made suitable friends in the village, mainly through the good offices of the tutor she'd employed for them.

'I'm very pleased with their progress, my lady, and am confident that they'll get their school certificate with flying colours next year. Joe wishes to take his higher certificate the following year and I expect him to pass that as well.'

'It's entirely down to you, Mr Barnaby. They received very little in the way of education before they came to me, but they're both highly intelligent young people and in a few short months are both now literate and numerate and eager to learn.'

'Your son has told me he wishes to join the RAF and become a fighter pilot,' the tutor said. 'As he can already drive a tractor and car, as well as handle a pony and cart, I'm certain he'll find flying any sort of aircraft an easy task.'

Just then, the house shook, as something large exploded on the base. There had been several air-raids there but as she no longer had any contact with the airmen and women who worked at Manston, she didn't know how bad the casualties or damage had been.

One thing she did know was that from the amount of aircraft landing and taking off so frequently, there must be squadrons from somewhere else in the sector using the base. She remembered Angus saying it was considered a forward base rather than an active one. She wasn't quite sure what the distinction meant, but it might explain why there was so much air traffic.

Mr Barnaby took his leave, and Joanna went in search of her children, who were now sitting on the terrace with the dog. She'd expected to see Elizabeth there, but the old lady wasn't with them.

'Ma, Grandma insisted that she was going to take a walk around the park on her own. She wouldn't let either of us go with her, and I don't think she should be wandering about on her own at her age,' Joe said as he pointed to the small figure quite some distance away, walking along the edge of the potato field.

'Oh dear, I'd better go and fetch her back.'

'No, we'll go. We could both do with the exercise after being cooped up all morning doing schoolwork,' Liza said with a smile, as she headed for the steps that led from the terrace to the garden below.

'Lazzy, go with them.' Her dog remained where he was. She pointed towards Joe and Liza, who were jogging towards their grandmother. 'Go with them. Find Grandma.'

This time, he understood what she wanted and with one leap was over the balustrade and racing after them. Joanna watched for a moment and then went in to speak to Jean. She found the new housekeeper busy cooking something that smelled quite delicious.

'Jean, I'm sorry to disturb you, but have you noticed anything odd about my mother-in-law recently?'

'I have, but didn't like to mention it to you in case you hadn't. I think she's getting a bit confused, sometimes she doesn't remember why she's in a room or what she's just been doing.'

'I feared so. I do so want her to be happy in her twilight years. If it wasn't for her help, we wouldn't still be living here.'

'There's the four of us to look out for her, Joanna, she'll not come to any harm,' Jean said. 'Now, do we know how many are coming to the party at the weekend?'

'The twins invited six young people from the village, and I invited the doctor and our solicitor. So, with the five of us that makes eleven in total. Just enough to have a party atmosphere without being too much trouble.'

'I thought I'd make a fruit punch, as there's plenty of soft fruit in the garden, as well as mint and borage. If we put a few bottles of pop into your silver punch bowl, the fruit and the herbs, and just one glass of brandy, they'll think they've got something very grown-up.'

'That sounds perfect. Nobody's going to get inebriated sharing one glass of brandy between six of them. Sandwiches and whatever cake we can find the ingredients for will be more than enough to go with it.'

* * *

The party was a huge success, and Joanna and Elizabeth had managed to purchase a record player as a gift for Joe and Liza. It was a tad old-fashioned, as you had to wind it up in order to hear the records, but it was better than nothing. July 28 would, in future, be a day of celebration in Goodwill House.

The youngsters had found some suitable records to dance to and the adults had left them to it in the ballroom. The fruit punch and the refreshments had been put out on a table for them to help themselves.

'I'm so glad, my dear, you decided to cater separately for us adults,' Elizabeth said. 'A glass of decent wine to wash down our sandwiches is preferable to the insipid fizzy drink you've given them.'

'I thought the fruit punch rather tasty, but I agree, it would have been greatly improved if we'd added a bottle of wine. However, they don't seem to mind and are all having a wonderful time. The next few years are going to be most enjoyable with a house full of laughter and hijinks.'

'The young doctor is waiting to speak to you. I'm going to enjoy my drink and talk to Mr Broome. When you're out of mourning officially – next year – you could do worse than look in his direction.'

'Good heavens, Elizabeth, I told you that I've no intention of marrying a second time. But you're right, Dr Willoughby's obviously waiting to speak to me. Excuse me, I'd better see what he wants.'

Jean was in the ballroom with the youngsters and enjoying the dancing as much as they were. She had proved a revelation in these past few weeks and, if the twins were barely recognisable as the two East End ragamuffins who'd arrived a few months ago, then so was Jean. Baxter, the sour-faced taciturn maid, had metamorphosed into a happy, smiling, much-loved member of the household. The fact that Jean was calling her by her Christian name showed how much things had changed between them all.

'Dr Willoughby, did you wish to speak to me about something?'

'I do, my lady. I've no wish to alarm you, but Smith has been seen in the neighbourhood again.'

'I thought he'd left for good when he was evicted. He has no friends in the village after the way he behaved after Betty's death. Why would he come back?'

He looked grave. 'I fear he's set on revenge against you for having him dismissed.'

'How could you possibly know that without speaking to him? I take it that you haven't?'

'Obviously I've not done so. I'm merely using the evidence before me to draw these conclusions. I just wanted to warn you to be very careful to lock up at night, windows as well as doors, and to make sure that your dog is running freely around the house.'

She'd never liked Bert but hadn't thought him a vengeful and dangerous man. There were no men living at Goodwill House, but they had Lazzy and he would take care of them.

24

Freddie had been devastated to be told by the medics that he was no longer fit to fly. The surgery on his face meant flying was now impossible. He'd been tempted to allow them to invalid him out and then find something else to do – he was interested to see if he could transfer to the army on an equivalent rank. He'd then be a major – he knew nothing about army strategy, but he was damn sure he'd soon learn. Not being able to fly would be no handicap in the army. If he couldn't fly, then what was the point in being in the RAF?

The Wing Commander who'd spoken to him afterwards had said that he was to take a month's recuperation. On his return to active duty, he was promised they would find him something useful to do if that's what he decided. He wasn't sure being in the RAF and being grounded would suit him, but he wasn't going to make any hasty decisions but give himself time to think.

He'd been staying with his parents in Guildford for two weeks, enjoying the sunshine, the rest, being able to get up when he felt like it and having time to go for long walks. He'd had three letters from Di but hadn't replied – he'd been too despondent to write anything sensible. She'd fallen in love with a flyer, a squadron leader, would she still want a ruined wreck of a man like him?

He was stretched out on a blanket on the grass, the two family Labradors sprawled beside him, when he heard a car approaching. He couldn't be bothered to sit up and see who it might be. Whoever it was, it wouldn't be anything to do with him, as only the most important people still had petrol.

Suddenly the dogs jumped to their feet and rushed off and he heard voices approaching. He recognised one of them and jack-knifed, surging to his feet.

'Di, darling, what the hell are you doing here?'

They ran towards each other and he snatched her up and swung her around. He kissed her and she responded, and a breathless and wonderful few minutes later they both came up for air.

'I thought you were dead. I rang Hornchurch and they said you were no longer there. I've not had any reply to my letters so obviously thought the worst. I didn't know what to do so came here to offer my condolences to your parents.'

'Bloody hell! I'm so sorry.' He held her away from him so he could look at her properly. She looked ten years older, drawn and pale, and this was entirely his fault. He'd been so mired in his own self-pity that he'd not considered her feelings.

'Your poor parents were so shocked, You caused a lot of unnecessary upset and anguish, Freddie, and although I'm so happy to see you alive and well, I'm not going to forgive you easily for what you put me through.'

'I don't blame you. But you haven't answered my question – how are you here? Shouldn't you be at your new posting?'

She sniffed, blew her nose and wiped her eyes before answering. 'That's another thing, I'll probably be put on a charge now for being AWL.' She wrenched herself from his arms and moved away, staring at him with anger.

'If you'd actually been dead then I'd have been given compassionate leave as your fiancée. However, as you're just lolling about at home, perfectly fit, then I'll certainly be demoted if not worse.'

'I'm sure I can smooth things out for you. Sit down with me and I'll tell you why I'm here.'

She listened without comment – another thing he loved about her was her ability to remain silent and attentive at the right time.

'You can't fly again?'

'Absolutely not.'

'I can hardly believe that I came here thinking you were dead, and now I discover that not only are you not dead, you're no longer active. I don't have to worry all the time that you might not return from a sortie.'

Now wasn't the time to tell her that he hoped to enlist in the army if he could. Her smile was radiant, she'd obviously forgiven him and when she rolled towards him, he gathered her close.

'I love you so much, darling, and I'm hoping that now I'm no longer flying, you'll agree to marry me.'

She snuggled closer and her reply was lost as his desire took over. If the family dogs hadn't decided to interrupt, it would have got decidedly out of hand. Making love to Di for the first time on the lawn in full view of the house was hardly appropriate.

He pushed himself up and gazed down at her. Her lovely face was flushed, her magnificent blue eyes positively sparkled. It took him a moment to find his voice.

'You didn't answer my question. Will you marry me immediately if we can get a slot at the registry?'

He stood up, offered his hand and pulled her to her feet, giving her a chance to gather her thoughts before answering.

'I'm not sure. We've only been going out for a few weeks, and rather than wanting to rush into things, now you're safe, why not get to know each other better?'

Somehow, he hid his disappointment. He also decided he'd definitely re-enlist with the brown jobs – maybe when he did that, she'd change her mind. Making such a drastic decision on so flimsy a reason probably wasn't a good idea.

'When we get married, my love, I want to do it properly in church and with your family and my friends there to wish us well,' said Di. 'I'd rather like a winter wedding – what about you?'

'This winter?' He was overjoyed that he'd misread the situation.

'Of course *this* winter, we'll have known each other for long enough by then to be sure we want to spend the rest of our lives together. As you'll be a free agent, we only have to worry about my leave.'

He was becoming enmeshed in his lies of omission and decided, before she left to take up her position, to tell her the truth. First, he had to make a telephone call to a chap at Victory House and get her off the hook.

'I'd better go and introduce myself properly to your parents and explain how the misunderstanding occurred. I got a lift here from your doctor – a charming elderly gentleman.' She clapped her hands to her mouth. 'Goodness me – he'll be spreading it all over the neighbourhood that you're dead.'

'Don't worry about it, darling, my parents will soon put everybody straight.'

* * *

Di couldn't believe how well Freddie looked for a man who was supposed to be dead. In fact, he looked better than he'd ever done and only then did she fully understand just how stressful being a fighter pilot was.

She glanced sideways at him and his eyes blazed. A rush of heat spread from her toes to the crown of her head. If she didn't want to do something she might regret, then it would be better if she didn't remain here too long. He'd always been attractive but now was absolutely irresistible – at least to her.

Mrs Hanover was on the telephone, explaining to somebody that she wasn't in need of any condolences as her son was perfectly well. Mr Hanover beckoned her into the sitting room.

'Please, my dear girl, don't look so worried. Thelma rang Dr Steiner and explained and he's speaking to those that he gave the erroneous information to. At the moment, she's conveying the message to the village gossip – that will ensure everybody's aware that our son's here and in perfect health.'

Di dropped onto a comfortable, floral covered sofa. 'I don't understand why anybody else would think he was dead. Freddie's been here for two weeks.'

Freddie joined her on the sofa. 'I've not left the house since I've been here, and I told my parents not to tell anybody. I really didn't want to socialise. As I explained to you earlier, I was thoroughly fed up about being kicked out of the RAF...'

'My dear boy, that's not correct, is it? It's your decision if you leave. There are hundreds of jobs you can do that are equally important in the war effort. What about intelligence?'

Freddie looked thoughtful. 'Become a spy? Now that does appeal. Analysing information is something I think I'd be good at.'

Mrs Hanover joined them and overheard this last remark. 'A spy? Oh no, Freddie, that would be just as dangerous – in fact more so – than being a fighter pilot.'

Di laughed, as did Freddie, at the misunderstanding. 'It's slang for being an intelligence officer, Mrs Hanover, he's not suggesting that he'll parachute into France and help the resistance.'

'How silly of me. That serves me right for eavesdropping. Forgive me for asking, my dear, but you appear to have arrived without any overnight belongings? We were so hoping you'd stay.'

'I left my kitbag and so on in the left luggage at Waterloo. I really didn't want to drag it all the way down here. I wasn't intending to stay overnight.'

Mrs Hanover was horrified. 'You can't possibly come all this way after the shock you've had and not remain at least until the morning.'

Freddie intervened. 'Mum, Di's AWL and has to return immediately if she doesn't want to be in trouble.'

'I thought you were going to speak to somebody on my behalf, Freddie?'

'I was just waiting for my mother to finish with the telephone. I'll do my best, but it's possible the only way to get out of this jam is for you to return today and just report a few hours late.'

Di's elation at finding him alive, and then her joy at discovering he was no longer going to be putting his life at risk several times a day, evaporated. She'd really not thought this through properly and he was right to be concerned on her behalf.

'I'm going to make lunch. I suppose you can remain for that.' Mrs Hanover shook her head and tutted and then left Di alone with Freddie's father.

He was a little shorter than his son, but the familial resemblance was striking. He also had that dynamic way of moving and when he spoke, he expected to be listened to.

'Mr Hanover, am I right in saying that you're a stockbroker?'

'I am, and because the younger members of my firm have enlisted, I'm busier than ever. It's only because it's Saturday that you find me here.'

'Saturday? I didn't realise it was the weekend – in the WAAF every day is the same. We work seven days and then, if we're lucky, we get a day off.'

'What exactly do you do, Miss Forsyth?'

'I'm sorry, Mr Hanover, I'm not allowed to discuss my actual duties.'

'Top secret? Good for you, my dear, whatever it is, I'm sure you're excellent at it.'

In the background, she'd been aware of Freddie talking to somebody on the telephone in the hall. He strolled in, obviously trying not to laugh. She wanted to get up and kick him hard in the shins. This wasn't anything amusing, as far as she was concerned.

'Don't scowl at me, darling, I've the best possible news. You're not AWL, you goose, you've got a three-day pass. You don't have to report at your new posting until Monday evening.'

She stared at him blankly for a second and then started to laugh. His father joined in, and his mother came in to see what the fuss was about.

'Mrs Hanover,' Di said when she was able to speak. 'If your offer for me to stay is still on the table then I'd be delighted to accept it. This confusion's entirely your son's fault. If he'd bothered to answer any of my letters, none of this would have happened. I was so upset, all common sense flew out of the window.'

Di wasn't entirely convinced that his mother was as pleased about her wanting to stay for two nights as she and Freddie were. She'd definitely heard a few more tuts.

Freddie showed her to a pretty bedroom overlooking the large, landscaped garden. She was rather surprised that there was still such an expanse of grass and that a family as patriotic as the Hanovers hadn't handed it over to a local farmer for the use of agriculture.

'There's a lock on the door in case you're wondering.'

She flushed at his frankness. 'I'm sure I don't need to use it. I told you once before that I'm not sleeping with you until we're married.'

'I'm sorry, that was crass of me. I wouldn't dream of coming to your bedroom uninvited and especially not under my parents' roof.'

She could hear Mrs Hanover on the phone again and then her hostess called out from the bottom of the stairs.

'Freddie, I've just spoken to your sister and they're all coming over for afternoon tea. Sylvia is bringing a few essentials for you, Di, my dear. I think you're more or less the same size.'

Di had no intention of holding a conversation about her personal garments conducted from the upstairs passageway. She rushed down, followed by Freddie, and took Mrs Hanover to one side.

'Thank you for thinking of me, it's so kind. However, I can't wear civilian clothes. I have to remain in uniform. I'll rinse out my underwear when I go to bed and hopefully it will be dry in the morning.'

'I'm sure nobody will ever know if you wear a frock for a couple of days. After all, Freddie was here for two weeks and nobody knew he'd come home.'

'Mum, I'm only in civvies because I'm possibly going to leave the RAF and I've got a month's leave. It's different for Di, she has to follow the rules.'

'Very well if you say so. I think it decidedly rude of both of you to be so ungrateful, Your sister will have to walk two miles pushing a perambulator with two small children in it, Freddie. Do you really think this is how she wishes to spend her afternoon?'

Di was revising her opinion of Freddie's mother – she wasn't the kind, accommodating woman she'd thought her to be. Di walked out of the front door onto the immaculate gravelled drive and hoped that he'd follow her.

She hastily moved far enough away so she couldn't overhear whatever was being said in the hall. Freddie came out a few minutes later, tight-lipped and obviously angry.

'I'm so sorry about that, darling. I've told my mother to cancel Sylvia's visit. Give me five minutes to get back into uniform, throw everything into my bag, and then we'll both head for London.'

'I'm the one who's sorry. I should never have come. I've now caused a rift between you and your parents...'

'None of this is your fault. I'll bring your haversack down when I come. You don't need to say goodbye. My father's locked himself in the study. It's what he always does when my mother behaves like this. He's a good chap but doesn't like any sort of unpleasantness and lets her get away with it rather than intervene.'

* * *

Freddie was grateful for the respite he'd received at his family home but although he was fond of his parents, he was well aware of their flaws. His kitbag was still packed, so it didn't take long to shove his shaving stuff and other personal items into it.

God knows where the two of them would go for the next two nights, but there was bound to be a cheap hotel or B&B available somewhere in the city. Separate rooms went without saying.

His mother was banging about in the kitchen. He'd no intention of speaking to her again – quite possibly not ever again, depending on how things were for him over the next few years. He'd only come back because he'd had nowhere else to recuperate. This house had stopped being his home years ago. He did stoop to pat the two dogs, who stared at him soulfully, as if understanding they might never see their favourite person again.

'Goodbye, old fellows, be good.'

Di was waiting at the end of the drive and her face lit up when she saw him striding towards her. The thought of spending two whole days in her company almost made up for the fact that he was no longer able to fly.

'Right, darling, I expect we'll have to walk to town. I doubt we'll be so lucky as to get a lift like you did.'

'It won't take us more than an hour, and it's a lovely day. You've got the short straw, my love, because you've got to carry your kitbag on your shoulder.'

She moved to his right side and put her hand into his. This meant she was walking closer to the traffic – if there was any. He wasn't comfortable with that, but with the inconvenience of his bag, there wasn't any other way of doing it if they wanted to walk together.

'I can't imagine you being in anything but that uniform, Freddie, I do hope you'll accept a desk job of some sort. Knowing that we're wearing the same grey-blue even when we're apart is really important to me.'

'Actually, I'm thinking of re-enlisting in the army. Not sure how I'll feel seeing my boys going up several times a day, getting shot down, dying, when I'm safe on the ground.'

Instead of being shocked, cross or horrified at his admission, she squeezed his hand sympathetically. 'I know what you mean. We all want to be useful, help the war effort in every way we can. I'd much rather you didn't join the army, but obviously it's your decision and I'll support you whatever you do.'

Before she could protest, he dumped his bag on the lane and pulled her into his arms. A vehicle of some sort pulled up behind them and hooted loudly. He stepped back automatically, trod on his bag, and they both went backwards in an undignified sprawl of legs and arms.

As they were untangling themselves, a forest of feet arrived at their side and they were hauled upright by willing hands. They were surrounded by grinning brown jobs.

'Blimey, mate, that was the funniest thing we've seen in a long while,' a cheerful NCO said. 'We're going to Guildford, want a lift? I reckon the blokes can squeeze up and make room for you and your missus.'

'Thank you, that would be really helpful. Sorry to have blocked the road but happy to have caused you and your boys some amusement.'

One of the soldiers picked up his kitbag and tossed it into the back of the lorry, which was full of soldiers of all shapes and sizes – no officers – but friendly enough. He lifted Di into the back, and she was greeted with whistles and rude remarks. Perhaps this wasn't such a good idea.

'I suggest that you remain silent if you don't wish to be put on a charge,' Di said. 'I might be a WAAF but I outrank all of you and that's all that matters.'

There was a chorus of apologies and Freddie smiled. He was always ready to step in and defend his lovely girl, but she really didn't need him to. He jumped into the lorry and winked at her and her eyes twinkled with appreciation. By some miracle, there was suddenly more than enough space for them to sit without being pressed against sweaty brown jobs. She sat on the end of the bench, and he sat closest to the soldiers.

The NCO who'd invited them was openly laughing as he slammed up the tailgate. There was no concealing canvas, which meant they could look out as they trundled along the lanes. Freddie put his arm around her shoulders and she rested her head against him. He closed his eyes and just enjoyed the moment.

25

Joanna wished that Dr Willoughby hadn't chosen to give her this worrying information about Bert Smith lurking in the neighbourhood on the very day that was supposed to be joyful for the family.

'I'm not quite sure what you're suggesting he might do, Dr Willoughby. Are you saying that he might break in and murder us in our beds?'

'Good god, of course not. I'm merely telling you that he's in the vicinity and might well try to get in and burgle your house.'

'Burgle? Yes, that makes more sense. The man's homeless and penniless, and stealing from Goodwill House would help his financial situation and also accomplish his goal of gaining revenge. I apologise if I sounded rather abrupt, Dr Willoughby, and thank you for telling me. I'll certainly make sure Lazzy is loose downstairs and not shut into the kitchen.'

'Good. Now, would you care to dance with me? I've seen your foot tapping to the music coming from the ballroom.'

She was about to refuse but then reconsidered. 'Yes, I'd love to, although it does seem rather livelier than anything I've danced to before.'

After a very enjoyable half an hour of dancing, first with the doctor and then with the solicitor, the adults left the youngsters to themselves. Watching Joe and Liza with their friends was a revelation. They were confident, popular and one wouldn't know that they hadn't been born into the Harcourt family.

The party came to a conclusion at six o'clock and the guests departed. Both Mr Broome and Dr Willoughby still drove cars and Joanna wondered how they had the petrol to put in them when it was so strictly rationed. They gave a lift to the three young people who lived in the same direction. The other three had come on their bicycles.

Elizabeth was asleep in an armchair in the drawing room. She seemed to spend a lot of her time sleeping nowadays.

'If we all muck in,' Jean said cheerfully, 'we'll get this tidied in no time.'

Joanna was quite prepared to pull her weight but was shooed away by the three of them. The telephone jangled and she smiled her thanks and hurried to answer it.

'Goodwill House, Lady Harcourt speaking.'

'Good evening, my lady, Mrs Dougherty here. I just wanted to confirm with you that you're ready to take my girls when they finish their two-week training.'

'Yes, as you saw when you came the other week, everything's ready.'

'There will be a dozen of them. They will be based with you and working mostly on your estate for your tenant farmers. I'll send you their names and so on next week.'

'Excellent news, Mrs Dougherty. My son has managed to cobble together four usable bicycles. Will the girls be expected to find their own way to where they're working, or will there be transport?'

'Transport? Good heavens, no – they have to walk if they don't have access to a bicycle or, in your case, a horse and cart.'

'I'm sure they'll soon adjust. We're all looking forward to welcoming them here. Someone in the WI told me that there's a hostel on the other side of Ramsgate where more than twenty land girls are billeted.'

'We put them wherever's suitable. Some girls will be living on the farms where they work, others in empty farm cottages, and a minority will be in luxurious billets at grand houses like yours. They'll be the lucky ones, I can assure you, even if they do have to walk two or three miles in each direction every day.'

'Thank you, I'm eagerly anticipating meeting our new guests.'

'Then I'll bid you good day, my lady. Remember, if you have any problems with any of your new boarders, don't hesitate to contact me.'

* * *

Despite the constant noise of aircraft landing and taking off, the frequent air-raid sirens from the base and the dogfights in the Channel, somehow Goodwill House seemed strangely removed from all of it. It was as if they were living in a protected bubble of some sort, a place where mayhem and chaos couldn't penetrate.

Whatever might happen on the base wouldn't impinge on their life at all – this was nonsense, of course, but the thought gave Joanna confidence as she prepared for bed that night.

The only member of the household that she'd told about the worrying conversation with the doctor was Jean. They'd both agreed it would be better to keep this sort of information to themselves and not worry either the twins or Elizabeth.

Joe and Liza were now on the family floor and Jean had moved into their rooms, delighted to have so much space of her own. Joanna, as always, checked that Elizabeth was comfortably settled.

'It was a most enjoyable day, my dear, and think it went splendidly. I've rather revised my opinion of Mr Broome and think that possibly Dr Willoughby is the man for you.'

'As long as you don't add the new Lord Harcourt to the list, then I suppose I can think myself fortunate. You seem to believe that all the unmarried gentlemen of my acquaintance are possible husbands for me.'

Elizabeth appreciated the humour and chuckled. 'Forgive an old lady, my dear, I do love to romanticise. It's just because you're far too lovely and too young to remain a spinster.'

'I wasn't happy with David, so why would I want to repeat the experience? You never remarried, why was that?'

'Good gracious, why would I give up my independence and my fortune for a man? I can assure you I didn't lack male company but never wished to marry any of my lovers.'

Joanna couldn't hide her gasp. She stared at her mother-in-law in astonishment. 'Lovers? In the plural?'

Elizabeth laughed. 'A ménage á trois was never something that appealed to me. I always had one gentleman friend at a time.' She raised an eyebrow and Joanna wasn't sure if she was being teased or deliberately shocked.

'This is a highly irregular conversation to be having at bedtime...'

'I think to be talking about lovers both singular and plural right now is the perfect time.' Elizabeth was enjoying making Joanna feel uncomfortable. 'One could do things in the south of France, my dear, without raising any eyebrows. Unfortunately, that's just not possible here.'

'I'm relieved to hear you say so, as I thought you were about suggest that I took a string of lovers.'

With that, Joanna smiled and said goodnight and headed for the adjacent bedrooms where the twins now resided. She knocked quietly on each door, didn't open it, and called out her goodnights and received sleepy replies from both.

Before entering her own room, she walked back to the end of the wide passageway to the gallery and leaned over the balustrade. As expected, the dog was stretched out with his head on the bottom stair. He was well behaved nowadays and wouldn't dream of venturing upstairs.

She was satisfied that in the unlikely event Smith attempted to force his way in, he would receive a very unpleasant surprise.

* * *

Later that night, something woke Joanna and it wasn't the dog barking. She sat up, listened carefully, but could hear nothing untoward. She was about to settle down again, thinking she'd woken for no particular reason, when Lazzy started to howl.

She tumbled out of bed, rammed her feet into her slippers and snatched up her silk dressing gown. As she burst out of her room, both Joe and Liza appeared, similarly dressed.

'I'll see what's wrong, Ma, he doesn't usually make that sort of noise,' Joe said and dashed off.

'Liza, will you get Jean please? I'm going to get your grandmother up.'

Her daughter didn't argue but raced up the stairs to the attic whilst she knocked on Elizabeth's door. 'Come in, my dear, and put the light on so I can get up without fear of falling over.'

Joanna did as requested. 'Joe's gone to investigate the reason for Lazzy making such a noise, but I think it better if we're all up, just in case.'

Elizabeth was out of bed and in her slippers and dressing gown in moments, moving with surprising speed for someone of her antiquity. 'There's only one reason we need to be up and dressed and that's if the house is on fire. Is that what you suspect?'

As soon as she heard the word fire, Joanna knew that was the reason she'd woken up and the reason the dog was so agitated. She ran to the window and opened it. 'My god, there's smoke coming out of the downstairs windows of the Victorian wing.'

Liza appeared with Jean and she left them to bring Elizabeth down safely. She fled down to the telephone and as soon as she was connected asked for the fire brigade and the police to be contacted.

Joe appeared at her side. 'Ring the base, Ma, they'll get here sooner. I'm going to find the stirrup pump and soak the curtains and boards that separate us from the Victorian end.'

He didn't wait to hear her reply but dashed off again. He was really a most resourceful and mature young man. As soon as she was connected to the base, Joanna explained the reason for disturbing them in the middle of the night.

'Don't worry, my lady, I'll have our tenders with you in double-quick time. I reckon we'll be there long before the local chaps who've got to come from Ramsgate. Can you make sure we've got access to your water?'

'I'll have my son do that. We have two wells – one for outside and one for the house. They're both accessible.'

'Good show.' The unidentified speaker hung up and she turned to speak to the three slowly descending the stairs.

'Manston are sending engines. Thank goodness it's a warm night and we'll come to no harm on the terrace.'

Jean had her arm around Elizabeth's waist. 'Come on, my lady, I'll get you settled outside and then find you some cushions and a couple of rugs.'

Satisfied her mother-in-law was going to be safe and as comfortable as she could be, Joanna rushed to the kitchen, followed by Liza.

'If you make the tea, Ma, I'll help me brother. I reckon I can throw a few bucketfuls of water at the boards easy enough.'

'Good girl, I think it might be wise to dampen the entire wall that adjoins the Victorian end. I'll make the tea and take it out to the terrace and then come and help you.'

Liza's speech had reverted but that was hardly surprising in the circumstances. Fire was the most terrifying of enemies in an old house – everything was so dry and there was so much wood everywhere. The panelling in the library and the study would burn like tinder if it caught.

Joanna almost dropped the kettle as a wave of something, she wasn't sure what, washed over her, making her feel weak. Was the house insured? Had David let this lapse? This was something Mr Broome hadn't mentioned, and she hadn't thought of until now.

With shaking hands, she somehow completed the familiar routine of making tea. She popped everything on a tray and dashed through the house, her inappropriate nightwear flapping around her. Maybe she'd rush upstairs and change into something more suitable.

'Here you are, Elizabeth, I have to leave you to serve yourself as Jean and I have to do what we can to save the house.'

Lazzy, no longer howling, but with his tail between his legs, pushed his cold nose into her hand. 'Good boy, you woke us up. Stay with Elizabeth and keep her safe.'

The dog padded across and flopped down beside her mother-in-law. 'At least there's no flames visible as yet, but I can smell the smoke and see it in the moonlight.'

'Run along, my dear, your dog will take care of me. Listen, I think I can hear the sound of heavy vehicles approaching on the lane.'

Joanna turned to look and, sure enough, two pinprick head-lights turned into the drive. They would be here in minutes, and she hadn't asked Joe to open the wells. She rushed through the house and as she reached the passageway that led to the Victorian end, her feet slid from under her in the stream of water. She landed with an undignified thump on her bottom.

Embarrassment had her on her feet in seconds. Her nightgown and peignoir were now soaked and clinging in a rather suggestive way to her body.

'Joe, the fire engines will be here from the base in a moment. Can you open the wells so they can get their hoses in?'

'I've already done that, Ma, and am going to help Auntie Jean and Liza douse the other walls. Blimey, you look like a drowned rat.'

'I know. I'm going to change; I can't stay like this and be of any use to anyone.'

She snatched the first items she could find in her closet and was dressed in a mismatch of jumper and slacks with her feet pushed into her garden shoes. She hoped her lack of a brassiere would go unnoticed.

Elizabeth would be perfectly fine in her night clothes on the terrace with blankets and pillows, but the other three needed sensible footwear and clothes if they were to continue with their strenuous physical work.

Instead of dashing back and probably getting in the way, doing something she wouldn't be good at, Joanna collected a change of clothes and outdoor shoes for the three doing such sterling work to save Goodwill House.

'Here you are, get out of your wet things. You'll be able to work better. Don't argue, it won't take more than a few minutes to do what I ask. I'll go and speak to the firemen from the base.'

A chorus of thanks followed her from the room. She picked up a torch from the shelf in the kitchen where they were kept, slammed back the bolts and turned the key in the back door and was outside just as the first engine pulled up at the front.

'One well is by the coach house and the other is in the courtyard outside the kitchen,' she told the tall man who hurried towards her.

'Is everybody out of the house, my lady?'

'Yes – that is, not exactly. The fire's not in the main part but in the Victorian wing. I hope your hoses are long enough to reach that end.'

'We carry gallons of water on our tenders. Everybody needs to be outside even from the main part.'

'My son, daughter and housekeeper are soaking the connecting wall on this side.'

'It's not a civilian's business to fight fires, my lady, I'll send them out to join you on the terrace. Leave us to do our job.'

Joanna wasn't sure if she was offended by his brusque manner or impressed by his authority. She was about to go into the house but decided against it. The place was now crawling with RAF firemen and there were more than enough of them to do what was necessary.

When she arrived on the terrace, the twins and Jean were already there. 'I think this side of the house will be all right, Ma,' Joe said as he embraced her in a very damp hug. 'There's a lot of smoke, but the walls weren't even warm.'

Liza joined in the family cuddle and Joanna revelled in the physical contact. David hadn't been an affectionate man and, once marital relations had ceased, he never willingly touched her. She and Sarah had followed his lead and neither of them kissed, hugged or touched each other very often, even though the bond between them was strong.

Lazzy, jealous of the interaction, shoved his considerable bulk between them and forced them apart.

'Stupid dog, we love you too and without your waking us up it might have been so much worse,' she said as she pulled his long, silky ears.

'I'd make us all another cup of tea, but we're banned from the house,' Jean said as she fussed around her former mistress.

'I don't need all these blankets and cushions, Jean, it's not me who's wet and cold. Here, share them out between you.'

They settled down to wait, not knowing what was going on or how bad the fire was. It occurred to Joanna that she should have given the fireman in charge the keys to the house, as it would have saved them having to break down the door.

The engine from Ramsgate arrived half an hour after the others but still had plenty to do. The young man who was in charge clumped up the terrace steps an hour or more after he and his men had arrived.

'My lady, the fire's out. It didn't reach the upper floors, but the damage on the ground floor is substantial. I'm sorry to have to tell you that the fire was set deliberately.'

'I thought it had been,' Joanna said. 'We were warned that a man, one Bert Smith, who'd vowed to hurt us, was back in the neighbourhood, but I didn't really think he'd do anything so drastic.'

'The police will deal with that. Have they been informed?'

'They have, Sergeant, but have yet to arrive. Thank you for your help. Without Manston, we might have lost our home.'

'Your children prevented the fire from coming into this side. There's a lot of water damage but better than the alternative. You don't want to go next door – it's not safe.'

'Can we go back inside? My mother-in-law has been out here for hours and she should be in bed.'

'Yes, the stairs aren't wet and are perfectly safe. I suggest all of you retire and leave us to arrange for the water to be pumped out.'

'I have to remain up to speak to the police when they arrive.'

'I'll speak to them. Forgive me for issuing orders, but we'll get on quicker knowing you're not out here shivering.'

'Thank you for your assistance. We'll do as you suggest. I know that you're a sergeant, but I don't know your name.' She shone her torch up into his face.

'I'm John Sergeant.' His teeth flashed white in his soot-stained face. 'I know. I'm Sergeant Sergeant and it causes a great deal of hilarity in the mess.'

Joanna had no urge to laugh. For some reason he was making her feel rather unsettled. 'I can imagine why. Forgive me for asking, but you're obviously a well-educated young man, so why aren't you an officer?'

'My choice, my lady. I got a scholarship to a local public school. My father's a carpenter and my mother's a cleaner in a house similar to yours. I'm more comfortable and better suited to being a senior NCO.'

'That was a most impertinent question and I apologise, Sergeant. I won't delay you any longer.'

'The blokes from Ramsgate are pumping out the water from your side, but we won't attempt to do anything next door until it's safe.'

'Thank you, I look forward to seeing you then. Good night.'

The dawn chorus had started before everyone was settled. Joanna lay restless and unable to drift off, despite being exhausted. For some inexplicable reason, images of the RAF fireman with mismatched eyes and a devastating smile was keeping her awake.

He must be several years her junior, came from a different background, but he made her pulse race in a way none of the suitable gentleman she'd met ever had.

26

Di spent the short journey to Waterloo Station sitting on Freddie's bag and leaning against his legs. She had time to digest and ponder on what had just happened and what might happen next. The fact that he was no longer going to be flying and would probably be based in London was all her prayers answered.

What was less pleasing was the fact that because of her uninvited arrival at his house, she'd caused a rift between him and his parents – not only that, she had cut short his well-deserved and much-needed month's recuperation. Also, she would be taking up her new post as a plotter and he would have nowhere to stay.

'Freddie, what are you going to do for the next two weeks?' She'd had to raise her voice in order to be heard and this meant that those squashed into the same corridor were also privy to their conversation.

A very rude soldier shouted back. 'If I was you, mate, I'd have it off with your lady love.'

Freddie dropped a hand on her shoulder, knowing she was about to say something that might provoke further unpleasantness. Instead, he just spoke in his usual, beautifully modulated tone.

'I'm going to shoot down a few more Germans – what about you?'

There was a general murmur of support for his reply and the offender muttered an apology and said nothing else.

Freddie leaned down so he could talk into her ear and not be overheard. 'Sorry about that, darling, and don't worry, I'm not actually going to be shooting anyone.'

There was no point in trying to converse and the journey was so short it didn't really matter. The train began to slow as they approached the station. As they were closest to the door, Freddie leaned out the window and turned the handle so it opened. He didn't swing out with it as she'd done the first time that she'd tried to do this.

Di got out first and he followed with his bag over his shoulder.

'I need to get my stuff from the left luggage office,' she said. 'I don't know London very well so have no idea where we can find accommodation for a couple of nights.'

'There're plenty of decent small hotels and B&Bs. I'm sure we'll find something.'

After collecting her belongings, they set out together, kitbags on their left shoulders, leaving their right hands free, but this also meant they couldn't walk side by side and still continue a conversation without raising their voices.

'Let's find somewhere to have a coffee and we can talk about what's happening next,' she suggested.

'Okay, there's a Lyon's Corner House over there. We can get a decent meal and decide what we're going to do.'

There were more civilians on the third floor, where they eventually found an empty table, than those in uniform, and all of them nodded and smiled admiringly as they wove their way across the crowded room. It surprised her how many people were still prepared to go out for a cup of tea and a cake when the inevitable arrival of the Luftwaffe was imminent.

The nippy – the usual affectionate term given to a waitress in this restaurant – took their order and was back in a few minutes with the tea.

'Finally, we can talk about the future. What are you going to do for the remainder of your leave, Freddie?'

'I'm perfectly fit and really don't need another two weeks lazing about. I'm going to report for duty and see if there's any chance of becoming a spy – if not, then I think I might quite like to be a controller, run things in a plotting room. You never know, we might end up working together.'

'That would be spiffing. Do you think you'd still be based at Hornchurch?'

'I haven't the foggiest, but no doubt, I'll discover everything I need to know when I get back to Hornchurch. My chaps are still at the forward base in Rochford but must be coming to the end of their stint. It will be good to catch up with them, and especially with Ted.'

'I've no idea where Millie went to be trained, as I've had absolutely no contact with her. I'm hoping that she'll have finished her training too so we'll be able to get together – or at least have an address we can write to.'

Their lunch arrived – they'd ordered bangers and mash with onion gravy. She looked at the plate with dismay.

'Golly, bangers means more than one, surely? Still, the mashed potato is lovely and smooth and the onion gravy delicious. Do you want my sausage? You need protein more than me.'

'I wouldn't dream of depriving you of your solitary banger. Let's hope the spotted dick and custard is a tasty but with a somewhat larger portion.'

They left the restaurant late in the afternoon and went in search of somewhere to stay for the next two nights. They were fortunate to discover a commercial hotel which had two single rooms vacant.

'You're lucky, ducks, I've had a couple of cancellations from two of my regulars, otherwise I'd not have a dicky bird. I don't do no meals apart from breakfast but there's plenty of caffs you can go to for a bit of supper,' the friendly landlady told them.

'We thought we might go to the cinema – will we still be able to get in if it's after nine o'clock?'

'Bless you, I don't lock up till eleven. Some of my blokes don't get here until late if they've been travelling. Them trains arrive when they feel like nowadays.'

The landlady, a small stout woman with her hair scraped into a bun at the back of her head, nodded as she spoke. Her several chins wobbled.

'Thank you, ma'am,' Freddie said politely.

'I'm Ethel to all me guests. Not never been called a ma'am before.' She handed two keys over from the hooks behind the counter. 'One of the rooms is first floor, back, the other second floor, front. There's a bathroom and bog on each floor by the stairs.'

She then vanished through the noisy beaded curtain, leaving them to find their own way. There was an overwhelming smell of kippers wafting from behind the curtain but apart from that the place was spotless.

'You take the first floor, darling,' Freddie said. 'Just dump your things and we'll meet here in fifteen minutes.'

The room was small but adequate, a tiny sink with a cracked mirror above it sufficient for cleaning her teeth and having a quick wash. The bed had a faded blue candlewick bedspread and an even more faded blue eiderdown on top. She'd boil if she slept under so much bedding tonight and wondered why Ethel hadn't put the eiderdown away for the summer.

There was a small clean towel hanging on a hook by the sink

and Di quickly washed her face and hands and put on another smudge of lipstick. Freddie had already kissed away the first lot.

She found the WC and was pleasantly surprised. With mostly men staying here, she'd expected it to be rather unpleasant. However, like the rest of the place, it was pristine and smelt fresh. When she pulled the chain, there was an ominous gurgling from the tank above but eventually the water flushed through as it should.

She rushed back to her room to wash her hands a second time, grab her haversack and gas mask, and was then ready to meet Freddie.

* * *

Freddie chucked his bag into the room, used the ablutions and headed downstairs. The guesthouse was quiet, probably because this was a commercial hotel. It was conveniently situated in Morley Street, a few streets away from Waterloo Station, and no doubt guests didn't arrive until after they'd finished work. He lounged against the wall opposite the stairs so he could watch Di when she came down.

The row with his mother was nothing new, which was why he rarely returned to his home. If he'd had anywhere else to go, he'd have gone there. He was grateful, however, for the two weeks he'd had in the peaceful countryside recovering his spirits and health.

There were several cinemas just across the bridge. He thought the nearest would be the Tivoli in the Strand. Only a short distance further on, there were bigger places in Leicester Square. He didn't know what films were current but there was bound to be something they'd both enjoy.

He heard the distinctive sound of a chain being pulled and then

Di was running gracefully down the stairs towards him. He pushed himself upright and reached the bottom step as she arrived. They were now at the same height and he rather liked being able to look at her lovely face so closely.

'I thought I'd be waiting an hour, darling,' he said with a smile. Before she could protest that she was never late, he closed her mouth with a kiss.

It was she who broke the embrace by gently pushing on his chest. 'Freddie, my love, you must stop doing this. I just put lipstick on and I expect it's gone again.'

He tilted her face and made a pretence of examining her mouth and he loved the way colour tinged her cheeks under his scrutiny. 'No, still there. Well, to be honest, there's only a smidgen left.'

'You're quite impossible, Squadron Leader Hanover. Fortunately, I actually have my lipstick in my bag today.'

'Don't put it on again, as I can guarantee it'll be removed in the same way before long.' He thought he'd better change the subject, as even talking about something as innocent as a kiss was making him uncomfortable.

'It's only a ten-minute walk to the Strand, and there are several cinemas to the left of the bridge.'

'I haven't been to the pictures since I joined the WAAF. I really don't mind what's showing; I do enjoy the newsreel and the cartoon, sometimes even the B film is enjoyable just because it's so dire.'

'It's a damn nuisance we have to appear fully dressed...' She giggled and he raised an eyebrow, which made her laugh even more. 'You know exactly what I mean. Don't interrupt a senior officer, or I'll be obliged to place you on a charge.'

She smiled at him and he was tempted to kiss her, regardless of the pedestrians around.

They exited the building, turned right and were soon at Waterloo Bridge. They marched briskly across and then turned left and stopped outside the Tivoli to see what was showing.

'*Cavalcade of Variety*, a musical with Billy Cotton. What do you think?'

She nodded vigorously. 'Oh yes, please. Just what we need to cheer us up.'

He insisted on buying the tickets, although she said she was quite prepared to pay her way. 'A gentleman always pays for a lady in the same way he always opens the door, stands up when she comes into a room—'

'And raises his hat when he sees her? Don't be such a fuddy-duddy, Freddie. Things are different now. If we can drive fire engines, fly aeroplanes and become officers in the armed forces, then we don't need to be mollycoddled or treated like a lady in a Jane Austen novel.'

They were just about to cross the foyer and enter the auditorium. 'I warned you not to interrupt a senior officer.'

He pulled her into his arms and, despite the presence of the ancient usherette, he kissed her thoroughly. To make sure she got his point, he then pulled off her neatly pinned hat and ran his fingers through her hair, dislodging hairpins in all directions.

This was meant to be funny, he'd intended to say something facetious, but said something else entirely. 'I've never seen you with your hair loose, darling. God, I so want to make love to you.'

'There ain't no room on the back seats here for none of that nonsense, young man. Well, I never did! What's the world coming to when a couple of posh folks like you want to use our Tivoli as a knocking shop?' The usherette, having uttered this extraordinary comment, carried on as normal by opening the doors and shining her torch on the carpet so they could follow her to their seats.

The door closed behind her. They remained in the foyer. He wasn't sure how Di felt about what had been said and he'd no intention of going into this cinema, even though he'd bought the tickets.

'What's a knocking shop?' Di asked.

'I think we'd better find somewhere else to go. I'll give the tickets to that couple who've just come in so they won't go to waste.'

'I can't go out looking like this. I'll find the ladies' room and get my hair back up. Don't look so worried, my love, I've got plenty of hairpins in my haversack.'

The recipients of the free tickets were overjoyed, and Freddie decided he'd wait on the pavement. The fresh air would do him good. He wasn't usually so impulsive, but he was so madly in love with Di, just being with her made it hard to breathe.

It didn't take her long to restore her appearance and she emerged into the sunshine, looking around for him anxiously as if she thought he'd abandoned her.

'Shall we walk along the river instead?'

'We'll find somewhere to sit down so we can talk. I'm really sorry for embarrassing you just now.'

She stretched up on tiptoe and kissed him lightly before putting her arm through his. 'I know you didn't do it deliberately. And in case you're wondering, I know exactly what that obnoxious old lady meant. I might be innocent, but I'm not ignorant.'

They strolled alongside the river, pausing to watch the water traffic occasionally, but neither of them felt the need to chatter. Just being together was sufficient for them both.

'Look, there's a bench over there and there's nobody on it at the moment,' Di said. 'If it wasn't for the sandbags, brown paper strips on all the windows, and the amount of people in uniform, you wouldn't know there was a war on at this precise moment.'

'I should have checked where the nearest shelter is, but like you, today seems a long way from the chaos we went through at Manston. You can't even hear the fighters taking off from Kenley and Hornchurch – just birdsong and seagulls.'

'Don't forget the pigeons. There are thousands of them in London. I wonder what they've got to eat now it's illegal to feed bread or anything else to wild birds.'

'Actually, I was wondering if any enterprising Londoner might start netting them and selling them as food when things get tough,' Freddie said.

'I don't see why not. I've had pigeon pie a couple of times and it was very tasty, a bit stronger than pheasant, but still palatable.' She smiled at him and he wanted to grab her hand and rush her to the nearest hotel and demonstrate just how much he loved her.

What a ridiculous conversation to be having when there was something so important to be discussing. He waited until they were seated and then swivelled so he was facing her and took her hands in his.

'Darling, you know how I feel about you, and I think you feel the same way. I know you don't want to sleep with me until we're married, so could I persuade you to bring our wedding forward from December to right now?'

He expected her to shake her head, repeat what she'd said about waiting, but instead she smiled. 'I've changed my mind about waiting. I will marry you immediately if that's possible. Spending time with you has convinced me that there's no need to wait. I love you and that isn't going to change. But only if you can get some of those prophylactics Millie was telling me about.'

He was grinning like a lunatic. 'I certainly can. Ted was married by the RAF padre. You don't need a licence for that. We're both serving members, so all we need to do is get permission from whoever's in charge at the moment.'

'I'm not officially based anywhere until Monday, so I don't need permission. Surely someone of your rank doesn't either?'

'I don't know if that's correct, but let's assume it is. Therefore, all I have to do is get in touch with the padre and arrange for us to be married on Monday. We can't do it on a Sunday obviously.'

'We passed a telephone box earlier. I'll sit here and enjoy the sunshine whilst you make the phone call. I'm not going to get too excited until we got a definite yes.'

The phone box was unoccupied and Freddie got out the loose change in his pocket and stacked the pennies, halfpennies and shillings on top of the box. He shouldn't need all of them, but he didn't want to be cut off if the money ran out prematurely.

He couldn't dial the base directly, only local calls worked like that, so he dialled the operator and told her the number he wished to be connected to. She asked him to put the money in and he heard it drop into the box.

As soon as someone answered the call, he pushed button A and was connected. He couldn't believe his luck when the chap he was speaking to told him that the chaplain was actually in the building. The pips went and he shoved a few more coins into the slot.

'Good afternoon, Squadron Leader Hanover, how can I help?' The chaplain sounded a decent sort of bod.

'My fiancée and I want to get married on Monday. I'm based at Hornchurch, although I'm on crash leave at the moment, and Corporal Diane Forsyth is between postings.'

'Then I see no difficulty. There's a small chapel on the base we can use. I've got my pen and paper ready, so give me all the details and then I can have the licence ready.'

By the time the formalities were completed, the stack of coins was almost down to the last few. Freddie replaced the receiver in the cradle, scarcely able to comprehend that in less than two days' time he'd be a married man.

* * *

Di saw Freddie sprinting towards her and knew he'd been successful. She was on her feet and ran into his arms.

'Monday, at eleven o'clock, you will become Mrs Diane Hanover. I don't expect you to use your married name whilst you're still in uniform, it would complicate things. I hope you'll want to wear your wedding ring, though.'

'I certainly will. It would be lovely if Millie and Ted could be our witnesses as we were theirs a few weeks ago.'

'That was the other piece of good news I was going to give you. My old squadron's back from Rochford and has a week based at Hornchurch, just flying the occasional mission unless something major happens. This means that Ted can certainly be one of the witnesses.'

'Did you actually speak to him?'

'I left a detailed message and I'm sure it'll get to him. Shall we see if we can find ourselves some tea, or perhaps something stronger, to celebrate?'

'Do you think anyone would notice if you came to my room tonight?' This was a decision she'd come to whilst she was waiting. They wouldn't have any time to consummate the union after the ceremony, so they could have a two-day honeymoon in advance.

His eyes darkened and a slight flush appeared along his cheek-bones. 'Are you quite sure?'

'One hundred per cent. As long as I don't get pregnant, I can stay in the WAAF and hopefully become an officer one day.' The thought of being Freddie's wife, of sharing the rest of her life with him, of having children when the war was over, filled her with joy.

His hands tightened over hers, the grip almost painful. 'Then we'll book somewhere decent as a married couple. I've been carrying a wedding ring in my pocket since we got engaged, in the hope that I might persuade you to change your mind.'

She was so excited, so happy, it was as if she'd swallowed a whole bottle of ginger pop in one gulp. 'I love you so much, Freddie darling, and can't wait to be your wife.'

ACKNOWLEDGEMENT

Writing about bombing, civilian deaths and the hardships of war in the twentieth century is what I do, but for this to be happening now, in Ukraine, is hard to accept. My thoughts and prayers go out to all those innocent civilians and brave soldiers suffering because of Russian aggression.

Fenella J. Miller, July 2022

BIBLIOGRAPHY

Hornchurch Scramble by Richard C. Smith

Chronicle of the Second World War edited by Jacques Legrand and Derrik Mercer

We All Wore Blue by Muriel Gane Pushman

A to Z Atlas and Guide to London, 1939 Edition

Oxford Dictionary of Slang by John Ayto

Wartime Britain by Juliet Gardiner

How We Lived Then by Norman Longmate

The Wartime Scrapbook by Robert Opie

RAF Airfields of World War II by Jonathan Falconer

Living Dangerously by Betty Farley

The WAAF at War by John Frayne Turner

A WAAF at War by Diana Lindo Woodfield

RAF Fighter Squadron by Anthony Robinson

First Light by Geoffrey Wellum

A Detailed History of RAF Manston 1931–1940 by Joe Bamford, John Williams and Peter Gallagher

Old Ordnance Survey Map Ramsgate 1905, the Godfrey Edition

MORE FROM FENELLA J. MILLER

We hope you enjoyed reading *Duty Calls at Goodwill House*. If you did, please leave a review.

If you'd like to gift a copy, this book is also available as an ebook, digital audio download and audiobook CD.

Sign up to Fenella J. Miller's mailing list for news, competitions and updates on future books.

https://bit.ly/FenellaMillerNews

The War Girls of Goodwill House, the first in the Goodwill House series, is available now.

ABOUT THE AUTHOR

Fenella J. Miller is the bestselling writer of historical sagas. She also has a passion for Regency romantic adventures and has published over fifty to great acclaim. Her father was a York-shireman and her mother the daughter of a Rajah. She lives in a small village in Essex with her British Shorthair cat.

Follow Fenella on social media:

twitter.com/fenellawriter
facebook.com/fenella.miller

Sixpence Stories

Introducing Sixpence Stories!

Discover page-turning historical novels from your favourite authors, meet new friends and be transported back in time.

Join our book club Facebook group

https://bit.ly/SixpenceGroup

Sign up to our newsletter

https://bit.ly/SixpenceNews

Boldwood

Boldwood Books is an award-winning fiction publishing company seeking out the best stories from around the world.

Find out more at www.boldwoodbooks.com

Join our reader community for brilliant books, competitions and offers!

Follow us
@BoldwoodBooks
@BookandTonic

Sign up to our weekly deals newsletter

https://bit.ly/BoldwoodBNewsletter